CHARLES BARBARA

STIRRING STORIES

TRANSLATED AND WITH AN INTRODUCTION BY
BRIAN STABLEFORD

Contents

Introduction

*H*ISTOIRES ÉMOUVANTES by Charles Barbara (1817-1866), here translated as *Stirring Stories*, was first published in Paris by Michel Lévy frères in 1856. "Le Rideau" (tr. as "The Curtain") had initially appeared in *L'Artiste* in 1846. "Héloïse" (1852), "Les Douleurs d'un nom (1853; tr. as "The Dolors of a Name") and "Vieille histoire" (1853; tr. as "An Old Story") had appeared in the *Bulletin de la societé des gens de letters*. "Le Billet de mille francs" (1853; tr. as The Thousand-Franc Bill"), "Les Jumeaux" (1854; tr. as "The Twins"), "La Leçon de musique" (1854; tr. as "The Music Lesson") and "Extraits des rapports d'un agent de police" (1854 as "Un drame ignoré; extraits des rapports d'un agent de police"; tr. as "Extracts from the Reports of a Police Agent") were initially published in the *Revue de Paris*. "Une Chanteuse des rues" (1855; tr. as "A Street Singer") first appeared in *Le Journal pour tous*.

The collection was followed some years later by *Mes petits-maisons* (1860; tr. as *My Lunatic Asylum*, a companion volume to the present one), issued by Hachette, but the stories in both collections were drawn from much the same spectrum of original publication dates, each volume including one story published before the 1848 revolution, while the remainder were from the first decade of the Second Empire, and thus produced in an era of strict political censorship. It is probable that the stories in the present collection were not published first because the author thought them better than the stories held over for the second collection, but because he thought them slightly less likely to attract the unkind attention of the censors, although one of them—"Extraits des rapports d'un police agent"—must have seemed a very chancy inclusion in both its periodical and volume publications, sailing very close to the wind in its savage sarcasm and its extremely unflattering tacit depiction of its narrator, in spite of the careful inclusion of dates setting the story under the previous régime rather than the current one.

The last-named story, in particular, offers a hint of what Charles Barbara might have accomplished, and would surely have attempted to accomplish, had he not been forced to write on a tight leash throughout the heyday of his career. Working within that restriction, however, his achievement was by no means trivial, and his contribution to the somewhat fugitive tradition of Romantic prose was more significant than history was long prepared to recognize.

Louis-Charles Barbara was born in Orléans, the son of a maker of musical instruments whose character was apparently tyrannical, and against whose pressure he rebelled with a resentment that seems to have lasted throughout his life—although his schooling in the violin sometimes provided the crumbs of a living in periods when his writing did not make enough money to support him; Barbara reluctantly turned performer with voice and violin when circumstances were tough, as they frequently were in a turbulent era of French history.

Barbara was still a child when the French Romantic Movement first got under way. Arguably, by the time he joined it actively in the early 1840s, it had already passed its heyday, even before it ran into the economic reefs associated with the upheavals of the 1848 Revolution and its aftermath. He arrived in the heart of "Bohemian" Paris, however, in time to be parodied in Henry Murger's *Scènes de la vie de Bohème* (1847-1849) as the churlishly antisocial "Carolus Barbemuche," and to form lasting friendships with Charles Baudelaire and "Champfleury" (Jules Fleury-Husson) in spite of his rather reserved character. Barbara edited two overtly political periodicals in his native Orléans during the brief interval of the Second Republic, *Le Démocrate* and *Le Constitution*, but that career was cut abruptly short by the consequences of Louis Napoléon Bonaparte's *coup-d'état*. He returned to Paris and continued writing throughout the 1850s, when the literary marketplace was under its greatest pressure from the censors.

Because Barbara shared Baudelaire's enthusiasm for the work of Edgar Poe—he made his own translation of "The Murders in the Rue Morgue"—the experimental aspects of his early prose fiction naturally took some evident inspiration from the American writer, but he chose not to reprint most of those early stories, and the endeavors collected in *Histoires émouvantes* are mostly experimental in a markedly different spirit, although Poe's influence is still evident in his use of psychologically idiosyncratic unreliable narrators in "Le Rideau" and "Héloïse." Barbara's experimentation with unusual narrative points of view might seem a trifle maladroit by today's standards, but in that regard, like Poe, he was a significant pioneer and his explorations produced several interesting exemplars that were probably influential in their day.

Barbara's first novel, serialized in the *Revue de Paris* before being thoroughly revised for its initial book publication in Belgium by the then-exiled Pierre-Jules Hetzel in 1855, *L'Assassinat du Pont-Rouge* (tr. as *The Red Bridge Murder*) owed a considerable debt to Poe. Antedating Paul Féval's *Jean Diable* (1861) and the early detective stories of Féval's ex-secretary Émile Gaboriau by some years, *L'Assassinat du Pont-Rouge* warrants consideration as the first significant work of the French genre of crime fiction that was gradually transformed into the *roman policier*, and it is undoubtedly not a coincidence that *Histoires émouvantes* (1857) followed closely on the heels of the Poe collection *Histoires extraordinaires* (1856), issued by the same publisher.

Mes petits-maisons was swiftly followed by *Les Orages de la vie* [The Storms of Life] (1860), labeled *première série* and containing two novellas, "Thérèse Lemajeur" (1855) and "Madeleine Lorin" (1857). No other volumes appeared under that umbrella title but those two stories can be seen as elements of a series of intense character studies of young women, which had begun with "Une Chanteuse des rues" and also continued with "Irma" (1858 in *La Revue française*; reprinted in *Mes petits-maisons* as "Irma Gilquin"). It is significant that the two novellas in *Les Orages de la vie* and "Une Chanteuse des rues," were initially published in *Le Journal pour tous*, the most downmarket of Barbara's outlets, which deliberately cultivated "popular fiction," by contrast with the "literary fiction" favored by the *Revue de Paris* and *La Revue française*. In slanting "Une chanteuse des rues" toward that market, the author seems to have felt obliged to give it a rather saccharine upbeat ending that contrasts sharply with the natural tendency of his work, as exhibited in the other stories in the present collection, with the exception of the sardonic comedy "Les Douleurs d'un nom." The tragic variants employed ironically in his work, with striking force in such studied laconic narrations as "Les Jumeaux" and "Extraits des rapports d'un agent de police," seem to have been much more in tone with his own frame of mind. His awareness of the unfashionability of that frame of mind is clearly reflected in "Vieille histoire," the narrative frame which offers an interesting fugitive glimpse into one of the *cénacle*s of the era, the ancestors of modern "writers' workshops."

The works Barbara went on to publish in the 1860s continued the sequence begun in "Thérèse Lemajeur" and "Une Chanteuse des rues," and were markedly less innovative than his earlier work, *Le Journal pour tous* then being his primary market, although "Françoise Cottier" (1866 in *La Revue française*) belongs to the same sequence. Censorship under the Second Empire eased somewhat in the 1860s, but Barbara was only able to publish a handful of further stories in that decade, although two of them are substantial in length; his last novel, *Mademoiselle de Saint-Luce* (1864 in *Le Journal pour tous*) only achieved book publication posthumously in 1868, the same year in which his fourth and last collection of short stories and novellas, *Un Cas de con-*

science, *Anne-Marie, L'Herboriste, L'Accordeur, L'Officier d'infanterie de marine* (the compiler evidently could not be bothered to improvise a title for it) was published.

In 1858 Barbara had produced a dramatic adaptation of *L'Assassinat du Pont-Rouge,* which was produced at the Théâtre de la Gaité and enjoyed some success, but he was not able to follow it up. In 1861 he married and had two children, in spite of his awkward financial circumstances, but his wife and daughter died in a typhoid epidemic in 1866 and the consequent mental distress led to his internment in a lunatic asylum, a fate of which he might well have been mortally afraid for some time; he swiftly committed suicide there by jumping out of a window—an end that can be compared and contrasted, with a certain macabre irony, with the conclusion of "Esquisse de la vie d'un virtuoso" (tr. in *My Lunatic Asylum* as "Outline of the Life of a Virtuoso"), which he had penned ten years earlier—and, indeed, with the entire ambiance of *Mes petites-maisons.* "Extraits des rapports d'un agent de police," which, although not straightforwardly autobiographical, undoubtedly draws very extensively on the author's own experiences, clearly reproduces similar anxieties—although the modern reader, in measuring the paranoid aspects of the story, needs to recall that it was written in an era when the Parisian "secret" police were indeed keeping many of the members of the Romantic Movement under active and hostile surveillance. Just because you're paranoid, as the popular saying has it, it doesn't mean that they aren't out to get you.

Although his career lost impetus after the publication of *Histoires émouvantes* and *Mes petites-maisons,* which assembled the best of his work—*Les Orages de la vie* draws material from the same period but is less ambitious—Barbara was undoubtedly an important and innovative writer, who would surely have been able to do more ambitious work had he not been operating in the shadow of censorship, and had he not been under strong pressure following his marriage to produce work appropriate to perceived popular taste. Like Champfleury and his fellow writer of Romantic prose fiction Charles Asselineau, Barbara has tended to be pigeon-holed by literary historians merely as a "friend of Baudelaire," but it would be grossly unfair if his work were to be eclipsed even by such a vast shadow. Barbara was a fine writer, as heroic in his innovations as he was in his tribulations, and he left behind some first-rate works, including the majority of those assembled in his two major collections.

This translation was made from the copy of the 1856 edition of *Histoires émouvantes* reproduced on the Bibliothèque Nationale's *gallica* website.

—Brian Stableford

STIRRING
STORIES

STIRRING STORIES

CHARLES BARBARA (1817-1866), the son of a luthier, became involved in Henry Murger's *Buveurs d'eau* group, before meeting Baudelaire and turning towards literature himself, though also playing the violin as an additional means of support. His first novel, *L'Assassinat du Pont-Rouge*, was first published as a serial in the *Revue de Paris*, before being published in book form in 1857. Other words include his collections *Histoires émouvantes* (1857) and *Mes Petites-Maisons* (1860), and the posthumously published novel *Mademoiselle de Sainte-Luce*.

BRIAN STABLEFORD's scholarly work includes *New Atlantis: A Narrative History of Scientific Romance* (Wildside Press, 2016), *The Plurality of Imaginary Worlds: The Evolution of French roman scientifique* (Black Coat Press, 2017) and *Tales of Enchantment and Disenchantment: A History of Faerie* (Black Coat Press, 2019). He has translated more than three hundred volumes from the French, mostly in the genres of *roman scientifique*, *contes de fées* and Romantic and Symbolist fiction.

His recent fiction includes the visionary science fiction novel *The Revelations of Time and Space* (2020) and its sequel *After the Revelation* (2021); the last in his long series of "Tales of the Genetic Revolution," *The Elusive Shadows* (2020); and the comedy fantasy *Meat on the Bone* (2021), all published by Snuggly Books.

The Twins

WHEN very young, prey to an indomitable curiosity, I witnessed a public execution. I felt simultaneously fearful and glad in thinking that I would never have to fear such a fate. What did I know, though? Who can foresee what the denouement of his life will be, and say: I shall die here or there, of an accident or a disease, at such a time, in such circumstances?

In an absolute detachment from the earth, no longer hoping for anything but death, uniquely in order to obey the urging of my defender, I shall recount the story of my life succinctly. If ever it is read, I challenge any man to say: "That is not true."

Personally, however, I still cannot understand how I have come to be confused with the worst rascals. When I oppose to my youth, my actions, and my incessant rectitude the ignominious execution to which I am condemned, my ideas are troubled; I seem to be the victim of a horrible nightmare, and it requires nothing less than an excessive mental tension to convince me that I am awake . . .

My father was a locksmith in a provincial town. At one time, he employed as many as a dozen workers. He had two daughters, one aged eight and the other nine when my mother, having remained sterile for ten years, became pregnant again and brought into the world, in the same hour, my brother Théodore and myself.

Both born, according to the physician, in the conditions of a long viability, we initially offered the particularity of a resemblance so extraordinary that even our mother, in the beginning, sometimes had to have recourse to a small birthmark that I had on my neck in order to distinguish us from one another.

As we grew older we did not cease to have the same height, the same hair-color, the same complexion, the same eyes and the same features, with the consequence that people who did not know that I had a brother and encountered him in one place, having just seen me in another, believed me to be endowed with ubiquity. No less notable was the fact that the resemblance in question did not stop at the epidermis. We had a similar character, sensibility and tastes. Whatever made my brother weep brought tears to my eyes, and what pleased him caused me pleasure. At school and college we gave evidence of an equal memory and an equal vivacity of comprehension. If my brother was the first, I never failed to be the second, when we were not *ex aequo*.[1] The solemnity of prize-giving was a day of triumph of which my brother and I had full measure. We loved one another enough to be unable to quit one another for a single instant.

That resemblance, however marvelous it appears, is, after all, not new. If nothing is less rare in a family, not to say among strangers, than two faces similar to the point of lending themselves to mistakes, it happens no less frequently that one encounters natures provided with

---

1 i.e. tied.

such analogies that it is permissible, with regard to our imperfect senses, to say, as was said of us: "Here are two identical natures."

Living the same life, under the constant empire of the same impressions, it resulted from our identity that at a given moment, an identical thought crossed both our minds. Among a thousand instances, I shall cite a characteristic one.

Our father was an eccentric man, carried away to excess, whose despotic humor isolated him from the bosom of his family, where he reigned without contradiction. Without saying a word, he endured the harshest contrarieties from outside, and came to relocate them and to rage against them internally. It was necessary for our mother to submit to scenes that he had not dared to make with their rightful object, and to assume the dolors of the despot's wounded pride; for he was not tranquil until he had, in a sense, decanted his annoyances from his own brain into the soul of the poor woman, unless he had a pretext, occasionally, for pouring out his wrath on our backs. He beat us: that entered into his theory of raising children. But, according to his mood, he belabored us with blows for something trivial, or let us off with a simple threat for misdeeds that were really punishable. We had an excessive fear of him. We were on the alert so long as we knew that he was in the house. He dressed at home in a manner that enabled us to recognize him as far as the eye could see. His red skull-cap, his ragged blue frock-coat and his green apron were sufficient to put us to flight. If he had, in addition to that, his arms folded over his breast, we were immediately convinced that he was in search of a victim.

The house of which we occupied the ground floor was made up of two wings separated by an immense courtyard. The family lodgings were situated on the street. At the back of the courtyard were the workshops and the sheds.

One day of leave I was idling in the workshops. I had left Théodore at the front occupied in coloring prints. I knew that my father was absent. A humorous idea suddenly came into my head. I put on the ragged jacket of an apprentice, knotted a red cravat around my neck, put on a dented and staved-in hat, fixed a handkerchief with the aid of a pin to the bottom of my trousers, and in that disguise, at which the workmen laughed joyfully, I went into the courtyard with the intention of going to find my brother.

I had not taken three steps when I stopped, as if struck by lightning. Raising my eyes I perceived the terrible red skullcap of my father, who, his head bowed and his arms folded over his breast, was coming straight toward me. A glacial frisson ran all the way to the marrow of my bones. My head spun. It would not have taken much to make me fall ill. I only just had the presence of mind to turn round in order to flee.

I was stopped again by bursts of laughter that resounded like thunder behind me and in the workshop. Nonplussed, I turned round and perceived that the person I had mistaken at first glance for my father was none other than my brother Théodore, who, at the same moment when I was disguising myself, had put on a red cap, a blue frock-coat and a green apron, and was coming to me as I was going to him. The fit of hilarity that took possession of Théodore and me is easily imaginable.

Dressed in our rags, we set about performing a pantomime. Théodore counterfeited the parental mannerisms perfectly, while I struck the poses of Frédéric Lemaître in *L'Auberge des Adrets*,[1] The workers, young and old, formed a circle around us and took a vivid pleasure in that free performance. But an apparition, really thunderous this time, suddenly troubled the parade and chilled the blood in our veins. Our father really had just emerged at the extremity of the courtyard. With terror in the soul, we took flight like wild geese frightened by a rifle shot. My father, throwing himself upon a knotted rope, was on our heels in the blink of an eye.

The house had several connecting staircases. Stretching our legs to the point of running out of breath, strewing our course with various parts of our disguises, we went up and we went down, only to go up again and go down again, until our father, harassed by fatigue, judged it appropriate to rest, after having administered a few strokes of the rope to us.

Those incidents, and many others of the same sort, did not prevent us from being happy to be alive. Even now, I cannot think about that without my eyes becoming moist. How I would like to return to that time, when I extended my back in order to receive blows destined for my brother, and when Théodore did the same for me. Oh, how beautiful the colors of the sky and the trees were, how quickly troubles and tears were forgotten!

---

1 The drama in question, by Benjamin Antier, first staged in 1823, starred the actor Frédéric Lemaître in the role of the bandit Robert Macaire. Conceived as a melodrama, Lemaître's performance transformed it into a picaresque comedy and made an archetype of its central character, laying the groundwork for the phenomenal success of a sequel, *Robert Macaire* (1834), and numerous imitations.

How brilliant and joyful the perspectives of the future were! How little it cost us then to admit that we were guilty when we were innocent, in order to summon upon us the paternal wrath ready to fall upon our mother or one of our sisters! We supported the pain of correction all the more stoically the more convinced we were that we were innocent. Less in testimony of that than to aid knowledge of my elder sister, who was subsequently to show herself so cruel in my regard, I shall report another anecdote.

We were not thirteen; my elder sister, Augustine, was over twenty. She was rather beautiful, but cruel and selfish; she did not love us. In her opinion, we could have dispensed with being born and eating away a part of her heritage. Unlike Sophie, her junior, who interceded for us when we were beaten, she watched the blows rain down on our shoulders impassively. My mother's sister, an aged spinster who lived with us and loved us tenderly, was sometimes scandalized by that indifference. My father was occupied in arranging a marriage for her, via the intermediary of Théodore's godfather, to a grocer in Paris. She nevertheless had a relationship with a young notary's clerk whom she had met in a house where we went on Sunday to play lotto. She had the imprudence to arrange rendezvous with him in the courtyard of our house. On determined days she went at night to open the small door within the coaching entrance. The young man slipped into a hangar in the depths of the courtyard, where my sister did not take long to join him.

One evening, our father, who had something to do in the workshop, heard movement as he passed the hangar. He plunged his eyes into the darkness and perceived confused forms. Obtaining no response to his interrogation, he went inside; immediately, the forms were animated, and disappeared like shadows. His myopia prevented him from distinguishing clearly silhouettes that he would have recognized immediately with ordinary eyesight. He hastened to go to the workshop to fetch the tool he needed, and he returned with a formal intention of clarifying the matter.

The family was complete; my sister Augustine had just returned, very pale and out of breath. My father was absolutely insistent on knowing who the delinquent or delinquents were. In a tone and manner that presaged a storm, he passed us in review, stopping before each of us and asking: "Is it you?" The denials he received irritated his despotism further. We divined that it was about to explode. My sister Augustine was trembling in every limb. Although my father did not have the custom of beating her, she knew that he was capable, in a fit of fury, of striking her as hard as us.

He appeared to be suspicious of her, and was darting oblique glances at her that were very disquieting. She blushed, paled, leaned against a chair and seemed to be on the point of losing consciousness. We saw the moment coming when her countenance would betray her. Without understanding very well what it was about, except a matter of being beaten, as my father advanced toward Augustine, with a threat in his mouth and his arm raised, Théodore and I, without any common understanding, cried simultaneously: "Father, it's me!"

We were literally put to the question, by the whip and the rope. My father doubted the verity of our assertion; he labored us with blows with the intention of extracting a confession of the lie, but we held firm until the end in spite of atrocious pains. You can judge the violence with which he struck us when you know that we had to stay in bed for three days, and bore the marks of his blows for nearly four months. Well, while we were beaten thus, while my mother, my aunt and my sister Sophie wept and begged our torturer, Augustine took advantage of it to repair the disorder of her costume and to look at herself in the mirror . . .

A few weeks later, my father married her off to the grocer from Paris, assuring her by contract of a sum of ten thousand francs, which was paid three months after the marriage.

I could say that for me, youth—which is to say, the age of insouciance and absolute joys—ended there. The mirages that smiled at us on the horizon and lulled us with happy dreams, were suddenly transformed into sinister clouds. At that time, our father's prosperity, previously increasing, commenced to totter. Dazzled by luck, which had not ceased to be favorable to him, he no longer limited himself to the profits of his estate. He wanted to increase his wealth tenfold rapidly, by means of speculations. He bought a plot of land and had costly constructions raised there.

A few successes emboldened him; he threw himself body and soul into that kind of commerce, and used the credit he had unsparingly. But the majority of the buildings were unfinished, because property suddenly suffered a steep depreciation. The entrepreneurs pressured him; in order to satisfy them he was forced to sell at a loss. Misfortune determined that, at the same time, a notary to whom he had confided his funds disappeared, leaving a considerable deficit. The fortune that he had taken twenty years to build crumbled in the blink of an eye, fatally, like a town under the effect of an earthquake.

In the midst of those disasters, my poor mother, who had been stifling for years under the weight of her husband's irascible humor, was devoid of strength under that avalanche of new dolors, and succumbed. Her death was, so to speak, the knell of the ruination of our house. My father, prey to an immense despair, delivered himself bound hand and foot to what he called destiny. After having glimpsed himself momentarily as one of the rich property-owners of the region, he could not resist the shame of seeing himself ranked among the bankrupt. I cannot write it without being dolorously affected: local people found him one morning drowned in a deep pond not far from the town.

The creditors naturally fell upon his property, which, divided in proportion to their credits, scarcely gave them twenty-five per cent. Our mother had been married under the regime of community of property. My aged aunt, my sister Sophie, my brother and I no longer had anything before us but a road darkened by the horrors of poverty.

Fortunately, we were not abandoned by our family. This is what became of each of us.

In Paris, we still had a maternal aunt who had a confectioner's shop in a prosperous quarter. The excellent woman had the generosity to come to the aid of our misfortune. Not content with taking my sister Sophie into her home in the quality of a shop assistant, she gave, of her own accord, an annual pension of three hundred francs to her sister, our Aunt Thérèse, and convinced her niece Augustine, not without difficulty, to do as much. Théodore's godfather, a merchant esteemed in Paris, showed himself no less generous. He took charge immediately of his godson's future. Charmed by his open and intelligent face, and prejudiced in his favor by the success he obtained in his class-work, he resolved to enable him to continue his studies in the meantime, and enrolled him, to that effect, in the Louis-le-Grand college.

I received the poorest share. My sister Augustine and my brother-in-law agreed to take me into their home with the intention of teaching me the commerce of grocery. Bitterness overflows my soul at the mere memory of the torments with which I was heaped during the brief sojourn I made in that interior, a thousand times more glacial than my cell.

Without counting the bread soaked with tears with which I was nourished and the cold brutalities of my brother-in-law, I was incessantly the target of my sister's shrewish humor. No negro ever had masters more demanding and more ferocious than mine. I carried out my commissions at a run; I returned from them covered in sweat, and yet they always found that I had taken too long. If one or other of them surprised me chewing a roasted coffee bean or a plum, I was pitilessly put on dry bread and deprived of wine.

The art of weighing, in particular, was for me a perpetual source of tortures. Ordinarily, dominated by an instinctive probity, I weighed accurately and forgot to throw the merchandise into the balance and remove it adroitly before the platen rose again. I cannot describe the vocabulary from which my brother-in-law and my sister drew the coarse insults they threw in my face then. But if I pushed forgetfulness as far as giving "extra weight", oh, I could be sure of receiving, for three hours, not to say half a day, thereafter, two or three leg-breaking kicks. By turns, I "stole my bread," or I "wasn't worth the rope to hang me" when my brother-in-law didn't cry "You'll die on the scaffold!" That man, evil as he was, certainly did not think that he was prophesying so truly. I never ceased having fear in my soul, or being bewildered.

From all that bad treatment, it resulted that I had inconceivable distractions, and I arrived, in a sense, at justifying their procedures in my regard. They finally decided, in the profundity of their judgment, that I was incapable of exercising their honest commerce. I was placed in apprenticeship with a man who fabricated iron wire netting.

Although still very young, what I had suffered had matured me rapidly. I already understood that Robinson Crusoe, on his island, at grips with necessity, was no more abandoned than I was in the midst of society. Free of an odious yoke, gripped again by hope, I felt reborn. I worked as few children work. Entirely given to the passion of being self-sufficient and independent, I was active and indefatigable; I solicited items of advice ardently, I collected them like pearls, and by dint of attention I divined what people disdained to teach me. My facility of conception, my manual dexterity and my energy earned me the amity and the encouragement of my employer.

In the meantime, Théodore, spurred on by ideas analogous to mine, justified the sacrifices of his godfather and became his pride, maintaining himself among the most distinguished pupils of his school. I saw him from time to time, on Sunday, in the home of my Aunt Thérèse, who, in spite of the modesty of her annual income, had taken up residence in Paris in order to be close to us. Our mutual affection had lost nothing of its vivacity. If I was glad of his school uniform, he did not blush either at my overall or my black hands. He told me that sometimes, on the benches, he was astonished not to see me by his side, and that he desired then to be a worker, in order to live my life.

We were always so very similar that we sought in vain to explain the difference in our destinies. In any case, I was sure of his sentiments and was confounded with him to the point that I felt as proud of what he was as I would have been in his place. We were truly one soul in two, comparable to a little river, on which we had often floated in our childhood, which, in order to bifurcate and hollow out two beds, did not cease to have a single source and remain nevertheless the same water.

I shall pass over those years of my life as rapidly as they passed, in effect, for me, for they were, if not happy, at least tranquil. I earned my living, and Théodore was about to leave school. The businessman, liberal by reason of the praise he received of his godson, wanted him to be initiated into the arts of pleasure and bodily exercise. Théodore drew, was a musician and played the flute, knew how to handle weapons, ride a horse and swim. He was not only well educated, he also had a most attractive exterior.

Many dissimilarities could already be observed between us. If it was still impossible for the least expert eye to be mistaken as to our common origin, it was nevertheless certain that my brother was much better developed than me. With broader shoulders, more solid arms and stronger hands, I had legs thinner than his. Instead of walking upright and braced like him, my torso leaned forward and my back increasingly ended to roundness. I will add that the fire of the forge, filing iron, and sunburn, had darkened my complexion singularly. Then too, his clothes had a cut that mine did not have, and that alone would have been sufficient to differentiate us considerably.

Neither proud nor ambitious for having made brilliant studies, Théodore obeyed his godfather's desires as orders. He accepted a position as a clerk in his organization, with a minimal salary, which, thanks to his zeal, soon rose to twelve hundred francs. He then became an integral part of the family. He ate at the employer's table, heard himself called "my son" by the mother, and talked about music and drawing with their only daughter, Hortense, who treated him as a brother while waiting to see him as a fiancé.

In our Sunday conversations, united more than ever in a similar future, we strolled in imagination through the new perspectives of happy days that had opened before us. He lent me a capital, I established myself, and both of us, separated for a time by hazard, at the head of a commerce of equal prosperity, recommenced going through life side by side, as in the fine days of our childhood.

Dazzling illusions, destined, in a way, uniquely to illuminate the depths of the abyss in which my existence was to be so miserably extinguished!

Without loving one another less profoundly, my brother had his friends and I had mine. The life of young men of our age is well-known. If, today, one does not usually find it bad that a young man goes to the café or the dance-hall, one gladly absolves a worker who frequents the taverns and the barrières. In any case, we only used those pleasures moderately, and both us had already put a brake on the disorders to which the ardor of our temperament might lead us. It seemed written that the events of our lives would unfurl perpetually in imitation of two parallel chains.

Like my brother, who, assured of the dispositions of his godfather, allowed the seed of a durable affection for Hortense to develop, I became fond of the sister of one of my work comrades. One cannot be any more in love than I was. At present, when I evoke her touching and pale image, my entire body quivers with emotion. Amour, in being revealed to me, enlarged my life and gave it a goal. It was a center around which all my thoughts rotated. I attest that, if my fiancée had not died, amour would have affirmed me forever in the straight road from which I had not yet deviated. Probably, without effort and without struggle, my actions would have succeeded one another in the bosom of an atmosphere of simplicity and honor, and perhaps I would never even have suspected the opportunity to fall.

She was not to live. Scarcely had I glimpsed her than a ferocious fate prepared to snatch her away from me. Although she was frail of constitution and before long she was having frequent spasms, no one suspected as yet that her illness was incurable and approaching the crisis that determined a rapid decline toward death. Ever more passionate as I got to know her better, after eighteen months of frequentation, I made a formal request to her family. They replied to me that we could only marry when I had accomplished the customary pilgrimage of the workman through France. I departed full of enthusiasm, not without having embraced my brother and kissed amorously the forehead of the woman that I already regarded as my wife.

But, wearily, my expression is languishing and rebellious to rendering what I feel, and it seems cold to me, to the chagrin that is invading my soul, to spell out, in imitation of a book-keeper, this, that and the other. I would like to say everything in a rush, in a flash, for the sentiment that fills me and penetrates me is all one . . .

I went from town to town; I was received as a companion. I remember. Because of my courage, my promptitude to render service and my probity, I was given a nickname. In the workshops, on my report book I was no longer called anything but Joseph the Glorious. Although people found in the double meaning of that epithet one more reason to abuse me, I was glad of it, for it was to spare my family name a stigma and my brother the despair of knowing about my ignominious death.

I was only a third of the way through my journey when alarming news struck me in the heart. My fiancée's health was giving rise to the most intense anxieties. Troubled and indecisive, wondering whether I ought to go forward or retrace my steps, I learned from a second letter, awaited for a month in the midst of mortal anxieties, that there was despair for her life.

I returned very quickly. I could not believe in my misfortune. I counted on saving her by means of the omnipotence of my passion. When I saw her I was struck by her paleness and the extraordinary gleam of her eyes. I no longer quit her room. For several weeks I lived in poignant alternatives. She got better momentarily, soon to decline again, until the day when I was convinced that she would perish. I was stifled by anguish; I emerged to shed floods of tears.

The convulsions of her death-throes finished crushing me. Truly, although I had a robust body, mentally, I was agonizing too. I wish to God that I had died at the same time as her. A frightful presentiment entered into my flesh like a poisoned dagger: the sensation that with that angel, all hope of happiness and repose in this world had flown away . . .

My unfathomable grief followed the course of all grief; it was exhausted of its own accord, and my tears dried up. Gradually, my chagrin turned to bitterness and heaped me with a sort of voluptuous sadness. My fiancée's charms received new perfections from absence. I felt so sadly proud of having had the love of a woman such that I could not imagine a second, and I placed her cherished image in a secret corner of my soul with a religious pride. However, there were times when life was insupportable to me. The need to talk to her and to hear, if only the murmur of a beloved voice, devoured me.

At that time I only saw my brother rarely; he was absorbed, on the one hand, by the duties of his position, and on the other by the pleasure that ran, in a sense, before him. I sometimes had the sad courage to seek in drunkenness an alleviation of my despair, but I only extracted from it one suffering more: that of being ashamed of myself. It was on one of those funereal days when my soul, mortally sad, wanted no longer to be, that I met a woman, the memory of whom will cause a blush to rise to my face and scorn for myself to tear my breast all the way to the scaffold.

One Saturday evening—how could I forget that detail?—I was returning from my workshop rather late, because it was pay day. Buried in the most somber ideas, I crossed the Rue Sainte-Anne. I was no more than a few paces from my lodgings when I suddenly heard the sound of labored respiration and the rustle of a dress. I turned round. A woman seized my arm, saying breathlessly: "Act as if I were with you, or I'm doomed."

Ignorant of what the matter was, but moved by the cry of distress, I acceded to that plea. Three paces further on, a man armed with a cudgel caught up with us, and was obstinate in staring at us with such affectation that I was on the point of speaking to him. The woman deflected me from that by squeezing my wrist with her clenched fingers and stammering familiar banalities. The stranger, discountenanced by the calmness of our attitude and our indifference in his regard, soon went away, with a marked displeasure.

I waited for an explanation of that scene. The woman, still on my arm, began to look down her nose at me and laugh. Finally, she said: "I've had a narrow escape. But for you I'd have got at least three months." I understood that I was dealing with a prostitute and that it was a matter of avoiding the police.

At her door, unthinkingly, I tried to continue on my way. She stopped me. "I'm alone," she said. "You aren't coming up to rest for a moment?"

There was nothing indecent in her tone or her manner. In spite of that, I felt a spontaneous repugnance. Then I hesitated. Subsequently, I felt the spur of an intense curiosity. The frankness with which she repeated her invitation caused me to dread passing in her eyes for a simpleton. I went with her. In the light, I perceived a woman who was still young, whose face had a remote resemblance to the woman I was mourning. That observation suddenly revived my wounds and nearly caused me to burst into tears.

She questioned me. "What's wrong?" she asked, with interest. "You don't seem very cheerful."

Would you believe it? My heart was so heavy, and I was having so much difficulty containing the grief that swelled it, that I seized with a sort of joy the opportunity to let it overflow. Into those ears, which could only lead to a miry soul, I did not hesitate to spill the story of the holiest amour there ever was. To my great surprise, I saw tears in her eyes.

"Poor boy!" she said.

I experienced relief.

She added: "Your tears only make her return. It's necessary not to think about her any longer."

For a few moments we didn't say anything more. Under the gaze of the woman, who was emboldened to the point of staring at me, emotion overtook me.

Suddenly, in a voice whose tone further increased my trouble, with her eyes still upon me, she said: "You're a handsome fellow, you know. You please me. I don't have a lover, would you like to be mine?"

I considered her with a mixture of astonishment and fear. That point-blank declaration determined a painful struggle in my soul. I understood, vaguely, the gravity of the response that I was about to make. By turns, yes and no strayed over my lips. My indecision was an infamy in itself, and I would be punished for it. Oh, morality cracks more easily than glass breaks. If a man could know all of its fragility, the slightest oscillation would frighten him.

My uncertainty deceived the woman, She thought I was hesitating out of timidity. Strengthened by my weakness, she came to sit down on my knees. I woke up the next morning in her home. And in spite of that admission, these confessions ought not to be rejected with disgust. I have admitted the fault; you shall know the torture. It commenced on the first day and will only conclude with the end of my life.

A sentiment had pursued me for a long time, which I had never combated energetically because I did not believe it to be susceptible to realization. When I perceived an actress in the theater who was applauded for her effrontery, or a young woman in a ballroom whose scandalous dancing provoked enthusiasm, I could not help feeling, deep down, a desire to be loved by one of those women. Now, while that despicable wish was partly realized in the most unexpected manner, how did it come about that I was sad, oppressed, and ashamed, that I wanted to hide and to bury my liaison in an impenetrable secrecy?

All those preventive measures against myself, with the aid of which I tried to delude myself! I never set foot in her bedroom. In an excursion to the country, I would not allow her to spend a centime; I insisted on supporting all the expense myself. I exhausted my purse with a view to pleasing her, and I did not want to receive a pin from her. She understood my scruples, however, and strove to protect them. It was not enough; twenty times I made the resolution not to see her again. That was because, in the confusion of my ideas, I sensed that, for an honest man, there is no motive capable of sanctioning relations of that sort. It was because my conscience, the integrity of which I was eroding, revolted, and forbade me to behave badly. I walked, so to speak, bowed down by the weight of my own scorn; I suffered all the more because, in spite of my incessant precautions, my work comrades had discovered my passion and sometimes made allusion to it in wounding terms.

One morning, I encountered my brother, who seemed to be standing sentinel in the Rue de l'Ancienne-Comédie. Before accosting him I could not resist the pleasure of walking in his shadow and consuming him with my eyes. On returning from my voyage I had found Théodore as the cashier in his godfather's business, on a high salary.

He seized my arms precipitately. "I'm glad to see you," he said.

"What are you doing here?"

"I'm waiting for my witnesses." To my astonishment, he told me: "A monsieur has insulted me; I sent him two of my friends; it's necessary for him to make apologies, or to fight."

I asked him the subject of the quarrel. Théodore made me wait for his response. Finally, he told me, in an embarrassed tone, that he was in love. I interrupted him in order to exclaim: "What about Hortense?"

"I still love her as much," he replied. "The other is only a caprice, a chance passion. She is truly adorable, my friend, maintained, it's true, but she has such a good heart. I stole her from a fop who is mad about her. Yesterday, at the dance-hall, in a fit of jealousy, he accused me of living at her expense . . ."

As Théodore spoke, cruel reflections flooded my mind. I could not ecstasize enough at that conformity of destiny. At the moment when I was linking myself with a prostitute, it was necessary that my brother make the acquaintance of a woman who was scarcely any better.

I did not understand how Théodore could be in love with two women at the same time, when, if my fiancée had lived, I was convinced that I would never have had any other amour.

In fact, I thought, *the mores of the people in whose midst he lives explain his conduct, if they do not excuse it.*

At any rate, I did not have the courage to sadden him with observations. His witnesses soon brought him, not only excuses written in the humblest terms, but also an invitation to breakfast on the part of the accuser. While being proud, privately, of the firmness of my brother, I thought that, among my comrades, the worker feeble enough to express such excuses would be considered the most cowardly of men.

Without hesitation, Théodore introduced me to his friends as another self. They immediately treated me with amity, and wanted to take me with them. I emerged from the table with my head slightly tipsy, but I nevertheless went to my employer's establishment with the intention of working there until the evening.

When I arrived, it might have been half past two. The workers were waiting in the courtyard for the work-bell to ring. Some, lying full length on the ground in the sun, were sleeping or smoking; the others, leaning on the wall of supporting themselves with their elbows on the ground, were chatting and laughing. My entrance occasioned a silence by which I was offended. I caught some of them looking at me with a knowing expression.

I had been subjected to the same mortifications twenty times over without taking any notice. At that moment, under the influence of I know not what nervous irritability, I was seized by impatience and stared boldly at a group more provocative than the others. They all lowered their heads, with one exception, who met my gaze with a menacing intrepidity. I marched toward him.

"Why are you looking at me like that?" I said to him.

He got up and looked at me with even wider eyes, in a scornful manner. I was ready to hurl myself at him, but a comrade deflected the quarrel with a word.

"Come on, Joseph," he said. "If he's looking at you like that it's because he finds you handsome."

A tall and robust worker, about forty-five years old, who was reputed to encourage the disorders of his daughter and to profit from them, had the imprudence to stimulate the dispute. "The fact is," he said, "that one doesn't see such a pretty fish every day."

All my anger, on the point of being extinguished, was reawakened against that man.

"As one might say, in talking about you, that one rarely sees one as old and as ugly."

The burst of laughter that my reply provoked exasperated the worker. He was, in any case, of a violent humor. Abandoning allusion for blunt speech, he launched at me the crudest epithet that can be addressed to a man, an ignoble insult under which, in the language of the marketplace, an associate of prostitutes, who lives on their infamous amours, is castigated. The blood rose from my breast to my head through all is channels with the rapidity of a rocket. It seemed to me that my eyeballs departed like bullets and that my temples were about to explode.

My muscles taut to breaking point and my fists clenched, I cried "Take that back!" in despair and ready to burst into tears.

Instead of responding to me, no less furious than me, he put himself *en garde*. Everyone formed a circle around us.

The contest was equal. If my adversary had strength superior to mine, I was much more agile than him. I avenged by the number of my blows the violence of his. The fear of being vanquished by me redoubled his rage. At one moment, collecting himself into a ball and bracing himself, he bounded like a stone from a sling. Counting on my resistance, he was no longer touching the ground; but I stepped sideways, he found empty air and fell. It was impossible for him to get up again; he had broken his leg.

That brawl and the accident that followed it were variously received in the surroundings. The wife and daughter of the wounded man went to complain to the police commissaire, who hastened to draw up an official document. I was summoned before the tribunal of correctional police on a charge of having inflicted voluntary wounds that occasioned an incapacity to work.

The majority of the witnesses that I cited, either out of malevolence or timidity, were confused in their testimony. The best disposed affirmed that they believed me to be drunk. Only my employer made a brief declaration in my favor. The public minister was nevertheless obstinate in establishing a comparison between "an aged man of irreproachable conduct, the unique support of a numerous family" and a worker of low morals who did not blush at living in concubinage with a public prostitute. My advocate, for whom my case was the debut, spoke at length but without succeeding in being heeded. I was sentenced to a month in prison, a fine of fifteen francs and damages of fifty francs.

I cannot express the anger provoked in me by that punishment, which I was well-founded in thinking unjust. For I no longer know how many days, subjected to all sorts of insults, I had given proof of a forbearance without example. That seemed to me to be all the more meritorious because I had great difficulty moderating the ardor of my blood.

My patience suddenly ran out at the worst of outrages. To a retraction that I demanded my adversary had responded with a provocation. He was much more robust than me. I had only succeeded in equalizing our strength by wearying his vigor. The accident could only be attributed to chance, if not to his clumsiness. Why was I condemned? Because I had a relationship with a prostitute. My conscience warned me well enough how shameful that was, but what had that to do with the results of the quarrel? Evidently, in the balance in which the judge weighed the actions of others, prejudice counted for more than the crime.

I understood in that the power that the law has to give a man a profound terror. It is better to come to grips with the waves of the sea than to fall into the hands of human justice. At the sentiment of revolt that rumbled in my breast I felt as mad as if I had tried to batter down the walls of my cell with blows of my head.

I emerged from prison misanthropic. My employer, inflexibly severe when it was a matter of probity and interest, was very flexible with regard to anything else. Not judging my case a hanging matter, he made no difficulty about taking me on again. Nevertheless, he said: "You're spinning a bad thread. People who have had dealings with the law are like those who have attempted suicide; people affirm that they always recommence, and end up fatally in consequence. My opinion is that you'd do well to redouble surveillance of yourself and break it off with your prostitute, or misfortune will overtake you."

That prophetic advice responded to my own sentiments, but, without perceiving it, I had become excessively attached to that woman. I could reason with myself, and combat her memory as much as I liked, my suffering was intolerable as soon as I ceased seeing her, always bringing me back to her. It happened frequently that I signified to her that she must choose either to break with me or to renounce her ignoble profession. In reality, with the firm desire to please me, she enumerated so many formalities to fulfill, so many obstacles to overcome, that I was convinced that I was asking for something almost impossible. I limited myself then to quarreling with her, to seeing her less frequently, to trying to ensure, by a redoubling of precautions, that no one suspected me of renewing my relationship with her, and finally by saying every time, as I quit her: "I shall never see you again."

Nearly nine months passed in the midst of those cruel pains. I was already mistaking for tranquility the sinister calm that precedes catastrophes. In the cloud of laxity in which I was asleep, the lightning was gathering that was about to complete my ruination. To tell the truth, recalling my uncertainties and struggles of that time, it seems to me that in our capital actions, we are only masters of the first, and that once the first has been committed, fatality connects the others.

It was not rare that, toward the end of the month, my employer, who kept his books himself, gave me evidence of an exceptional confidence by sending me to settle invoices. One afternoon, he confided me a bill for the sum of three hundred francs, payable by a proprietor who lived in the vicinity of Chaillot. He instructed me not to waste any time, because he had a great deal to pay out the next day.

The length of the journey and the obligation I had to wait some time for the signature of the note, meant that I returned rather late. I had about my person two hundred-franc banknotes fixed in a side pocket by means of a pin and a hundred francs in gold, carefully wrapped, in one of my fob pockets. By comparison with the sums I had already handled, that amount was not very much.

Although I was marching with my head down, with the appearance of a man carrying a treasure, my preoccupations were elsewhere. I traversed the Champs-Élysées at the height of the roundabout. I heard my name pronounced, and shivered. Raising my eyes I perceived my mistress in company with two women and three men. Truly ashamed to have encountered them, I gave her a glacial welcome and quit her abruptly. She ran after me.

"You're jealous," she said to me, "but you're wrong. That man is paying court to me, but he means nothing to me."

At first, I did not have the sentiments that she attributed to me. I had fled for fear of being seen with her. From the fact that there were three women and three cavaliers I had not drawn any consequence. But her insinuation disturbed me, and the intoxication of jealousy suddenly went to my head. She told me then that the women were old acquaintances who, encountering her that morning, had persuaded her to spend the day with them, and added that it was only up to me to join the party.

I looked at the man who was laying claim to the heart of my mistress; he was better dressed than me, albeit in a somewhat slovenly manner; he looked me up and down with an expression of superiority and scorn that wounded me cruelly and inspired a resolution contrary to the most elementary prudence. Saying to myself that my employer only needed the money between then and the next day, and that I had no lack of excuses to justify my lateness, I obeyed blindly the hand that drew me away ...

I was, however, taciturn and in a state of mind near to desolation. I only went reluctantly into a barrière tavern. At first I refused to drink. The people with whom I found myself inspired in me, if not mistrust, at least a profound aversion. They were madly cheerful, and filled the establishment with their bursts of laughter and songs.

My presence did not seem to inhibit in the least the individual who had awakened my jealousy. He put his arm around the waist of my mistress and kissed her in front of me. The feeble resistance that she opposed to that boldness gradually threw me into a muted irritation.

I thought I saw that she was encouraging the pretentions of my rival, and I was gripped by a violent chagrin.

Soon determined to get the upper hand and separate myself from her irrevocably, I drank under the pretext of giving myself courage, although it was only with a view to numbing myself. I did not cease to empty my glass, which was constantly full.

Gradually, drunkenness overtook me. Nothing any longer escaped my lips but divagations. My head was heavy, I was incapable of standing upright. I ended up losing my memory, and even the sentiment of my own existence.

Thus, the next day, when I opened my eyes, I tried in vain at first to understand how I came to be lying in my mistress's bedroom. Scarcely was it permitted for me to reassemble two memories, however, than I leapt to the floor and bounded to my garments, which were lying on a chair. I plunged my hand into my side pocket: nothing! With jerky and feverish gestures I explored all my pockets. Rapidly, I visited my fob pockets, turning my clothes over and over. Nothing! Nothing!

I felt large drops of sweat filtering through my flesh on my forehead and my dace. A hypothesis electrified my mind. I turned to my mistress. Half-dressed on the bed, as motionless as a block of marble, she was looking at me with wide-open eyes. A question and a response emerged simultaneously from our throats, which resembled two cries of despair.

"What's the matter?" she said.

"My employer's money?" I cried.

I became as pale as her, and was frightened by the fearful expression that she had.

Our reciprocal attitude revealed the truth sufficiently in all its horror. Without meaning to, that woman, to her inexpressible dolor, had led me into a trap.

Mute and bleak, while I sat on a chair, holding my head, which was ready to split, in my hands, she got dressed in haste and went out. I don't know how long she remained outside. Throughout that time, I remained motionless, plunged in a sort of dolorous torpor. I floated between life and death. I had lugubrious visions, and felt that I was collapsing into a gulf. I did not budge until my mistress returned. I fixed my eyes upon her. The sight of her multiplied my tortures a hundredfold. She was fearfully white, panting, dragging herself along rather than walking. She could scarcely sustain herself, she no longer dared to look at me.

For a part of the day she had run around in vain, trying to find her friends of the previous day. With the greatest effort she had been unable to discover the tracks of those who had robbed me. One can only imagine approximately the state that the unfortunate woman was in. The inventory of her bedroom and her chest of drawers made her prey to the delirium of dolor. Like the majority of her peers, she lacked savings and order. A large fraction of her clothes and underwear were in pawn. Her jewels, her rings, her watch and its chain, half silver and half copper, did not have an intrinsic value greater than twenty-five francs. As for her furniture, of which she could dispose, since she paid her rent in advance every week, she would not have obtained more than a hundred francs for it from a second-hand dealer. She knew, in any case, that she occasioned me too much expense for me reasonably to suppose that she had any savings . . .

Suddenly, the word "thief" exploded in my brain like a pistol shot and made me jump. I fled. I only succeeded in calming down slightly after having written to my brother to meet me that same evening, at the home of my Aunt Thérèse.

My brother loves me as much as I love him, I said to myself. *He is ready to die for me, as I am ready to die for him. That I can rely on him it would be odious to doubt. He is housed, nourished, and earns two hundred francs a month; he must have money put aside. At the worst, supposing that he has not, it will still be possible for him to ask his godfather for an advance.*

Like all people that want something passionately, I exhausted all the hypotheses susceptible of opposing me, and, putting things at the worst, I did not even glimpse the possibility of a failure. I forgot that events almost always deceive our previsions, however profound and subtle they may be. One is utterly surprised, at the moment of the denouement to see an objection surge forth of which one has not thought.

The profoundly desolate and ashamed fashion in which my brother came toward me immediately threw me into a great disturbance. I examined his face with amazement. Pale and distraught, with his eyes reddened by recent tears, he lowered his head and seemed fearful of meeting my gaze. The negligence of his costume struck me immediately.

I threw my arms around his neck. He received my caresses without returning them and burst into sobs. Clawed by anxiety, I asked him what was wrong. For a few moments he gave evidence of the most violent chagrin. I begged him to have compassion for me. He told me, in a voice punctuated by tears, a story—oh, a story to make one die on the spot, even more horrible than mine.

His passion for the maintained woman, over whom he had nearly fought a duel, had drawn him to commit a truly blameworthy action. I have heard it said that nothing is costlier than a mistress who does not traffic her favors. Although he did not give her money routinely, she was nevertheless a cause of ruin for him. A salary twice his own would not have sufficed for the minor expenses of superfluities, such as carriages, plays, excursions to the country and garments, that are necessary for those women. He was still in debt for rather large sums.

The woman had turned his head by dint of beauty and coquetry. She no sooner appeared in a dance-hall than she was immediately surrounded by courtiers and assailed with the most brilliant offers. My poor brother loved her madly, he lost his head. A frantic jealousy made him impatient to be her sole possessor. She consented, in a moment of generosity, no longer to draw gold from all purses and to limit her luxury to my brother's resources. She pushed abnegation as far as liquidating some of her jewels and dresses. But her sacrifice, to which she did not glimpse an end, did not hold up before the apprehensions of the end of the month. She had bills to pay, she owed three months' rent on her apartment, she needed clothing, etc.

"Unless I have a thousand francs immediately," she said one day, "I shall find myself on the street tomorrow."

For my unfortunate brother that was an order to bring her that sum or not to return. Prey to despair, he spent an entire night seeking a solution to an impossible problem, and finally resolved to take an action of which his frantic passion hid the indignity from him.

In the three years that Théodore had been his cashier, his godfather, who had a boundless confidence in him, had only looked at the books two or three times. My brother, in his fever, calculated that it would be easy to extract a thousand francs from the safe and to replace them in less than six months, without anyone noticing. In any case, admitting a premature discovery of the deficit, pretexts flowed from his mind to give acceptable reasons for it.

He had been mistaken in all his calculations. On the one hand, the woman took the thousand francs and disappeared; on the other, at the same time, his godfather, who had no work to do, took it into his head to check the state of the safe and the books. The surprise of the employer at the conclusion of his task, the impatience with which he awaited the return of his son-in-law and the mysterious fashion in which he summoned him to his study were clearly remarked by the clerks.

The scene was long and terrible. My brother, incapable of sustaining a lie, confessed everything. Shame and remorse threw him at his godfather's knees. His throat full of sobs, his face streaming with tears, he begged him for a long time not to be pitiless. He showed that he understood the extent of his fault; he swore that no punishment would approach the one that the memory of his action would inflict on him perpetually.

The indignation and anger of his godfather gradually ebbed away before the sincerity of that repentance. He decided not to expel him, and to keep his dishonor secret, but after reflecting momentarily, he said, with the expression of a judge:

"You understand, Monsieur, that you can no longer remain in your post. You are no longer to be anything but what you were when you entered here, a simple clerk with a salary of a thousand francs. You will cease, until further notice, to eat at my table and spend your evenings in my home. See whether that suits you."

All in tears, Théodore added: "At the same time I have lost my future and poisoned my life forever. I was almost the equal of my godfather, and now I am reduced to the lowest rank. To complete my shame, my comrades, who have vague suspicions, are showing me scorn and distancing themselves from me. They cannot succeed, however, in despising me as much as I despise myself. May it please God that I have the strength to support such a horrible existence! I might obtain my pardon from others, but I shall never obtain it from my conscience."

Breathless, thunderstruck, I listened to my brother and forgot myself. When he had finished, two despairs instead of one lacerated me and tortured me. I was gripped by terror at the aspect of those two destinies, which were obstinate in unfurling in parallel. I began to believe that I was doomed to misfortune, and thought that my brother doubtless was also, and that idea further stimulated the fire that was burning in my breast.

Théodore thought of asking me what I wanted of him. There was no point in adding my suffering to his own. I replied that I had simply asked him to come because I felt the need to see him. I tried to revive his courage and I quit him. I was already prey to a new hope.

In a few strides I was in the street where my sister Augustine lived. The shop was closed. To have an idea of my night it is necessary to suppose something impossible, for example, a man suspended by his fingernails for twelve hours above a gulf of four hundred feet. In the morning, I ran into my sister's shop. The establishment had grown to the point that two errand-boys had become necessary. My sister was at the market with her maid. Her husband was still asleep.

When I returned, my brother-in-law told me that his wife was visiting a sick neighbor. The stings of a thousand wasps pricked my heart. Finally, I caught up with Augustine. It was past noon. I begged her to come with her husband into the back room of the shop. There, in a voice strained by anguish, I told them succinctly what had happened to me. I only omitted one thing: the shameful condition of my mistress.

Scarcely had I said that my employer's three hundred francs had been stolen than my sister cried: "That's a lie!"

From white I became red. "Augustine," I said, with a contained anger, "I have only ever lied once, and you ought to remember the occasion."

It was my sister's turn to blush. But she recovered promptly. "I thought that was Théodore," she stammered. "But no matter. What do you want?"

"For you to lend me three hundred francs."

"We don't have them."

"Think," I said, with an energy in which there was fear and tears, "that it is a matter for me of prison and a dishonor that will reflect on you."

"All our funds are placed," replied my sister, coldly. "We don't have a hundred francs in the house."

"You won't borrow in order to save me from infamy!" I cried, my fists on my temples.

50

"Come back in a few days; we'll see whether we can let you have fifty francs."

"It's three hundred francs that I need, and right away!"

"Oh, then go look for them elsewhere."

I doubt that any man, whoever he might be, could have as much eloquence, heart and soul as I had during the following two hours. I would have succeeded in convincing a tiger and making it weep. But there are relatives compared with whom hyenas have entrails. I might as well have been addressing myself to the bones of a sepulcher.

Her husband, less pitiless than her, allowed himself to be touched by my despair. She froze his pity with a glance. I was on the point of reminding her that she had had ten thousand francs from my father when we had not had a sou. I understood by her face that it would only irritate her uselessly. In any case, hope had no sooner vanished within me than a new one was born.

I had wasted precious time. Perhaps it was already too late. I ran to the home of my aunt who kept the confectioner's shop. I hardly knew her, but she had the reputation of being sensitive and generous.

Admire the genius of misfortune when it has sworn to crush a man! On entering the shop I learned the most disastrous news; my aunt and my sister were not there; they had left the day before to attend the wedding of a distant relative who lived in the Aube. They would not be back for at least three weeks.

At that last blow I was seized by a terror comparable to that of drowning. My mind near to going astray, I made a sort of tour of myself, hoping to discover a rope on to which to cling. If I had felt guilty, I would not have hesitated to have recourse to suicide. But to die while an accusation of theft weighed upon me would have been to condemn myself; that was impossible.

I went to the home of my master; I should have commenced there.

"Ah, there you are," he said, in a mocking tone. "I thought you were dead. Your description is already with the commissaire of police."

I lacked air; I was stifling; my knees were knocking. Forced to catch my breath at every syllable, in a stammering tone, I told him about the theft of which I had been the victim.

"You've certainly taken your time to bring me this strange news," he said.

I justified my delay by the steps I had taken with a view to making up the sum that had been stolen from me.

"Are you at least bringing me my money?" he asked.

"No," I said, "but I've come to offer to work for you without receiving a centime until the three hundred francs are repaid."

The man, although full of probity, was, as I have said, ferocious as soon as it was a question of interest.

"Pooh! A fool's bargain!" he cried. "You might fall ill and die. Who would pay me then? In any case," he went on, "how do I know that you haven't eaten that money? You live with a prostitute. I've warned you."

I spoke about my error as a crime and I swore to renounce the creature forever.

"It was necessary to come immediately," he said. "It's too late now. You've caused me to miss a payment. It's a credit of three thousand francs that you've caused me to lose. Then too, I'd be setting a fine example to my workers! What's done is done. Go see the commissaire. Make your deposition there."

Ignorant of the trap that he was setting for me, and not thinking, in any case, of fleeing, I went to the police officer the following day.

First of all, he asked my name. I told him. He read a piece of paper that was on his desk.

"You've arrived just in time," he said. "I was about to mount a search for you." After having scanned the piece of paper again, he said: "You live with a prostitute. You've stolen three hundred francs from your master."

I protested energetically against that accusation. He listened to me willingly. After a long interrogation he summoned my mistress before him, and confronted us. The explanations we gave him doubtless did not satisfy him, for he told us that he found it necessary to keep us under arrest. I was conducted by two agents to the Prefecture depot . . .

I understood that I had nothing more to do than recommend myself to God's mercy. I was caught in a machine that seemed to be to me what a mill is to a grain of wheat. Plunged in a sort of lethargic prostration, I obeyed the people in whose power I was mechanically. I had no more tears in my body; my fibers were slack and limp; even my faculty of suffering was worn out.

I had one moment of reawakening and hope, however. That was when an officially-appointed advocate visited me in my prison. He invited me to tell him my story. Sitting on a bench with his legs crossed and his eyes closed, he never ceased, while I was speaking, to rotate his thumbs in opposite directions. He finally interrupted me to say, winking slyly: "Yes, yes, I see how it is. Far from being the author of the theft of which we're accused, we sustain that we've been robbed. It's not new, but it still succeeds sometimes. There's hope."

The man's face respired nothing but sordidness. He was already old and entirely bald. His inferior lips formed a projection like a bowl into which his red nose, as long and mobile as a trunk, seemed to be dripping two or three black teeth. His large pale blue bulging eyes and his flat ears, like two oyster shells, completing making him a nightmarish individual. Well, at that moment I envisaged him with the enthusiasm that must transport a saint at the sight of an archangel.

"Save me," I cried, "and my gratitude will be eternal!"

"Hmm," he said. "Do you have relatives or friends?"

Under the threat of the most cruel torture, I would not have named my brother. "No, Monsieur," I said.

"Do you have any money?" To my embarrassment, he hastened to add: "It's not that I'm asking you for any. My devotion is gratuitous. Your affair isn't bad, we'll obtain the minimum."

I fell back into a bleak dejection.

From the examining magistrate and the interview with my defender it resulted that the day of the assizes delivered me to the most sinister anticipations. I acquired therefrom the sad experience that the misfortune one foresees arrives sooner than the good for which one hopes. Moreover, after having heard the speech of the public prosecutor and my advocate's reply, I confess that if I had been called to testify, my mind would have been very perplexed. Twenty arguments were raised against me. I frequented bad places. I had a public prostitute for a concubine. It was not the first time that I had sat on the bench of the accused. I had already been imprisoned for having, in my fever of doing harm, broken the leg of "the respectable father of a family." I could not stop there. Evil engenders evil. Once engaged in the ladder of crime it is necessary to descend all the steps. When one lives in disorder, when one has no other law than evil passions, resources do not take long to be lacking, and one has recourse to theft. That is what I had done. Did not the nickname of Glorious that I had received in the workshops indicate in me the excessive vanity that impels a man to all crimes? At a first fault I had found the judges indulgent; I had not been touched by that magnanimity of justice. By recidivism, I seemed to be in haste to prove that I was incorrigible. One could not, without peril for society, protect its indefatigable enemies; a severe repression was necessity, etc., etc.

What could a man who had not listened to me reply to all that? Nothing, except lies or commonplace rebuttals. In fact, he recounted a life that was not mine and threw himself into banal considerations that had no relationship with me. It was with a stupefaction neighboring on despair that I heard my defender declare that I had nobly admitted my crime and exhibited a profound repentance. Instead of invoking the impartiality of the law, he recommended me as a guilty man to the mercy of the judges. I had a desire to stand up and defend myself, but shame and dolor nailed me to my bench. I heard myself sentenced, attenuating circumstances being admitted, to five years in prison and ten years of surveillance. My mistress—or at least, the woman who had been, for she was no longer—was acquitted.

The incessant victim of the ruses of I know not what power, it was not sufficient that I be ripped apart by wounds, it was also necessary that I live with my scars. My heart was no sooner filled with suffering and ready to overflow than an invisible hand made an incision, so to speak, by which it was emptied. Thus, by dint of suffering, I had come to believe that I could not be any more unfortunate, and to that belief I was resigned. I was nevertheless obliged to acquire the certainty that there is no man so unfortunate that he cannot become more so.

Like many people, I had floated before then between good and evil, not because I was inherently vicious, but for fear of becoming a saint. I presumed that once having set foot on the road of scruples, one cannot turn back, and that from one exigency to the next, one arrives at a relative perfection that excludes all happiness. Without suspecting that in that state one extracts a calm that substitutes in large measure for the paltry joys that one is losing, I was presently resolved to despoil the old man, with all the more ardor because, like a clumsy person who breaks everything he touches, it seemed that I was incapable of moving without doing harm. I will add that the revolting disproportion between my fault and the punishment that was inflicted on me inspired sentiments of victimization and caused me a kind of bitter sensuality.

Under the influence of an exaltation of martyrdom I experienced an imperious need not to justify in future even the appearance of a reproach. My destiny, it is true, was to decide otherwise. Nevertheless, those dispositions rendered prison life bearable to me. I gradually wearied the hatred of my companions in captivity, who ceased attempting to educate me and elevate me to their level. By my assiduity in labor and my submission the despotism of the rules, I avoided punishment and earned the benevolence of my guardians. To the letters and the money that my mistress sent me, I had opposed an inflexible refusal and silence. She no longer existed for me. If it had been possible for me to have news of my brother and to know that he was happy, I would have enjoyed a perfect tranquility . . .

My love for Théodore had increased by reason of the vivacity and profundity of my chagrins. It was the only thread that still attached me to life. Toward the end of my detention, my desire to see him had the violence of an irresistible passion. I awaited the hour of my deliverance in a state of devouring impatience, and I heard it sound with an ineffable joy. Interned in the département of the Loiret, after having received my roadmap, at the risk of being punished for deviating from my itinerary, I set forth without delay for Paris.

My design was not to approach my brother; I simply wanted, in passing, to satisfy myself with the sight of him. I prowled by night around the house where he lived. Hazard favored me. I soon saw him come out, and my poor heart beat violently. How much it cost me not to throw my arms around him! I only contained myself by means of a supreme effort.

I followed him, with a thousand precautions. As soon as he went directly in front of an illuminated shop window I gazed at him intently. He was pale and thin, and seemed to be absorbed in sad thoughts. I would gladly have given the days that remained to me to know the subject of his preoccupations.

Suddenly, he stopped in front of the window display of a merchant of prints. A gas jet illuminated his face fully and permitted me to consider him as I wished. That was nothing yet. His eyes fell upon an object that caused him a powerful emotion; so I judged, at least, by the contraction of his features and the persistence of his gaze in the same direction. Beyond a doubt, I even perceived two large tears forming in his eyes and sliding down his cheeks.

Stirred in the depths of my soul, it was necessary for me to know the secret of those tears immediately. I approached the display. I was suffocated by an infinite wellbeing. All my dolors vanished in that indescribable impression.

I acquired the conviction that what had made my brother weep was precisely the memory of me. The engraving that moved him so profoundly represented two beautiful children, with blond curls, of a marvelous resemblance. Our mother had once bought it and hung it at the foot of our bed, so that in the morning, when we woke up, the first thing that struck our eyes was the children in that print. How many times Théodore and I had remained in contemplation before those two lovely faces! My entire youth was in that image. I saw myself again in my mother's arms, and I felt her caresses on my cheek.

I could no longer master myself. Without knowing how, I found myself next to my brother.

"Théodore!" I said, in a faint voice.

He turned round. We fell into one another's arms. Our two souls were confounded in a long and passionate embrace . . .

My poor brother, by dint of being anxious for me, was no longer living. I had a frisson on learning that he had taken steps in order to have news of me. Something as singular as it was fortunate, my sister Augustine had not told him about my adventure. The fear she had of Théodore's reproaches and anger now rendered her silence explicable to me.

I was reduced to drowning my life in fables and reassuring him on my account by means of lies whose aim rendered them innocent in my eyes. He had no reason to be as discreet. I glimpsed with pleasure that he was progressing rapidly toward a complete rehabilitation, and that he was able again to have hope for the future. He had succeeded in reimbursing his godfather completely. The latter had gradually returned him to his esteem and affection. He had demanded that his godson recommence eating at his table and spending his evenings with his wife and daughter. It was evident that he had not abandoned the project of marrying him to Hortense and giving him his establishment as a dowry.

Unfortunately, Théodore had not found as much grace before his own conscience. The remorse of his fault had weakened him slowly. In addition, out of jealousy, the clerks who had witnessed it never missed any opportunity to make allusion to it and remind him of it. One of them, in particular, who had been an officer in a line regiment, conducted himself as an implacable enemy. Quarrelsome and boastful, although genuinely brave to the point of intrepidity, he always had some epigram in his mouth that turned to insult.

Théodore was impatient with such an existence; he wanted at any price to impose silence on those mockers and raise himself in his own eyes by exposing himself with premeditation to a danger adequate to a decisive expiation. In spite of my desire to know the plan that he was mulling over in his head, he did not want to be more explicit for the moment. On the other hand, he promised to write to me.

On the pretext of the demands of my condition as a worker, I gave him my address as *Monsieur Joseph, poste restante, Beaugency*. Then we went to the house of our Aunt Thérèse. The worthy old lady, who had thought that I was dead, nearly died of joy when she saw me. She covered me with caresses and tears, mingled with reproaches in which the vivacity of her tenderness for me was obvious. I departed the next day for the place of my internment. I took with me a provision of enjoyment sufficient for many days.

It is more difficult for an unfortunate submissive to surveillance to bury his past in proportion to the number of inhabitants his abode has. Too many people know his secret. Even supposing that those with whom he has dealings are incapable of indiscretion, his periodic comings and goings to the offices of the mairie or the prefecture always end up giving him away. After having submitted several times in workshops to hearing my comrades say that they did not want to work beside someone under the supervision of the law, and that of being ignominiously dismissed by masters, I tried, with a view to sparing myself those insults, to earn my living by means of commerce; but I exhausted in peddling the few resources that remained to me. I made it a scruple, at that time, not to address myself to Théodore, who was depriving himself of necessities in order to extinguish his debts more rapidly.

To all my misfortunes I then joined that of making the acquaintance of a wretch who was to have his share of influence in my horrible destiny and doom me irrevocably. That man, a Piedmontese named Feretti was a businessman of a singular species. He possessed seven or eight barrel organs, which he hired out to his compatriots or to men like me. Scenting my misery somehow, he sat down next to me one day in an inn where I was lodging, in Beaugency.

Thickset, with the neck of a bull and the muscular limbs of a Hercules, thick black hair in the disorder of the branches of a pomegranate tree and large hard eyes as brilliant as balls of agate, he had oily jaundiced skin, angular features and, in addition to all that, a sly and malevolent manner that rendered him extremely antipathetic to me. However, necessity, stronger than my repugnance, determined me to enter into conversation with him.

I had no hesitation in telling him that I was in need and that I had no work, and for his part, he hastened to offer me one of his barrel organs. While drinking, he gave me a few details of the métier in his patois. I went to bed prey to indecision. The next day, he renewed his offers. I accepted, only to repent of it immediately. At the moment of delivering the instrument he demanded my papers in warranty. He immediately guessed the reason for my confusion and insinuated to me that he would take no consequence therefrom. I did as he asked.

As soon as he had the proof of his conjecture in his hand an atrocious smile lit up his face. "Known, known," he said.

I concluded therefrom that among the number of those to whom he hired out his organs, there were some no less unfortunate than me.

A few weeks later, one evening, after a day of fatigues, hazard put a newspaper in my hands. I scanned it mechanically. Suddenly, a news item stirred my gibers to breaking point. I read and reread:

> *An encounter with swords has just taken place in the Bois de Vincennes between sieurs Théodore F*** and Eugène T***, two clerks in the establishment of Monsieur L***, a merchant of paints. Sieur T*** received a wound in the chest of which he died a few hours later. The law has been informed.*

I could not sleep that night.

In the morning I went to the post office. My presentiment was not mistaken; I was handed a letter from my brother. I soon had the secret of the duel. On the day when I had quit Theodore he was premeditating risking his life and tempting the judgment of God. That was what he had hidden from me. He wanted to be able to raise his head boldly or to die. The ex-soldier, his hateful enemy was known as a duelist no less skillful than fortunate. It was known that he had had numerous affairs, from which he had always emerged successfully. After a characteristic insult, my brother had sent him firm witnesses of whom he had made sure in advance.

Théodore had written to me before the encounter, which was to take place at noon, not far from Saint-Mandé. He confessed that, without being a coward, he was not free from terror, and that in anticipation of the presumable result of the duel, he had spent a horrible night. Sensing that he was incapable of struggling against the skill of his adversary, he regarded himself as doomed, save for a providential hazard. Although he doubted that the vigil of a man whom the following day would lead to the scaffold could be troubled by tortures as poignant, he would have liked that voluntary torture to be even more cruel, since his conscience would become tranquil by reason of what it was suffering. In case of misfortune, he embraced me passionately and begged me to forgive him.

The newspaper had just given me the second part of the drama. Contrary to his expectation, whereas he thought he would be killed, he had killed his adversary. But what would become of him? The mere idea of seeing him at the discretion of the law terrified me. Twenty times, I was on the point of breaking my ban and running to Paris. I lived in an intolerable anxiety.

A letter from my Aunt Thérese calmed me slightly. Theodore had been wounded rather grievously in the shoulder. He was being cared for in the home of his godfather, who was presently showing him an affection even more intense than in the beginning. The businessman had employed all his credit to obtain assurance that his godson would not be troubled. It was agreed that Théodore would surrender himself to imprisonment on the eve of the assizes.

Meanwhile, my relationship with Feretti was becoming more impossible by the day. If I had listened to the anger that the resentment of his injustices provoked in me I would already have argued and fought with him several times. He soon demanded to be paid in proportion to my daily receipts. In consequence of those new demands I scarcely had enough to live on. He completed his bad faith by means of accounts of revolting iniquity. Claiming that I had damaged his instrument, he demanded so much for the damage and so much for the repair. He got drunk, and had me settle his bill on the condition of paying me back, which he always forgot to do the following day, and he would not suffer being reminded of his odious failures; at the first words he closed your mouth by means of oaths, insults and the offer to conclude the argument by means of fists. My companions trembled and bowed their heads before the wretch. As for me, foreseeing the moment approaching when I would no longer be able to contain myself, I thought seriously about separating myself from him.

The waitress in the inn where we habitually lodged was a stout country wench, honest and obliging, whose father was a locksmith. She showed a marked preference for me and frequently spent the evening chatting to me. My chagrin in knowing Feretti and my aversion for the man had not escaped her. As soon as she knew that I was a metalworker and locksmith she thought about her father and told me that he would probably give me work. She soon told me, in fact, that the matter was arranged. I did not hesitate for an instant.

I settled up with Feretti and asked him for my papers, I employed infinite precaution in the dread of irritating him against me. While confiding to him that I had decided to change estate, I feigned indecision on the subject of what I was about to undertake, and tried to make him believe that I would return to his employ if I failed. We quit one another on seemingly friendly terms.

Six weeks went by. I was as satisfied with my new employer as he was with me. I did not think I could ever be happy, but I hoped once again for a repose analogous to that of the tomb. You can imagine my despair when, one morning, as I went into the workshop, I saw the locksmith come toward me with an embarrassed expression and say to me: "My boy, here is what I owe you. Take your things and get out. I'm truly sorry, because you have a knack for the work, but in sum, I can't keep someone under legal surveillance in my establishment."

I left crushed by the weight of an immense dolor. I did not take long to discover where the blow had come from. The locksmith's daughter, who I met shortly thereafter, told me with a desolate expression that Feretti had gone to see her father. That man, whom nothing could move, who did harm for the sake of it, had perceived me in the forge in passing and had decided coldly to have me dismissed. That new infamy completed the measure. Rage filled my soul and made me prey to an irresistible desire for vengeance. Entirely given to that sentiment, incapable of reflection, I went to the inn that evening. I found Feretti at table before a bottle of wine and occupied in settling his accounts with two of the poor devils that he exploited.

Scarcely had I gone in than I said, furiously: "What you have done is cowardly and infamous!"

He attempted to feign astonishment, but in his eyes and on his lips the joy of a wild beast burst forth, which betrayed him.

I repeated my first remark in even more energetic terms.

"You're going to shut up!" he said to me, with a menacing smile.

"You might be strong," I said to him, closing my fists, "but I'm not afraid of you. Come on!"

"As you like, my lad," said Feretti. He got up and added: "Follow us, the rest of you, and see how hotheads are corrected!"

Accompanied by the two individuals present, we drew away from the town. On the way, a presentiment traversed my soul. I stifled the sinister glimmer, saying to myself: "How can I be more unfortunate?" And, in fact death would have been mild to me by comparison with what I was feeling.

We stopped at a bend in a deserted path bordered on one side by a wall and on the other by a steep slope about a hundred feet deep, ending in the Loire. The moon illuminated us fully. No other noise could be heard but the rippling of the water through the stones of the banks.

The fight did not last as long as the shortest story. Without saying a word we fell upon one another with an equal fury. Our breasts did not cease to render dull sounds under the blows. The hatred by which I was animated multiplied my strength tenfold. Feretti seemed astonished to find such a terrible adversary. He tried several times, but without success, to knock me down or to seize me round the waist. Far from reckoning with me, as he had expected, he understood, on the contrary, that he was about to be beaten.

Foaming with rage, he drew a knife from his pocket, slyly. In the moonlight I suddenly perceived the blade, which was heading straight for my face. I deflected the blow. At that new perfidy I lost my reason. I took two steps back and armed myself similarly. I was absolutely beside myself; a fiery gulf would not have stopped me.

"Traitor! Assassin!" I cried between two breaths. "Woe betide you!" And I rushed at him.

The combat became savage. Our bruised faces were streaming with sweat and blood. Both free even from the fear of being hurt, we struck out this way and that. Suddenly, Feretti fell, uttering true howls. Writhing on the ground in convulsions, he cried with all the force of his lungs: "Murder! Murder!"

Echoes repeated that formidable cry in the distance. It was only then that I remarked that the witnesses were no longer there. I approached Feretti. He was agonizing in a pool of blood.

I recovered my reason. As cold as marble, stronger now because destiny could no longer do anything against me, all that remained in my soul was an obsession: to see my brother one last time and learn his fate. After that, my life belonged to whoever might want to take it. I fled, therefore, but with the composure of a man master of himself.

Calculating that my description would not take long to be transmitted in all directions, I limited myself only to traveling by night; I avoided the roads and frequented places. I nourished myself on fruits and roots, and I slept by day in thickets or behind hedges. Several times, skirting farms, at the appeal of dogs barking at me, I was disturbed by rifle shots. My strength would not have been sufficient for such a journey if my body had not been electrified, after a fashion, by my fraternal passion.

Because of the detours and the by-roads that I took, I extended my journey to at least thirty leagues. I arrived at my Aunt Thérèse's house half-dead of fatigue. The worthy old woman, having taken my head in her hands to see me better, almost fainted at my lividity and the ravages hollowed out in my features. I lulled her anxieties with fairy tales. She told me that Théodore was to be judged the following day.

Lost in the bosom of the crowd that filled the vicinity of the court of assizes, I saw the jurors and the judges take their respective places successively. My brother came in, supported on one side by his defender and on the other by his godfather. He was exceedingly pale and had his arm in a sling.

The trial was, from beginning to end, a veritable triumph for him. I read his acquittal almost immediately in the eyes of the jurors. The witnesses were unanimous in rendering justice to his sentiments of moderation. It was established that Théodore, of mediocre strength with the épée, found himself facing a kind of professional assassin, redoubtable because of his skill and self-confidence. My brother's godfather declared in addition that the victim had persecuted his godson for a long time, on the basis of rumors that had no serious foundation. He added that he prized in that regard the character, the probity, the conduct and the intelligence of that same godson, for whom he destined his daughter and his establishment. He did not think a young man could be found more capable and more worthy to succeed him.

In the presence of that evidence, the public prosecutor abandoned the accusation. The president of the court summed up in Théodore's favor. The jury scarcely deliberated; it returned after a few minutes with a verdict of acquittal rendered unanimously. Like a hero, my brother was surrounded by friends and heaped with congratulations. His godfather's face respired joy and pride.

As for me, is there any need to say it? Sobs rose to my throat, I was inundated by joy. How sweet it would have been for me to die at that moment!

I returned to the place whence I had come and placed myself in the hands of the law. My confession rendered the investigation facile. I recounted my quarrel with Feretti and how I had killed him. The witnesses, who had abandoned us at the commencement of the fight, could not give any precise information. To complete the misfortune, they searched in vain for Feretti's knife, while mine was found in the wound of which my victim had died. The public prosecutor's deputy had ample material for a crushing speech. Searching through my file, he recapitulated my life, and, with evidence in hand, demonstrated how, from one crime to another, I had finally ended up accused of murder. My advocate, although a man of talent, could do nothing against the facts that mapped out, so to speak, the stages of my criminal career. I did not even have the benefit of attenuating circumstances. Declared guilty of all the charges, I was condemned to the death penalty.

I believe that humans are born to suffer, and it seems to me that happiness only exists to mask the traps of misfortune; but I suspect that, among the unfortunate, there are many who could, as legitimately as me, find life a bitter mockery. So I only appealed reluctantly, and obstinately refused to sign the plea for mercy. To trade for a convict prison the sad days that remain for me to live would have been as ridiculous as cowardly.

Far from that, I shall die in a state near to enthusiasm. I have been given a letter from my brother in which he informs me of his marriage and urges me to come and take my part in his happiness. He added five hundred francs to his letter. On rereading it, I am convinced that on the day and at the hour of my execution, Théodore will conduct his bride to the altar. For having lived in a different environment, after having committed faults analogous to mine, he had been able to repent and find his forgiveness, whereas I have encountered the scaffold.

No matter; my brother is happy; my God, I only have thanks to offer you. May what I have suffered unjustly be poured over his head in felicity. At the present moment, without boasting, I attest that I am impatient to see the dawn of the day when I shall no longer exist, when I shall wash away my sins in my own blood, and when I shall recommence a new existence . . .

The Music Lesson

THE pure and penetrating sounds of the cello reached me, albeit faintly, as I went into the small town house where my master lived. On the second floor I waited before knocking on the door until the vibrations of the instrument had ceased.

The disorder of the room responded to the musician's singular exterior. Schenk had just laid his bass down on the bed. Ruled paper, pens, ink, a tuning fork and rosin littered the green cloth of a table. Musical scores, printed and manuscript, garments and underclothes, encumbered randomly an upright piano placed between the room's two windows. I perceived a stove in the fireplace, *proh pudor*,[1] on which something or other was cooking, for the lid was on. That culinary detail, seemingly puerile, was to take on in my eyes the proportions of a proof of the influence of external things on the sensations that music causes.

Schenk, a small man of thirty-some years of age, was standing with his hands on his hips. His dull, stiff hair was bristling like the fur of an angry cat. He looked in my direction but did not seem to see me. Without quitting

---

1 O shame!

that distracted air he asked me, in an indecisive tone of voice, to go on his behalf to inform one of his pupils that he was no longer indisposed.

For want, in the town, of anyone who could be called a violin teacher, Schenk had consented to direct my studies on that instrument. By virtue of his excessive irritability, I never enjoyed before him the plenitude of my means. There were days when I only heard the hour of the lesson sound with a sort of fear. At every omission, at every false note—and God knows how many I made!—he abused me, moderately at first but soon unsparingly, and if fear increased my awkwardness his wrath would be unleashed like a tempest. Nothing was lacking in that regard; lightning departed from his eyes, and the blows that he delivered with his fist to his bass or with his feet against the wall were an indisputable match for thunder. I often wept, and I could show to this day on the surface of my violin the furrows that the warmth and bitterness of my tears designed there.

That did not prevent me from liking him a great deal. He drew sounds from his cello that penetrated me, awakening mysterious, magical things in my imagination, of an intoxicating charm, and that alone sufficed to absolve him in my mind for his bizarre humor and his impatience.

The people to whose home I went saw me almost every day. Susanne, their only child, initiated to music by an old professor who, remarkably, had taught her something, was only happy at her piano. Although I was a mediocre player, she was always content to have me accompany, as best I could, sonatas by Haydn, Mozart or Beethoven. At other times I played my part in trios that

Schenk composed and in which he reduced the violin to my strength.

I went up to the first floor, where the family habitually resided, and I did indeed find the father, the mother and Susanne around a large fire. It was autumn. The father and the mother each occupied a corner of the fireplace; the young woman was between them, some distance behind, leaning against a grand piano, on the lectern of which a score was open. A gray daylight blurred the contours of the three individuals, whose pinched faces attested to sad preoccupations, with soft shadows.

Presumably they heard me, but no one paid any heed to me, which disconcerted me. I stood in a corner of the drawing room, fearing to be importunate, not daring to move.

At a sigh from the young woman, the father and mother turned their heads simultaneously in her direction. Their eyes passed over me without deciding to see me.

"What's the matter, my child?" asked the mother, tenderly.

Susanne responded with a tear, which trickled along an eyelash and fell on to her cheek.

The father repeated the question, but in a tone of impatience. A second tear sparkled on the young man's other eyelid and slid over her epidermis like a drop of water over the satin corolla of a flower.

I was ill at ease, and I would have experienced relief if my presence, having been noticed, had put an end to a scene whose details I was observing reluctantly. In addition to that, I was surprised by Susanne's tears; I knew that she was spoiled by her parents. Incapable then of imagining that a thwarted dream is sometimes sufficient to engender mortal pains in the soul of a young woman enslaved by her impressions, like the father and the mother. I wondered with astonishment what was wrong with her.

The father, a tall man and proportionately stout, of luxuriant health, quit his armchair and strode back and forth. Then he stopped in front of his daughter, with his arms folded, and addressed very harsh words to her. As far as I can recall, among other things, he said that he was heart-broken to see her repaying with ingratitude the affection of parents who loved her more than themselves; that the obstinacy of her mute chagrin was inconceivable, since they gave in to her merest whims; that if it was her impending marriage that was affecting her in this way, she should not hesitate to admit it; she ought not to fear breaking once again the hearts of a father and a mother whom she had incessantly made the victim of her caprices.

In spite of those bitter reproaches and the caresses of her mother, Susanne did not budge. She was as motionless as a rock through which spring water was filtering drop by drop.

They finally deigned to perceive me. I hastened to say why I had come. The father asked after Schenk with interest, and handed me over to his daughter for the rest; after which, he went out. The mother, for her part, told me that the lessons had been suspended because her daughter was about to marry; she added that if Susanne, at the moment, felt disposed to make music, she saw no inconvenience in it; that she would even be pleased, since it would procure her the pleasure of seeing Monsieur Schenk, etc.

In the meantime, Susanne passed from torpor to a vivid agitation. My master's name had resuscitated her, in a way. To her mother, who feared that a lesson might fatigue her, she replied that she felt better and that a little music would certainly do her good.

I reported these details to Schenk. When I mentioned the marriage, his eyes, which had been fixed on me, were suddenly lowered toward the floor, and I saw the melancholy of discouragement imprinted on his face.

I accompanied him . . .

Although lacking regularity in her features, Susanne was nevertheless thought to be beautiful, her physiognomy was ordinarily so lively, her eyes contained so many things and her smile had so much grace. Since she had not seen Schenk she had paled considerably; her red eyelids denoted the frequency of her tears, and her inclined head seemed to be weighed down by funereal thoughts.

Beside her, Schenk made a striking contrast, by virtue of his short stature and the awkwardness of his gestures. His eyes were charged with sparks; his angular, passionate face, in which suspicion and pride, and sometimes also a memory or a word, hollowed out profound creases, scarcely awoke anything but antipathy. He was always dressed like a man who thinks about clothes what others think about style, that the depth prevails over the form.

He opened the case that the domestic had brought and took out his bass, an old instrument of a dark and energetic coloration. That bass, although devoid of an author's name, had an inestimable value. The admirably chosen wood, the beauty of its forms and the finish of its details all announced the work of a master. Schenk attributed it to Duiffoprugcar, a Tyrolean instrument-maker of the sixteenth century.[1] The bottom, above all, was splendid; the waves of the maple escaped from the middle toward the wedges like the flames of a hearth. The *fas* had that clarity and elegance that distinguishes Cremona violins. The head of the neck was worked like an item of jewelry. Moldings of a bizarre design, and of an exquisite delicacy, took root in the cheeks of the pegboard and were developed over the spiral of the scroll. Although not having the same workmanship, the head, mounted in a new shaft, far from lowering the price of the bass, completed making it a magnificent and precious instrument.

I perceived that the father and the mother had gone, and I was pleased, for I knew that indifferent or bored listeners importuned Schenk and paralyzed him. A performer is only entirely comfortable in a sympathetic milieu; he has that in common with a magnetizer, whose operations proceed poorly in the presence of hostile people.

I sat down in a dark corner, like an inert object, no longer having anything alive in me, so to speak, except the strings that vibrate under the action of works of art. It seemed that I had a presentiment of hearing my master's bass for the last time. Schenk put into his execution more soul, fever and vigor than I had known him do before, and stirred me exceptionally in such a way that the impression is still as fresh in my memory as if it were yesterday.

---

1 Gasparo Duiffopruggar (1514-c1570), whose name was spelled in many different ways, including the variant employed by Barbara, is credited by legend to have been one of the first instrument-makers to produce violins in their modern form, in Lyon, but no such instrument of his manufacture survives.

An andante of a few bars served as an introduction. Against a background of low notes, threaded with an inconceivable artistry, the succession and harmonious progress of which caused a presentiment of a change of tone and movement, Susanne, parading her fingers over the full extent of the keyboard, sowed rapid strokes, *leggiermente*, comparable to the perforated arabesques of a Gothic church, or the points of lace. The effect produced was analogous to one of those morning fogs that agitate at the approach of twilight in a thousand confused forms. The feverish interest that attaches to the fantastic objects that the imagination evokes so easily in the half-light, immediately enchained the attention.

Suddenly, an allegro of deafening amplitude burst forth. From the entrails of the andante, like a chaos in which phantoms floated randomly, the friction and swirling of which filled the ear with a monotonous psalmody, a motif sprang of a splendor reminiscent of that of the sun. The shadows disappeared like large clouds chased away by the wind, unveiling splendid landscapes where the meanders of a river played, framed by flowery bushes, where blue lakes sparkled like ardent mirrors; where picturesque mountains, white at the top, black and torn in the sides, stood up straight and proud on the horizon, while, nonchalantly crouched at their feet, hills slept, some draped in the golden robes of wheat, others in the green scarves of vines. Impenetrable forests, whose masses of verdure undulated like the waves of the sea, framed that magical landscape magnificently, inundated with light and color.

And that sunlight, that sky, those waters, those woods those mountains, those hills, having become by enchantment the instruments of an orchestra, executed, with a fabulous ensemble, under the direction of an invisible master, a symphony to make one die of joy.

I was dazzled, swimming in enthusiasm; I grew wings; I plunged into the space where worlds orbit, where suns burn, I went further and further, without finding a limit, spurred on more sharply at every moment by the desire to touch with my finger the solution of the terrible problems that awaken pain in us . . .

At the paroxysm of my ecstasy, an abrupt cadence blew over that mirage and recalled me to myself. It seemed to me that something broke in my breast, so energetic and painful was the sensation . . .

From the beginning of the adagio I was drawn into a world of heart-rending realities. The volume, the roundness and the suavity of the sounds had created belief in the vibrations of a magnificent voice. Of a profound tenderness, the song gradually attained pathos and brought tears to the eyes. One found no trace therein of the febrile, poignant, tearing sentiment that flows in floods in the unhealthy compositions of a few modern Italians and the enervating melodies of the tender Schubert; it was the strong, healthy melancholy of the robust genius that, far from disdaining life, accepts its dolors and tries to console itself and then to console others for them with the aid of touching laments, a melancholy that is notably imprinted in the works of Beethoven. In that passionate song, I disentangled an entire story; I thought about Schenk, about his obscure existence, his isolation, the hatred of ignorant musicians that pursued him, and also the reputation for madness that they tried to make for him, without him even deigning to contradict them, even though his soul was swollen by bitterness in consequence.

He seemed to extract his only enjoyments from the profundities of the musical art. He scarcely warmed up except in regard to the cello, of which he always spoke with an extraordinary enthusiasm. For him, it was simultaneously the most difficult and the foremost of string instruments, and the one that merited being treated with the most gravity and nobility. He wanted nothing so much as to see it better understood, and did not have sarcasms enough for those who played it without appearing to suspect that Duport had ever existed.[1] In his opinion, the majority of cellists, by virtue of the paltriness of their playing, their lack of aplomb and accuracy, and their empty and ridiculously difficult compositions, denatured the character of the instrument and merited it being said of them that they were failed violinists.

It is not a matter of juggling with notes, of stupefying the listener with passages of runs and perilous leaps; it is necessary that the sequence of sounds, the entanglement of chords and modulations, results in an ensemble capable of moving profoundly; otherwise the artiste descends to the level of a juggler and only occasions an analogous pleasure, or boredom. Let the instrumentalist devoid of the creative faculty refrain from torturing his imagination to extract absurd morsels therefrom piece by piece; let him limit himself to the interpretation of the work of masters; a man of talent can still obtain, in that career

---

1 The cellist and composer Jean-Louis Duport (1749-1819), best-known for the twenty-one *études* making up the final part of his "Essay on the fingering of the cello and the conduct of the bow" (1806), a seminal work on the technique of the instrument.

incontestably preferable to that of an acrobat, enough success to content his ambition.

As for him, as soon as it was a question of mounting a stage before indifferent individuals who demanded that they be astonished by *tours de force*, he felt an invincible repugnance. He only had the free exercise of his faculties in the presence of people whose sympathy he had acquired and those people were rare, so he avoided opportunities to perform.

Only once, by force of obsession, it had been obtained that he would make himself heard in concert. No heavier fall had perhaps been observed in human memory. After having disposed minds to enthusiasm by a debut bursting with strength and beauty, he was suddenly troubled, lost his head and stopped dead. A nervous fever paralyzed his fingers; the arm holding the bow had the rigidity of an iron bar; sweat inundated him; despair distressed his features; large tears formed in his eyes; an inexpressible anguish rent his breast. Despairing of conquering his disturbance, he got up and quit the hall. The compassion that was shown to him on that occasion did him more harm than anything else. The memory subsisted within him in the condition of a bloody wound that was irritated by the slightest thing; it was sufficient to make allusion to it, even innocently, to render him furious and put him to flight.

The sustained attention that Susanne and I lent to him, and the emotion by which we were penetrated and to which we abandoned ourselves naively, gave him an imperturbable assurance and overexcitement to the point that he had the appearance of an illuminate. Crouching over his bass, his eyes on fire, outside himself, he had one of those moments of inspiration that he scarcely knew except when he was alone. He improvised a culmination so rigorously deduced from the motif, possessed of a logic so compact in its development, that it appeared to be an integral part of the written piece.

Schenk did not know what difficulties were, as difficulties. If he went from one end of the shaft to the other with a lighting rapidity, by means of staccato, of chromatic scales, like strings of pearls, clear to the point of perfection, one did not think of being astonished by his mechanism. The ever-present *idea* deflected attention completely from preoccupations of form. Without any trace of effort appearing, his fingers, bones and sinews, long and tapering, like those of a hunchback, flew over the keys like the great feet of a spider. More perfect trills and more accurate double chords could not be imagined, nor passages in octaves more rapid. Modulations spread color over the sparkling medley, from which escaped unexpectedly the song of the adagio, which Schenk took up again surreptitiously, accompanied by *pizzicati* or arpeggios. The effect of that melody, rendered with sounds of an incomparable accuracy, beauty and power, was prodigious.

At the sight of his pupil, whose head was bowed and weeping, Schenk, at first tender in his expression, then bitter and energetic, soon moderated his extravagance and gradually diminished the splendor of his sounds. Insensibly, the notes, running through all the nuances of descrescendo, scarcely made the air vibrate and became undetectable to the ear. The young woman, whose sensation seemed to be obeying the same law of decrease, calmed down.

There was a new pause.

The finale, *presto* in double time, departed like an arrow. With a staccato rhythm and an electric vivacity, he threw the reverie into nightmare. The notes, in their rapid succession and their fugal intersection, designed for my mind the arcades of a fantastic hall, shimmering like the architecture of dreams, of which the walls, because of the gilt, the paintings, the draperies, the mirrors and the innumerable candles, were as resplendent as the walls of a furnace. In that interior, which vacillated and offered new perspectives at every moment, through a forest of colonnettes, sometimes extending as far as the eye could see, sometimes shrinking to the point that one could touch the vault with one's hand, a host of women were crowded, chosen from among the most beautiful blondes, brunettes and redheads in the world. The imagination of a Muslim stimulated by fasting had never attained the splendor of that paradise. The majority had large expressive eyes, which realized unsurpassably the image of the Persian poet: *Your eyebrows are the bows of which your glances are the arrows.* Clad in silk, velvet or gauze, the colors and the forms of their robes fitted their genre of beauty marvelously. The head of this one was inclined under flowers; the breast of that one sparkled with diamonds; others floated in clouds of lace; all walked enveloped, so to speak, with passion; one unique thought appeared to preoccupy them.

A rumor suddenly rose up amid the groups; all eyes were steered simultaneously toward a black dot that grew visibly and put on human form. I recognized Schenk. He was almost handsome by virtue of being joyful. He was holding his bass in one hand and his bow in the other.

Too passionate to be coquettes, the women, without fear of crumpling their robes, tearing their lace, losing their diamonds, or deranging their hairstyles, hastened around him with a sort of jealous fury and disputed his smiles. It seemed that that fanaticism filled the unfathomable gulf of his ambition. His breast was not broad enough to contain so much happiness; he pressed one of his hands to it, as if to prevent it from bursting . . .

The duration of a lightning flash, and there was a disaster. A strange modulation reminded me, I don't know how, of a memory that sufficed to throw disorder into the phantasmagoria. Schenk was abruptly abandoned by the perfumed arms that were enlacing him. He became the center of a circle of wan, frightened faces, the radiance of which did not stop increasing. A mirror seemed to be the cause of that revolution. It had placed a cotton bonnet on his head; his cello, his admirable cello, had changed into an ignoble cooking-pot and his bow into a wooden spoon. His despair was as profound as his intoxication had been. A hoarse cry emerged from his throat. The circle was still growing, and also the fear on the faces, and also the fury in the soul of the poor musician. Gripping the spoon angrily, and plunging it with a feverish gesture into the cooking-pot, from which something like molten metal overflowed, he strode from the center to the circumference that enclosed him, and bore the fiery spoon to the faces of the women he had been adoring shortly before. A terrible clamor resounded. That was the signal for an indescribable confusion. The women fled in all directions, pursued by the fear of the burning pollution by which they were menaced.

The fantastic engendered the fantastic; a legion of individuals identical to Schenk and as terrible as him sprang from the walls. The fear of the women surpassed all measure. With heart-rending plaints on their lips and eyes full of tears, they huddled together, gathering in a cluster in the manner of bees, and then elongating in a dazzling scarf, and tumbling like a torrent into a sunken path where it became increasingly impossible to distinguish any precise form. Behind them ran an army of scullions uttering frantic cheers. And the movement of that indecipherable host accelerated with every passing moment, the cries increased in strength, in acuity and discordance.

The candles had been snuffed out; the edifice had crumbled; nothing could any longer be seen but ruins and rubble. It was cold. In a pale twilight, that human chain passed before my eyes with an increased speed, and sobs, its rings describing an immense ellipse, rotating on its axis like a piece of cloth in a glazing machine . . .

I was bewildered. The torrent brushed me and tried to draw me away. Devoid of strength against the paralysis of vertigo, I finally fell into the turbulence. With the rapidity of a rifle bullet, I went up and down, stifled by the dread of falling and breaking my head. The figures that I clutched vanished in my arms; and the movement of rotation was still increasing. The acceleration became such that I could no longer feel anything, and it seemed to me that I was reposing in the immobility of annihilation . . .

When I opened my eyes again, Schenk was replacing his bass in its case. Susanne, who was sitting with her back turned to the piano, seemed crushed by the force of her emotions. Her mother was examining her anxiously. Then the lady turned to Schenk and told him about her daughter's marriage. She continued, with a great deal of affability: "My child has made great progress with you, Monsieur, and there are debts that money cannot acquit. I hope that we shall not cease to see you. I assure you that you will always find devoted friends here."

So saying, she put in his hand the price of his lessons. Susanne stood up. Trembling, ready to faint; she opened her mouth to speak, but dolor cut off her voice. Her pallor, her tears and her pantomime spoke for her. Her forehead in her hands, she threw back her head, which, almost immediately, fell back on her breast, from which sobs suddenly escaped. Before her mother, who went to console her, had had time to take her in her arms, she went out and ran to shut herself in her bedroom. Schenk bowed sadly and left, never to reappear.

Two or three months later, Susanne was married to a young man of her own age, with a fortune equal to her own. Never perhaps had a bride so frail, so pale and so bleak marched to the altar. Many people thought that the discolored child, at grips with somber chagrins, would not be long delayed in seeing her wedding veil changed into a funeral veil. Even the parents were sad, and now seemed to fear the consequences of a marriage whose conclusions they had been in haste to sign.

However, it was to prove once more that there are no dolors so cruel that time cannot weaken them, and even cause them to be forgotten. I only saw Susanne again a few years later. My astonishment was profound. Instead of the delicate young woman as white as a lily, inclined like a reed under the wind, I perceived a stout lady whose face, full of a vivid redness, illuminated by two brilliant eyes, was smiling with the happiest expression. She had beside her two superb children over whom she was watching tenderly.

I was assured that she only touched her piano rarely, and sometimes even gave evidence of an aversion to music.

I will add that a hazard has very recently reawakened these details in my memory. Leafing through the music exposed for sale on the parapet of the quays, my eyes fell upon a *Trio* for piano, violin and cello, opus 7, composed by L. Schenk, printed and published in Paris in 1839. After seeking information I learned that a cellist named Louis Schenk, a baroque composer and an antisocial individual, after having sought his fortune for some time in Paris, had gone to bury himself in a small town in Germany.

An Old Story

"... A month later, they were married. *Finis coronat opus.*[1] The wedding celebrations lasted a week ... And bring on the violins!" cried Prosper, out of breath, throwing his manuscript on the table.

That manner of concluding a tale made some smile and scandalized others. Anselme, whose turn had come to amuse or bore the circle, as they might wish, put an end to the scandal with this beginning:

As might happen to anyone, I returned from a voyage. I was welcomed with an item of news that made me prick up my ears. During my absence, a tenant of the house, a young man, had hanged himself from his window, and that because of a woman who was almost my neighbor. I had some difficulty at first in remembering the young man, a Monsieur Paul, it was said, a chubby young man whom a word succeeded in rendering red in the face. As for the woman, Madame Clémence, by an ironic hazard, I remembered very well having crossed paths with her fre-

---

1 "The end crowns the work," traditionally attributed to Ovid.

quently on the stairway, and even having remarked more than once her bright eyes, her dark hair, her shoulders, her stature, and her youthful and cheerful expression . . .

That denouement, not only tragic but also singular, would have stimulated the most dormant curiosity. The house, at the corner of a square and a street, had five stories. The wall of the last two, slightly oblique in order to facilitate the flow of water, was covered with slates. At intervals, one of the iron hooks emerged from it that serve to attach the scaffolds of roofers. It was from one of those crampons, solidly sealed into the woodwork, that the young man had hanged himself, during the night. From my apartment, without a support bar, by reaching out with my arm, I could have touched that hook. It was to my right, a little below me, between one of Madame Clémence's windows and that of the room occupied by young Paul.

The difficulty alone of suspending oneself from it caused a shiver. He must first have passed the rope around his neck, then successively climbed out of his widow, walked along a very narrow lead gutter, reached the hook by standing up on tiptoe, hoisted himself up to a certain height by the strength of his wrists, maintaining himself in that position with one hand, and fixing the loose end of the rope to the curved iron with the other, and then let go. Was that not fabulous? What a steady gaze, what sang-froid, it must have required! A slightly bigger man would not have been able to hang himself. The death of the unfortunate fellow had only depended on a few inches.

Who knows? Without that hook, perhaps he would never have thought of suicide. The traces of his feet were still visible on the wall, and the broken slates that testified to the efforts of his death-throes, were still in the gutter . . .

I had not ceased to be importuned by the desire to know the story of that catastrophe when, one morning, I saw Madame Clémence come into my apartment. I was all the more surprised because that lady, until then, had hardly seemed concerned to make my acquaintance. The day before, between eleven o'clock and midnight, I had found her, all dressed up, chatting on the first steps of the staircase with the sergeant-major of a line regiment. I cannot describe the extent to which I was amazed. She had moved aside to let me pass and had returned my greeting while studying my expression slyly . . .

Her presence caused me a considerable disturbance.

"My God, Monsieur," she said, in a wheedling tone, "I've come to ask you if you'd be good enough to write a letter for me."

I had no sooner replied affirmatively than she sat down, took a letter out of her pocket, and added: "But first, I beg you to reread this letter for me, because I can't read very well, especially not handwriting."

It was only then that I perceived her drawling and common accent. Under the elegant exterior of the woman, I discovered a Norman peasant.

The letter, three pages of stilted writing in a grotesque style, unsteady in its orthography, of mediocre interest, in sum, was from the sergeant-major whose mature age, enormous moustache and chevron I had clearly remarked the day before. I no longer remember very clearly what it contained, except that there were charges laid at full tilt against the bourgeoisie, which collided with protestations of amour, making a noise comparable to that of twenty sabers clashing, and in the middle, a proposal of marriage resounded like a cannon shot.

I also know that, at that proposal of marriage, Madame Clémence, who was listening with the most serious expression, burst out laughing. I asked her what response she desired me to make. "Anything you like," she said, with vivacity, "provided that I never see him again. The monsieur has lost his head. Can you see me as a camp follower? It's quite enough to have had dinner with him. If *Monsieur* learned that I had had dealings with a soldier, he wouldn't be pleased, for sure."

We chatted, and in response to my plea, she explained to me how she had met the sergeant-major.

"I have a friend," she said, "whose suitor is in the regiment. They invited me to dinner and I found that sergeant with them, who seemed at first to be very amiable. He paid court to me and escorted me back to my door in the evening. I didn't know how to get rid of him. He never finished telling me stories and swearing that he adored me. I was bored to death, asleep standing up, when you saw us together. That's it."

The response that I promised Madame Clémence required another visit the following day. I had no need of any pretext to retain her; she sat down and talked to me about herself without being asked, with a complete abandon. She told me that *Monsieur* was a tall, stout man of thirty-eight who, in addition to a personal fortune and great expectations in regard to his mother, also received five or six thousand francs as a professor in a faculté. He was mad about her and gave her everything in profusion. With a view to distracting her and teaching her about society, which he was keen to do, he had taken her to respectable houses several times, but she had shown herself so gauche, and had committed so many gaffes, that he had been obliged to renounce that system of education. He had demanded that she take lessons in French, dancing and music, and had, to that effect, bought a piano. It was as much sterile expense; by her own admission, she did not understand anything; she was too stupid. *Monsieur*'s mother, very proud of her son, was thinking of marrying him off, but she, Clémence, would not hear of it. At the first rumor of a marriage, she had decided to make a scandal such that its conclusion would become impossible.

While listening to her, I got up to close the window, because the noise of carriages sometimes prevented me from hearing her. She stopped me. "Leave it open," she said. "If everything were closed, your neighbor would be able to hear what we're saying."

Encouraged by that benevolence, I tried to broach the subject of her amours with Paul. Her obstinacy in not understanding my allusions to that subject ended up making me impatient. At the risk of appearing brutal, I took her by the hand and tried to draw her to the window with the objective of placing the nail before her eyes. I don't know how it happened, but she divined my intention.

"Oh," she said, recoiling in a fearful manner, "what horror!"

I had a fit of repentance.

"I see what it is," she added. "Someone has told you that frightful story."

"Yes," I said, "but in passing. I'd like to have more details."

"Another time, we'll see," said Madame Clémence. "For now, close the window."

She was standing up and had resolved to go.

"You didn't want that just now," I observed.

"I want it now," she replied, going toward the door.

"What harm can it do you?" I said.

She became extremely animated. "What!" she cried. "You don't know that I've had my window on that side sealed up! You don't know that I feel ill and have attacks of nerves simply on looking at that hook."

I closed my window.

That awkwardness did not prevent Madame Clémence from making me regular visits of a sort from that day on. I was scarcely any further forward. She eluded my questions, or replied with impatience that I knew everything, that she had nothing new to tell me. On the other hand, about herself, her past and her family, she never shut up.

She came from Normandy, where there are so many beautiful women and magnificent blood. She was the eldest of three daughters of a worthy man who made full value of a small farm of which he was the tenant, in the vicinity of Caen. Decried in her village because of a few adventures, she had come to seek her fortune in Paris. From time to time, in order that she would be remembered, she sent money to her father and gifts to her sisters. They, moreover, came to see her once a year. For a fortnight, she gorged them with pleasures and then sent them back charged with all the toilette items capable of flattering their taste. So, not content with sending her baskets of big red apples for the winter, her younger sisters had created a reputation for her in the region of supernatural beauty, and it was necessary to admit that she was provided, with a fabulous luxury, with everything that could excuse such an enthusiasm. Her splendid hair would have been a burden for a frail woman. Thick eyebrows designed a dark and expressive line above her dark eyes. Her pallor did not prevent her from being fresh. She had the most beautiful teeth in the world; her body seemed as firm as marble; her feet were well made and not too large, a notable thing in a girl who had been brought up in the fields. In addition to that, she had an instinct for dresses that suited her as sitting on eggs suited a chicken.

By dint of looking at the woman, I had come to dream about her often. I recognized her footsteps by my sudden palpitations. If a day went by without her coming, I experienced a profound ennui, but, curiously enough, as soon as she was present, I became preoccupied and sad.

She questioned me about that sadness. I responded evasively. I no longer talked to her about young Paul, at first out of lassitude, and then because of personal sentiments that absorbed me. It was at one of those times that Madame Clémence, to my great surprise, told me at length a story that I had requested fruitlessly many times. My curiosity had tied her tongue, it seemed that my indifference had loosened it.

At this point, Prosper, who was thought to be asleep, suddenly repeated, in a low voice, the unsuitable exclamation with which he had concluded his own story. All eyes turned in his direction. Several people raised their voices at the same time to reproach him. Once again, Anselme drowned out the rumor by resuming his reading thus:

✳

By combining her story with what I had learned elsewhere, I understood the drama precisely as if it had passed before my eyes. I had succeeded in recovering from my memory the exact image of the young man. He was of medium height and somewhat replete. Twenty years of life had not yet affected the vivid red of his cheeks. Chestnut hair, long and neglected, was turned up over his nape like a bird's tail. His blue-gray eyes, buried under ever-lowered eyelids, rarely dared look anyone in the face, and his humble manner and the sadness of his garments bore the indelible imprints that seminary life engraves on every individual.

With a view to utilizing the time that separated him from the age when he would be able to purchase an advocate's office, he had come to Paris to study law. Devoid of friends and relationships, reluctant in addition to make any, by virtue of taciturnity and mistrust, he lived in a complete isolation and scarcely appeared to suspect that women, cafés, dance-halls and theaters existed. He did not love anything in the world profoundly except for his mother, an aged widow with a heart of gold, whose unique weakness he caressed by means of heroic economies and weekly reports of his expenditure. His neighbor, whom he encountered every day, seemed not to exist for him. He paid no heed to her.

That was not to the liking of the young woman, who was offended by the indifference of a young man bursting with health, who edified and embalmed the entire house, so to speak, by virtue of his tranquil life and his laborious habits. She had taken it into her head to force his attention. She succeeded only too well in that. Her beauty and her bold and provocative gaze inundated the young man's breast with disturbance, where a profound and incurable amour soon germinated.

But Clémence had to struggle against prejudices all the more tenacious because they grew roots of a new and robust nature. Timidity and ignorance immured the mind of the student more fully than his eyelids veiled his eyes. He had formed of women, whom he judged by his mother, an idea so noble and so elevated that he could not think of his unworthiness without blushing. His neighbor finished crushing him under the prestige of a pitiless coquetry. He was obstinate in believing her to have a nature far superior to his own.

Although he allowed amour to grow within him and enabled it to prosper in his dreams, it was without hope. Passion, which is almost a law, multiplied his pusillanimity tenfold and dictated fashions of acting to him that one might have thought inspired by hatred. If Clémence jogged his elbow in passing, he turned his head away; if she greeted him in a loud voice he turned a deaf ear; if, by chance, she saw him in the concierge's lodge and went in, he picked up his hat and escaped, with an abruptness that bordered on impoliteness.

The extravagance of his conduct, which she could not explain, would inevitably have put her off, if she had not had the presentiment of new and keen pleasures in the education of the young savage. Her stubbornness increased by reason of the obstinacy of her neighbor. Bold in her weakness, she knocked on his door and solicited insignificant services. Under the pretext of thanking him, she went into his room and hung on there with the aid of a conversation of which she bore the expense. At other times, she drew him into her apartment, where she kept him prisoner for entire hours. The student kept his head down and his eyes lowered, like a wolf trapped in a ditch. Clémence teased him about his girlish mannerisms, and reproached him for living like a bear—and for hating women, with whom she set out to reconcile him.

All of that turned the young man's head. He began to open his eyes wide and to go away pensive. The significance of those provocations began to penetrate his mind. It was only an imperceptible glimmer, but that gleam, like a drop of oil on a piece of cloth, spread so rapidly that it invaded his entire body.

To be loved by her—him! He had transports in his brain and nearly went mad. The shock that he felt is more easily conceivable because the blood was burning in his veins, his calm attitude hid a passionate soul, and it was his first amour. Clémence, by that time, could read his heart more easily than a book. Fatigued by three months of the comedy and resolved to end it, she finally extracted from his soul the secret of his passion, and then mocked him because he had not divined sooner that she also loved him . . .

An inexpressible happiness, dolorous by virtue of being intense, filled the student's days. His physiognomy took on an entirely new expression. He was incessantly penetrated by such joy that his entire body was radiant.

The beauty of his mistress maintained a perpetual hearth of enthusiasm within him. He had surges of passion of a stunning impetuosity. Inexhaustible follies, of which Clémence did not sense the facility, emerged from his lips, electrified by the fire of embraces. The poor fellow had alienated all the treasures of his soul to her, exclusively and irrevocably. More taciturn than ever with strangers, even his filial love descended rapidly to the level of a banal respect. His mother's letters importuned him; he no longer had time to read them; he did not reply to them. He had even lost the memory of the good woman's weaknesses, or, at least, those weaknesses no longer appeared to merit anything but disdain, for, at present, he spent more money in a month than he previously had in a year.

That rapid analysis, I ought to warn you, only exists in view of a denouement that, in the very old and ever-new story of the affinity of men of soul for statues in living flesh, only offers curious particularities. The student's amour was bound to follow the irresistible slope of these abnormal passions. Already, that amour, which was desiccating within him the roots of his oldest affections, no longer had the security of the first days. Jealous and umbrageous, he was alarmed by trivia, and Clémence did not always take the trouble to reassure him. So, for fear of losing her, or merely of seeing her cool, he exhausted all the resources he judged to be capable of attaching her to him.

A new eccentricity of intention or action marked each of his days. For instance, he wanted to realize his fortune and go to live with his beloved mistress in a forgotten corner of the world. Clémence smiled. Another time, in a paroxysm of excitement, he proposed resolutely that they die in one another's arms. The woman frowned and became icy. Paul, in despair at having saddened her, accused her of having no soul and offered nothing less than to jump out of the window in order to rid her of him. She only succeeded in calming him down by composing a laughing face.

To complete the measure, he nearly killed himself in front of her one day. They were having breakfast together. The young man, playing with his knife, affirmed that he would wound himself if she demanded that proof of his amour. She challenged him to do it, as a joke, and he stabbed himself in the chest. Clémence, frightened by the blood that was flowing from the wound, nearly fell backwards. She ran to fetch a doctor, who, after inspecting the wound, declared that a rib had fortunately caused the blade to deviate.

Such scenes went directly contrary to the student's objective. Clémence, very pleased in the beginning to inspire such an exclusive passion, did not take long to weary of it as a yoke. She was already seized by fits of ennui that she was unable to overcome. Paul reproached her for them as the equivalent of a crime. That was the point of departure of endless quarrels, which exasperated the woman and increased her distaste. She did not fail, on such occasions, to exaggerate the expression of her repugnance. The young man's passionate transport soon buckled under that implacability. He fell to his knees and begged for mercy. His pallor, his tearful eyes, and the irresistible eloquence that his passion produced, triumphed again over the rigors of his mistress.

It was in the aftermath of one of those reconciliations that he threatened her with a horrible vengeance. Beside one another at the window they were gazing vaguely into the street. Raising his eyes, Paul suddenly perceived the iron crampon that projected between Clémence's window and his own. He indicated it to his mistress with his finger and said, in an energetic tone: "You see that nail . . . well, if the time comes when you no longer love me, I swear to hang myself from it, in order that, when you open your window in the morning, you'll find me dead."

"That threat made me laugh out loud," Madame Clémence added. "However, I was paid for knowing it . . ."

Their sentiments with regard to one another had not ceased to be modified in an inverse direction, to the extent that one could say that the temperature of the woman's heart descended to zero while the student's rose to boiling point. The result of that was that Paul, without being more exigent than in the beginning, appeared to be excessively demanding. Twenty times she had warned him, refusing the door to *Monsieur* of her own accord. Presently, she took no account of a pretention that she could not even imagine. It was the jealousy of a young man who had previously amused her, but of whom she could not now even bear the appearance.

She told me that with a naïve cynicism that chilled me to the bone. "Oh, God in Heaven, I have no reproaches to make to myself. I loved him for three months as much as possible. By virtue of no longer quitting me, any more than my shadow, he ended up being taken in horror. I was bored, I had the desire to yawn; it made me feel ill. If I tried to talk reason to him, there were cries, tears and nervous twitches, just like a cat that has eaten arsenic pellets. I was wasting my time. I was a thousand feet over his head, and all those stupidities, I ask you, what do they mean? What's the point of hurting oneself? Because a woman no longer loves you! Love is like nails, one drives out another. Then again, I don't know how many times I annoyed *Monsieur*, who ended up having doubts about my relationship with Paul. Imagine, monsieur, if I'd lost my estate! I couldn't, however, be unfortunate for him!"

For a long time already, Madame Clémence had been slyly meditating introducing a new actor on to the stage. As a prelude to that *coup d'état* she closed her door to the student from time to time. Unable to recover the key that she had confided to him, she drew the bolts, and Paul, in spite of the scandal with which he filled the house, in spite of passionate letters, eloquent merely by virtue of the tears with which they were stained, could not always succeed in opening it. From her alcove she heard him sobbing or writhing in convulsions, or proffering death threats against her. It was no longer sufficient to have an aversion for him; now she was afraid of him and thought seriously about assuring herself of a solid arm, in view of the violence she thought she had to fear.

Long before knowing Paul, she assured me, she had not ceased to have a penchant for the artiste who enjoyed the exclusive privilege of dressing her hair. For some time she had been going to see him more frequently than usual. He was a fellow of twenty-eight, tall and robust, with a fresh and pretty face, always well groomed and perfumed. His name was Achille. His sign bore a Greek translation of his name and profession, because a few Hellenes were shaved in his establishment. He was implacably cheerful. His quips and puns made Madame Clémence roar with laughter. The attraction she felt toward the fellow developed rapidly under the influence of the ennui and fear that Paul caused her.

It did not take long for her to have in hand something analogous to those scarecrows that are used to frighten birds. The devotion of the hairdresser could not be put in doubt. However, what had more charm for him than anything else in the adventure was having the opportunity, knowing Latin as well as Greek, to parody Caesar's saying: *Veni, vidi, vici.*

From then on, Clémence broke entirely with the student and refused obstinately to receive him. In vain he begged her, spent nights at her door, wrote her ardent letters; she remained inflexible. Paul was drowning in tears; he was as fleshless as an old man; his hollow eyes had a strange fixity, and momentary flashes that presaged something terrible . . .

At this point, the incorrigible Prosper put the lid on his impertinence with an ambiguous observation that revolted people of the most moderate character. A grave man told him hotly that no one was forcing him to listen to the reading, which was tantamount to telling him that he ought to keep quiet or go away. Sensible to the reprimand, Prosper did not say another word, and Anselme finished his story in the midst of the utmost calm.

The student put himself incessantly in the path of his mistress. Clémence, no longer daring to go home alone, had herself escorted by Monsieur Achille, who, with an air of sovereign scorn, limited himself to pushing his rival aside with his hand.

One evening, Paul changed tactics. In the absence of his mistress, instead of waiting for her on the landing, he penetrated into her apartment with the aid of the key that he was obstinate in retaining, and hid in a closet next to the alcove. It would be difficult to specify his motive, unless he hoped to find himself alone with Clémence and, in that case, to extract a little pity from her. Previously, he had gone downstairs to give the concierge a letter for Madame Clémence.

At about eleven o'clock, from the place where he was, the young man must have heard the footsteps of his mistress. Unfortunately, as usual, she was returning home accompanied by the hairdresser. She was holding Paul's letter in her hand. Glad not to have encountered the student at her door, she said to Monsieur Achille: "It's another letter from the madman; read it to me. We'll have a good laugh . . ."

She lay down. Monsieur Achille sat down next to the bed and opened the letter.

"In all my life," Clémence said to me, "I had never heard anything so extravagant . . . I didn't know he was there . . . I laughed like a lunatic, especially because of Achille's comical remarks. I'm sure, Monsieur, that you would have done the same."

I asked Madame Clémence abruptly if, by chance, she still had that letter.

"I think so, yes," she replied. "Are you really curious to see it?"

"Very curious, I swear to you," I said.

"Wait," she said. "I'll go down and fetch it for you."

She soon came up again and said: "Here, read it yourself and see whether I'm not right . . ."

Very slowly, because tears had dampened the ink in a
number of places, I deciphered this letter:

*I have a body full of tears. Sobs are sti-
fling me. The warm and bitter tears that are
falling in large drops on my fingers, would
hollow out stone but have no effect on your
heart. You no longer want to see me or speak
to me; you hate me. I could die without extracting a tear from you; perhaps my death
would give you pleasure. But was it me who
sought you out? Why did you not leave me
to my mother, to my books? Who jogged my
elbow? Who said to me:* Look at me? *Who
said to me:* Love me, I love you? *Who lit
the inferno in my breast? Who poured the
poison into my veins? Who stifled my filial
sentiments? Who riveted me to a woman,
so firmly that I can no longer think about
anything else? Who has absorbed, devoured,
annihilated me? I find you strange. You grip
like a vice my limbs, my mind, my will, my
soul, and you say:* Let me go. *You have covered me with an incurable leprosy and you
say:* Get rid of it. *Do you imagine that I can
fold my arms, that I can stiffen myself against
the invasion of evil? Do you think, then, that
it is so sweet to love you? It would be necessary to know you less. I have only stirred the
mud in your soul, I have only displeased you
by opposing your crapulous habits; morally,*

you are more a monster than a woman. I am scorned because of this amour, and rightly so. If misfortune overtakes me, they will say: That's good; why love such a creature? Why did he not reject that infamous amour? *They speak about it at their ease. They blush for me, and they do not know that I blush even more for myself, that the scorn in which I hold myself only equals in depth and extent my monstrous passion. Amour is not a coat that one puts on and takes off at will. I would soon have uprooted it and trampled it underfoot. It is a coat of flame stuck to my skin; the shreds that I tear off are full of my flesh and my blood, and my body is no longer anything but a wound. I have at least the right to pity. I did not have much, but I have given you everything. What have I harvested from that? Endless tortures. The further I go, the more I suffer. It seems that the saying was made for me*: Either suffer, or die. *I spend nights at your door; I am on the floor, my ear to the wall, while you are in another's arms, and I hear you say to him what you said to me, and kiss him as you kissed me. I have red-hot coals in my entrails. Those caresses, which you lavish on anyone who does not care about them, you refuse to me, to whom they are life. In sum, for having loved you too much, my life is only hanging by a thread, and I hope that it will soon break. No, it is not for vain ostentation that I allow these horrible pains to accumulate within me, which are burning and killing me. I frighten those who see me. The neighbors no longer recognize me. The woman downstairs said to another*: What's the matter with that fellow? I've seen him as chubby as a cherub; now one can see daylight through his body. *My legs can no longer support me. One might think that I were dissolving in water. And I fear that only the sight of you can return me to life. Your love was my breath, and you know whether it will ever return. I only ask to see you. If you have anything dear to you in the world, I implore you, let me see you one last time; one last time, do you hear? To those condemned to death nothing is refused. Will you be more pitiless than an executioner?*

Monsieur Achille's clowning and Clémence's bursts of laughter were suddenly interrupted by the fall of a body that made the partition creak. The woman shuddered and uttered a scream simultaneously. The hairdresser, who had not heard anything, asked her whether she was mad.

"No," said Clémence, pale with terror. "I'm sure there's someone hiding in there." She indicated the partition separating the closet from the alcove.

Bewildered by such an energetic assertion, Monsieur Achille picked up the candle and went into the closet. He was struck by stupor on perceiving his rival there, who, collapsed against the wall, seemed devoid of life. A few moments later, he cried, brutally: "What are you doing here?" but Paul did not move, any more than a dead man.

Clémence had ice in her veins. "Who is it?" she asked, in a faint voice.

The hairdresser seized Paul by the arm and dragged him into the room. A little compassion mitigated the woman's fear, for, as she said, the student was a sorry sight. His face had holes big enough to contain a fist. His paltry limbs, which had the mechanical mobility of a child's toy, were floating in overly large garments as if in a sack. One could not say, at that moment, where dolor had drawn his soul.

The voice of his mistress suddenly extracted him from his lethargy. Raising toward her a gaze from which floods of melancholy flowed, and extending his imploring arms, he said with sobs in his throat and his soul on his lips: "Don't you want me to talk to you?"

Monsieur Achille interposed himself. He felt brave. Apart from the fact that Paul was small in stature, he was at that point so thin and so weak that it appeared that a breath could knock him over. At the moment when he took a step toward Clémence, the hairdresser grabbed him by the collar of his coat and shoved him with so much force that the poor lover fell to the floor against a piece of furniture. The woman made a gesture of pity.

Paul came to his knees and said, in a tearful voice that would have stirred the entrails of a hyena: "I'm meek, you see; I allow myself to be beaten." He added, animatedly: "It's not that I'm a coward, at least. One word, one gesture, oh, and you'd see my strength!"

Monsieur Achille, outraged by the threat, closed his fists and ran toward Paul. The latter, with the bound of a wild beast, was on his feet in the blink of an eye.

Throwing his fists backwards like two menacing slings, he nailed the hairdresser to the spot with a magnetic gaze comparable to two red-hot sword-points. But that superhuman muscular tension only lasted for a few moments. The flames he had in his eyes were immediately extinguished by the indifference of his mistress.

"Come on," said the latter, "be reasonable, Monsieur Paul, and go away."

Then there was a scene of ignoble pathos. Monsieur Achille, ashamed of having been afraid, took hold of the student bodily and tried to throw him out. The resistance that the amorous individual opposed, by clinging on to the furniture, rendered him furious, and Clémence completed exasperating him by addressing Paul two or three times with tenderness. He struck his frail adversary indignantly. After a quarter of an hour of that revolting fight, if it can be called a fight, he finally succeeded in pushing the student outside, bruised by punches, like an inert mass.

"Nothing was moving any longer," Madame Clémence added. "I thought Paul was already unconscious or dead, when I heard him going back into his room and turning the key in the lock. I thought I could finally sleep tranquilly. Sleep was already overtaking me.

"Suddenly, Paul opened his window, the one alongside the room where we were. I shoved Achille, who was asleep, and said to him: 'Listen!' By the sound, he was sure that Paul had climbed out of his window and was walking along the gutter. I was afraid. I imagined that he had heard me barricading my door and that he was coming back through the window. I was also afraid that he would fall into the street. I had all the trouble in the world holding back Achille, who wanted to get up. What do you expect? I was a thousand leagues away from the thing . . .

"But we couldn't hear anything any longer. There was a silence to make you shiver. The blood froze in my veins. We were still listening. Then something extraordinary and frightful happened. I can't think about it without my hair standing on end and my heart lurching. It still seems to me that it was only yesterday. At first one would have sworn that Paul was climbing along the slates. Then, for perhaps two minutes, he didn't budge at all. Then he fell like a stone, and started jigging about so forcefully that one might have thought that he was trying to demolish the wall. It was a rumble that went on and on. My windows trembled and slates flew to the right and left as if in a big wind. I leave you to imagine the state I was in. I stuck out my neck and opened my eyes. Not to mention that the sweat was flowing over my face like water. I could have been punched in the chest and I wouldn't have suffered so much. I was more than half dead. Achille's arm bore the mark of my fingernails for a long time . . ."

"And you didn't suspect, after his threat . . . ?" I exclaimed, suddenly.

"Yes," she interrupted, "you're astonished today, because you know that he's dead. But I didn't even remember his threat any longer. I only thought of it afterwards. At the time I was so far from the truth that I used all my strength to prevent Achille from going to see what it all meant. I squeezed his neck so tightly with my arm that I strangled him.

"We heard a man who stuck his head out of the window and said: 'Will they soon have finished knocking, whoever it is?' Unfortunately, the sky was so cloudy that he couldn't see anything. He went back inside almost immediately. In any case, the noise had stopped suddenly. One could only hear the thumps at longer and longer intervals. But it had all been finished for at least half an hour when we were still there, like statues, listening. Achille went back to sleep, though. As for me, it was impossible to close an eye. I didn't suspect anything, I swear to you! Only, without knowing why, I was devoured by anxieties; I felt something like two leaden hands on my breast, which were weighing on me and stifling me.

"It was only after dawn that I went . . . not to sleep but, so to speak, to float between two slumbers. When he woke up, Achille didn't take long to make me open my eyes. He had no sooner gone than a horrible dread took possession of me. I made great efforts to chase it away. I would have liked to have some laudanum to drink. I shifted in my bed as if it were a sack full of thorns. Not being able to stand it any longer I got up. An invincible force drew me toward the window. I opened it . . .

"Oh, what I saw . . . I'll never, ever forget it. I uttered a scream that must have been heard a league away, and I fell backwards . . ."

Madame Clémence drew breath and concluded thus: "Oh, that Paul knew very well what he was doing. I can't count the nights I've spent without sleeping, and the bad dreams I've had. In the early days I couldn't remain alone for a minute. Even now, even though I make arrangements in such a fashion that I never see the frightful nail, it sometimes enters into my eyes and wakes me up at night. I see Paul again as I saw him when I opened my window, hanged, with his face stuck to the wall. I can only hope to have repose when I've quit this house. And the gossip of all the neighbors! And the scenes I've had with *Monsieur*! Don't you find that abominable? Yes, that's what I've reaped for my excessive generosity. But what do you expect? I'm made that way; I'll never correct myself, I'll always be the same fool of the good Lord . . ."

Etc., etc.

Everyone knows the ardor with which we ordinarily lay claim to the faculties that we lack. After that speech, it was necessary not to doubt that Madame Clémence would have applied to herself the dictum, if she had known it, that sensitive people are fatally unhappy. Their hearts are too voluminous for the space in which they beat; one bumps, bruises and wounds them without noticing, as one detaches a wisp of straw in going past a laden cart; and if they complain and protest, one turns round and asks, with surprise: "Why are you screeching like that?"

Prey to a dull irritation, I quarreled with Madame Clémence one day, I don't know on what subject. She quit me, throwing in my face the original epithet, and never came back.

Three years later, from Saint-Germain, where hazard had taken me, I was going to Passy through the forest to see a person of my acquaintance. I sat down outside the railway station just as a passenger train went by, going from Paris to Rouen. The noise of the machine made by the steam did not prevent me from hearing someone calling. I raised my head and I perceived the smiling face of Madame Clémence in the frame of a window.

I approached. Her health was more flourishing than ever. She had filled out. With her milky whiteness, her ample bosom, the finesse of her linen, the necklace of hair she had around her neck, fastened with a miniature portrait of a man, she gave the impression of a rich bourgeoise, or, even better, a beautiful and worthy mother of a family. She seemed charmed to see me again. The train was about to pull away again, so we scarcely had time to chat, and she brought me up to date with her affairs in a few words.

"Monsieur is established," she said. "He gave me thirty thousand francs. I've married in my homeland a worthy man who adores me. We've bought a pretty house where we live on our income. You can see that I'm as healthy as a charm. I have a magnificent child. I'm happy."

I'm happy. What was so strange, then, about those few syllables, that they resonated in my ear like an unexpected drumbeat, and threw me into a whirlwind of sad ideas? *I'm happy . . .*

After all, why not? Where there is neither knowledge nor intention, there cannot be any crime. A person who meditates a murder silently is nevertheless culpable even if, thinking of the talion, he does not combine action with the thought. But can one cry *assassin* at a roofer who falls from a roof and conserves his life at the expense of a passer-by that he crushes?

Once and for all, it is for those whose jealous souls who have the privilege of durable affection and exclusive devotions to beware of these mechanical dolls, full of seduction but cold, treacherous and cruel, who, in the fashion of the gears of a mill, hook on to your coat-tails and then, stupidly and fatally, break your legs, arms, body and head.

The audience protested somewhat against the taste and ambition of that final image. Nevertheless, there was unanimous agreement that, all things considered, it was no worse than the concluding sentence of the turbulent Prosper. After which, in view of the advanced hour, the other story-tellers were adjourned until the next session.

The Curtain

IT was not even a curtain, unless one can call by that name a rag of green lustrine devoid of rings or a rail, nailed externally to the four corners of a window. After all, why not? Such a scruple, in these days? That much fuss about a word? Let's pass on.

In the Rue Bleue, on the same floor as me, alongside my bedroom, lived a petty rentier very attentive to the actions of others. "Neighbor," he said to me one day, putting his grizzled head through the sweet peas and nasturtiums that brightened up his window, "you worry me. For a fortnight you've been camped day and night at your window, your eyes fixed on that shred of green cloth opposite. I could understand your patience if, instead of that, there were some pretty girl perched there like a bird in a cage, but . . ."

I quit my window abruptly in order not to listen to the old man any longer. I was furious to know that someone was spying on me. Of course, if that window, instead of being hermetically blocked, had served as a frame for the most attractive of faces, I would probably have looked at it two or three times, and everything would have been said. If there is no woman so beautiful that she does not fail in some regard, there are, on the other hand, men amorous of perfection to the point the slightest flaw suffices to give them distaste even for a marvel. Those sympathetic and passionate men, moreover, are reduced only to loving pure chimeras. Cloistered women, of whom one only perceives the edge of the veil, inspire them with violent desires that claw them or stifle them, but they are made of bronze before a naked woman.

"Those shutters conceal a masterpiece," a cicerone says to you. If you do not blush with enthusiasm, you emerge from your apathy, your pulse has more activity, and your eye shines more than usual; in your memory, all the sublime symphonies of some colorist awaken, your soul rises to the temperature of admiration. Click-click! The shutters are folded back, and you are in the presence of an odious pastiche, shrill, garish, poorly mounted, dirty, restored by a painter-decorator. In all conscience, is it not better to leave the shutters closed?

Can one be astonished, given that, that I quit my neighbor unceremoniously, good fellow as he is. I feared his officious compassion as much as the scalpel of a materialist; I was afraid that he might tear the mysterious green taffeta and allow me to see the wrinkles of some duenna, or the hump or madness of a poor young woman. Oh, if curiosity had been the cause of my fever, I had no need to be obliged to the old fellow for so little; any door-keeper could have cured me. No, of my own free will, a magnetic atmosphere circulated around me in which my fantasy floated at ease. I only wanted to emerge from that milieu as late as possible. By that shred of lustrine my horizon seemed limited; all my loving and passionate being was concentrated on it; behind it, I saw my dream dwelling:

my ideal, the composite of my blood and my soul, the distillation of the best of myself. I was mad, if it pleases you to think so, but I execrated in advance anyone who would return me to sanity.

Every night, nailed to my observation post, I saw shadows passing back and forth, quivering, over the curtain, behind which burned a pale light. None, thus far, had moved me then more than any other; no voice, while those shadows passed back and forth, had cried: "That's her!" I suffered from her indifference; I thought myself disdained by that creature formed, in a sense, from one of my ribs; melancholy, that gangrene of the soul, prowled around me as around a sure prey. But one evening, at the hour when I least expected it, the chimera hatched in my brain; the strange vapors exhaled by the inextinguishable furnace that burns resplendently within me congealed, crystallized in the form of the most beautiful of women.

The atmosphere was stifling, the darkness profound. Up above, there was no moon or stars, only, at intervals, lightning cracking the thick black crust of clouds. A shadow, confused at first, was agitating behind the curtain; as it drew closer, the contours were designed more neatly on the transparent fabric. Soon, I could see very distinctly the silhouette of a young woman leaning on the window sill. I was breathless, choking; a frisson ran over my skin. By her movements, I understood that she was looking in my direction.

Our eyes met. The same electric shock struck us both at the same time. As I shuddered, I saw the lines designed by her body tremble. It was not in our power to turn our heads away; a superhuman force immobilized the direction of our eyes. A continuous jet of flame emerged therefrom, the encounter of which established between us, for a few moments, an intimate and profound union, a veritable fusion of our two existences. It was a magnetic current of sorts, which went from one soul to the other and resolved the problem of amour, so obscure for me until then, and, by virtue of that very fact, so absurd: two in one.

Such enjoyments are ineffable. I don't know how long that ecstasy lasted; I don't know what came to break the charm of that mysterious conversation, during which we said so many things without opening our mouths; at any rate, the memory of that moment will never leave my mind.

At first I could have believed that I was in love with a fiction, and yet my amour had as much energy as if its object had been real. Now that the fact had given reason to my presentiments, and behind that curtain truly respired the undiscoverable *dimidium anima meae*,[1] my passion set aside what was vague and imaginary in order to become practical, so to speak, and gained in logic what it lost in extent. Strange thing! I had only seen the silhouette of the woman, but neither her beauty nor her soul had any mystery for me any longer. The nuances of her hair, the tones of her flesh, the perfection of her forms and all the rare sentiments for which her body served as a screen, had been revealed to me in a simple glance. So I was certain that when the curtain fell, I would see the incomparable face of which the mold was my own mind.

In the milieu of the progress of that singular amour, the little old man who was my neighbor inspired an increasingly serious aversion in me. I shivered at the

____

1 "Half of my life"—Horace's tribute to Virgil.

sight of him, like a patient at the sight of the surgeon who is disposing to cut off his leg. He spied on me with an irritating obstinacy. I could not put my nose outside my window without immediately perceiving him at his. His little gray eyes sparkled with malice. He looked at me with an expression of false bonhomie, and tried to engage me in conversation. I withdrew without replying to him, but he did not let go; he continued to observe me and to renew his advances every time he perceived me.

In order to avoid his importunities, I sat two feet away from my window. From that place I could at least consider the folds of the curtain without fear of being disturbed.

One day, the cling-clang of my doorbell extracted me from my feverish contemplations. I ran to open the door. It was my abominable neighbor. I would gladly have exploded in anger, but time was pressing; I shut the door in his face. I went back to sit at the window.

Something strange was happening behind the curtain, on which the sunlight was falling directly. The overexcitement of my senses and the plenitude of my wellbeing informed me that *she* was there and that her eyes were in communication with mine. In fact, I thought I could see, through two almost imperceptible holes, the gleams of her dark eyes. With her finger, which she drew over the curtain, she traced bizarre figures in relief. Gradually, she replaced those figures with letters. In the first I distinguished without difficulty a J, in the second an E. I saw the finger hollow out successively a T, an A, and I, an M and an E. *Je t'aime!*

Joy wrenched a cry from me, I launched myself at the window; but I was interrupted in my surge by an enormous ivory ball that was agitating to my right. I turned my head and I perceived with horror the bald and shiny cranium of the infernal old man, who saluted me amicably and said to me in a honeyed and sardonic tone: "Ah! Neighbor, could you accord me two minutes of attention? I'll tell you the story of that curtain . . ."

I recoiled three paces as abruptly as I had advanced. The curtain had become motionless again; its surface was no longer undulating under the pressure of a charming hand; and yet those two syllables—*je t'aime!*—were still dancing before my eyes like characters in precious stone.

All things considered, even supposing that I had been the dupe of a hallucination or the caprices of a gust of wind, did not the happiness that inundated me and penetrated me compensate fully for the chagrin that a disappointment would cause me? In the final analysis, is it not always true that realization is suffering, and dreaming enjoyment?

And besides, if it were possible that I still had some doubt, the following night I was to acquire irrefutable proof that I did not have for a mistress a phantom emanated by the seething of a sick brain.

The night was as bright as twilight. The curtain, equally illuminated from both sides, had lost its transparency; for me it was an opaque and mute veil. But suddenly, I know not by what enchantment—I thought it was nailed down—it folded back upon itself like a theater curtain. I perceived then, drowned in light, the upper body of a strangely beautiful woman. Thousands of rays of light emerged from it, which, like white-hot iron wires, attached themselves to my epidermis and drew it in the same direction with an invincible force. I did not even seek to remove myself from the pangs caused by a delectable dolor; my body went toward that powerful attraction. I thought for a moment that my eyes might emerge from their orbits. Almost entirely leaning outside, sustained in the air by I know not what, I devoured the charms of the woman with my gaze; I would have liked to absorb them entirely.

In my reveries, I had laboriously imagined a model of Eve of a perfection and a richness of colors that I believed to be unrealizable, but now I had before me something altogether more perfect and more harmonious than what I had dreamed. The moon, on one side, and the candlelight, on the other, inundated her shoulders and her semi-naked breasts with reflections of silver and gold, the mixture of which produced a fantastic aureole around her flesh. Her dark eyes, which stood out against the mat whiteness of her face, formed a marvelous contrast with the gilded hue of the waves of her hair.

She moved her lips and her voice vibrated in a melancholy fashion, like the chanterelle of a bass. No song more plaintive or passion more true had ever stirred my soul.

Promised by her mother to a man whom she saw at first with indifference, since she had recognized me she envisaged death with less chagrin than that marriage. But, in the power of an inexorable bad mother, she had to marry or die. Her choice was not in doubt; a white shroud would be her nuptial bed; she would await in her virginity the day when our free souls could be united in an eternal embrace.

Such is the substance of the story that I believed I heard, during which I passed through the alternation of extreme sentiments. I lacked air, I was choking; confused thoughts seethed in my brain; I felt simultaneously the sharp pain of a wound and all the sensuality of a fortunate passion.

When I awoke, I ran to my window. The curtain had fallen back. My heart was squeezed when I remembered that behind that curtain a drama was being played whose denouement, whatever it might be, would be fatal for me.

I admitted, without any great effort, that the nocturnal scene had only been a vision; but that vision had shaken me with too much violence to be devoid of a reason for being. I accepted it as a copy, or rather a tracing, of reality. I finally had the key to the enigma. That fixed curtain, the shadow of the young woman who was profiled there every evening, those eyes that I had seen shining behind it, those letters in relief that I had read—everything, in sum—appeared to me to be as simple as a solved problem.

Thus, I was in a state to render a saint jealous. If had been laid down naked on a thorn bush, I would not have suffered as much. It is better to be bitten by a rabid dog and to sense a red-hot iron on the wound than to be attained by jealousy; the Inquisition, with its cords, its wedges, its hooks, its pincers and the entire apparatus of torture, is only a paltry executioner by comparison.

The exaltation of suffering troubled me to the extent of delirium; I gave the impression of a furious madman.

I opened my door to run I know not where. My neighbor blocked my passage.

"La la," he said to me. "Where are you running to like this, scarcely dressed, without a hat and your eyes bulging?"

I looked at him with a stupid expression.

"Come on, listen to me," he added. "You're ill, go back inside; I'll cure you with a word."

"Eh!" I cried at the paroxysm of fury. "What makes you think, you old wretch, that I want to be cured?"

I shoved him aside brutally and I went downstairs, leaving him to grumble at his leisure. In four bounds I was in the street. I placed myself on watch outside the door of number six, the house in which my mistress lived. A coupé with two horses stopped there at that moment. Several men got down from it, dressed in black as if for a ball or a burial. Immediately, I noticed one younger than the others, whose pale face caused me such a furious surge of hatred that I had the certitude of seeing my rival. I do not know what invisible force paralyzed my limbs and prevented me from yielding to the need I experienced to leap at his throat and strangle him. It was impossible for me to move before having seen those men descend.

Their visit lasted half an hour. Then they climbed into their carriage and drew away.

"Ah!" I said to myself with despair, returning to my bedroom. "They doubtless came to sign the contract!"

On my landing, the pitiless old man was waiting for me, his head passed through the gap in his doorway; but when he perceived my haggard gaze and the distress in my face, he was afraid. He drew back his head swiftly and turned the key twice in the lock.

Heart-rending and terrible screams suddenly rose up behind the curtain. Night had fallen only a short while before. I perceived shadows coming and going with an extraordinary vivacity. Evidently, they were trying to stifle the screams, which were becoming increasingly intense. The heads of curious individuals flooded to windows in the surrounding area; conversations were engaged between houses. In the midst of the voices I recognized that of my neighbor.

"It's my neighbor who is dying," he said. "The poor young woman . . ."

I blocked my ears in order not to hear the rest. When I took my hands away from my head, the screams had ceased. I was shivering, as if in ten degrees of frost. My slumber was nothing but a long and painful nightmare.

What a night! And what a day was to follow it! If the weather had at least been in harmony with the somber tint of my thoughts! But no, it was sunny; with perfumes; the wind brought me a vague noise of distant songs; all around me there was a festival atmosphere that reminded me of cherished memories, as if to make me sense more forcefully the bitterness of the present moment. In a state of complete prostration, I lent myself with a sort of sensuality to those cruel comparisons.

A slight tremor of the curtain recalled me to a sentiment of reality. The wrinkling of the cloth informed me that a finger was running over the interior surface. The indecisive movement of the hand that was tracing those furrows chilled me with fear. I understood clearly, by the softness and irregularity of the lines, that strength was lacking the poor seamstress, and it was with a constriction of the heart of which no physical torture can enable the comprehension that I read, in the succession of the letters the word "Adieu!"

I wanted to convince myself that I had not seen clearly, that an agitation of the wind had produced those characters by chance; but that same evening, the curtain was torn away, and I could see several persons in the room who were shedding tears around a bed.

I stayed at my window until daylight, my eyes fixed on the shroud that enveloped my dead mistress.

The next day, when I quit my room, workmen were extending a white sheet over the door of number six. I took pleasure in examining the details of those lugubrious preparations. Two undertakers soon brought down a coffin, which they placed on trestles, parallel with the street. It was covered with white serge. Candles were arranged around it; a woman came to deposit a bouquet of orange blossom with silver leaves.

I followed the procession, which paused at the church before going to the cemetery.

There, I could not reach the grave, so numerous was the cortege. I heard weeping, heart-rending sobs, fragments of the funeral oration. "We are all mortal . . . sooner or later, she had to die . . . she will live eternally in the memory of those who knew her . . . adieu, O most gracious and most tender . . . on high!"

Then there was the dull and sinister rumble of spadefuls of earth falling upon the fir-wood planks.

When the crowd had flowed away, approaching in my turn, I knelt down on the fresh grave. I was prey to the sadness that the absence of a beloved person causes. Large tears trickled from my eyes.

"Oh, my love," I said, in such a fashion as not to be heard by anyone, "My grief is great; but I am robust and I love to feel the blood flowing in my veins. Have no fear that I will drown in tears, or that my flesh will turn to parchment by dint of abstinence. No, there are less vulgar means to prove that I love you. Unlike the incredulous, who believe that you lie entirely in this tomb, I do not believe that you are dead. The spirit, although escaping the vase whose walls it breaks, nevertheless exists. It wanders freely through space, visiting by turns the objects of its hatred and those of its affection. It caresses the latter and torments the former. You will visit me frequently, dear shade! You will mingle with all my dreams, you will aid me to live, and perhaps I shall succeed, by means of the torture of a long life, in conquering a place beside yours."

I ran to shut myself away in my home in order to nurture at my ease all the developments of a woe that I loved. By means of the expression of my despair I had frightened my neighbor so much that he had entirely renounced the pleasure of making my acquaintance. I therefore have nothing to fear from his impertinent zeal, and I hope to die with the certainty of having been loved for my soul, once in my life.

Extracts From the Reports of a Police Agent

I

Paris, 10 November 1843.

IN conformity with the orders that you have done me the honor of transmitting to me, I went on the twenty-ninth of last month, at about five o'clock in the morning, to maintain surveillance on the Débarcadère du Nord. An obstinate driving rain was making every street into a small river. I was scarcely able to discover my man in the crowd of travelers. He was carrying a rather heavy package wrapped in a piece of gray lustrine and tied up with a sort of narrow belt of green wool with a buckle.

In the description given to me, that package was perhaps the only thing designated scrupulously, because, with regard to the individual himself, the employee of the passport office had made a diabolical portrait. I have, however, been informed that the monsieur in question is a painter, and you will probably tell me that a pen is not a brush. I cannot stress that too much. In numerous affairs, when success does not respond to our zeal, we are taxed with incapacity, although, most of the time, it is only necessary to blame the negligence of those messieurs. It seems essential to me to put before your eyes this derisory description:

Thirty years of age. Height one meter seventy centimeters. Light brown hair. Uncovered forehead. Blue eyes. Average nose. Average mouth. Black beard. Round chin. Oval face. Uniform complexion. Distinguishing features: none.

Without mentioning the name, which is spelled Hégésippe Vannier and not *Vanier*, one of two things must be true: either the maker of that portrait is blind or he is trying to make fun of the administration.[1] The aforementioned package notwithstanding, I had a very perplexed mind. While the said Hégésippe awaited the end of the deluge at the extremity of the eastern gallery, I scrutinized him carefully, and that examination put me beside myself. It is necessary for you to know that the hair is dark and not light brown, that the eyes are gray and not blue and that the nose and mouth are large rather than average. But what it is notably to be put under glass is the epithet *black* applied to a beard that, unless I am blind, could be mistaken for chips of rosewood. I will add that my indignation was boundless when I perceived on sieur Vannier's forehead, when he removed his hat momentarily, a scar the size of a haricot bean. How, then,

---

1 Although this character is fictitious, save for reflecting many of the author's own experiences, it is worth noting that Barbara would have been familiar with the work and biography of "Hégésippe Moreau" (Pierre-Jacques Rouillot, 1810-1838), a Romantic poet and short-story writer who had died young (of tuberculosis) in Paris shortly before Barbara arrived there. As a trivial noun, *vannier* means "basket-maker."

under "distinguishing features," has monsieur written *none*, with the final flourish of his pen? Those unquali-fiable inexactitudes could have caused me to commit a blunder, and earned me in consequence a remonstration from my chief. On my honor, I would hand in my resig-nation were it not for my duty, to which I am a slave, and my passion for the profession to which I have devoted myself.

But I am taking too long to tell you about the mea-sures I have taken with a view to reaching directly and promptly the objective that you have indicated to me. I believe that I have surpassed in conception my most celebrated colleagues and have truly extended the limits of the art.

Sieur Vannier, three months behind in his rent, only returned from traveling in order to receive a regulation notice to quit. My good fortune permitted that there was, alongside the room recently rented by him, a small room that is only separated from it by a thin partition. First I obtained the good graces of the concierge by means of an advance of five francs. The man wanted nothing less than to give me the secret history of all the tenants in the house. I did not ask as much as that.

I visited Vannier's lodgings with the most scrupulous attention. That room is small and obscure; the window is low down. Beams produce in the ceiling a series of in-tervals full of shadow. All these observations suited the project that I was forming very well.

Enthusiasm not permitting me an instant's delay, I arrived the next day with a bed, chairs, an armchair, a table and the implements necessary to the edification of my masterpiece. I had observed the day before that the smooth ceiling of my room—which is a recent annexe—was higher than that of the room of my future neighbor. Perched on a scaffold constructed with my table and my chair, with the aid of a drill, I made a hole at the junction of the ceiling and the wall of my man's room. Thanks to my keen observation, that opening was between two beams, in a place where daylight never penetrated. I rounded it out in the form of a funnel by means of a milling-tool and I applied my eye to it. I observed with an indescribable joy that I could see Vannier's interior no less clearly than if my body were within it.

Illuminated, so to speak, by that first result, I pursued my task, which was only half done. I had recourse to a tinsmith whom I commissioned to make a small tube, the model of which was inspired by knowledge I had obtained from lectures at the Sorbonne. I no sooner had the instrument in my hands than I ran to my little room. In the same partition, very close to the first hole, I pierced an opening of the diameter of my tube, destined in my thought to fulfill the functions of an acoustic pipe. I was constrained to make use of it several times. Vannier, gradually arranging his books, did not stop going back and forth. Then, tools of an unusual form became indispensable to me. My patience and my courage reckoned with all the obstacles. It was now only a matter of devoting myself to a decisive proof and discovering whether, in the final count, I had more vanity than merit. My plan was no less rapidly realized than conceived.

I went down to the lodge and told the concierge that my profession required the greatest calm, that I feared troubling my neighbor, and that I desired him to help me in a little experiment.

He hastened to follow me.

First we went into Vannier's room, where I made sure that my two openings, situated in a dark corner, could not be perceived. "Stay here," I said to the concierge. "I'm going to shut myself in my room. First you'll speak in a loud voice, then in a quieter once, and then in a whisper, very softly; finally, you'll utter a sigh." Then I went to my scaffold and applied my eye to the opening

I perceived the concierge with satisfaction; walking around the room, he seemed to be calculating the value of the furniture and rummaging curiously through the cupboards. That examination even extracted a rather ugly grimace from him.

"Are you there, Monsieur?" he suddenly shouted, at the top of his voice. Then, not as loudly, in accordance with my instructions: "Hop! Can you hear anything, Monsieur?" Finally, in a gradually decreasing tone, he repeated the phrase and concluded with a deep sigh. It goes without saying that, while I lost nothing of his gestures, I collected even the slightest inflexions of his voice.

Did I have reason to be proud of myself? In imitation of a spider, I had woven such a marvelous web that the slightest movement of the enemy could not escape me. Do you think that any more efficacious means have ever been devised for entering so far into the heart, brain and conscience of a man? I applaud myself all the more willingly because the subject submitted to my analysis, suspected—rightly, I am convinced—of tenebrous thoughts and culpable projects, is as unfathomable as the sea, as discreet as the tomb, and seems to take pleasure in misleading the eyes that study him. Oh, he can play a clever game in future, shut himself away with a triple lock, refuse to put even the appearance of a confession on paper, suspect his most intimate friends, and even his mistress; I say with pride that I have him! He's mine! And I shall have his secret, no matter where he hides it!

N.B. For all that—rent, deposit, tips, furniture, tools, etc.—I have only spent, in addition to my daily wage, the modest sum of a hundred and fifty francs. So, Monsieur, I assume that you will not refuse me what I value most in the world, your esteem and your support, and that you will deign to continue your benevolence toward me.

II

Paris, 13 November 1843

While waiting, Monsieur, for the enemy to rip the veil that doubtless hides his rascality, I shall give you, for what it may be worth, a perception of the interior of the individual and a few details of his way of life. I shall add to it the copy of a letter of which I have made communication to the Cabinet, availing myself of your signature. But for your precise orders, which constrain me to note religiously the slightest actions of sieur Vannier, I would have passed over all that in silence. At least, if the present report lacks administrative interest, you will have a specimen of the excellence of my apparatus, and an approximate idea of the services that one has a right to expect from it.

The room, almost square, is lightly paneled on the side of the window. An iron-framed bed is placed along the wall facing me, in such a fashion that from my observatory I can see my man close his eyes and open them. At the head of the bed, which is to my left and facing the window, there is a black crate, which forms a night-table by means of a board encumbered with papers and books. On my side, in a corner, there is a large pot that I divine by the sound that it renders when water is drawn for it. I count in addition two chairs and a table as large as a hand, on which is arranged everything necessary for writing. My opening is so cleverly contrived that I even perceive, imprinting on my eyes the most perpendicular direction possible, the strings and the red belly of a large violin, attached to the wall that separates us. Finally, at the foot of the bed, a cupboard open, the shelves of which are laden with a heap of books, newspapers, blackened papers and a little underwear. I think that is the entirety of the furniture.

It is scarcely daylight when Vannier gets up. He makes his bed and sweeps his room, just like a housekeeper. I hesitate to continue, so incongruous is the circumstance. He half-empties his water-jug into a zinc bucket and commences a ceremony that would stupefy ducks. I certify to you that he does not beat around the bush and has no fear of wearing away his skin. Such a rage of ablution is new to me. I scarcely wash myself except on shaving days; it is twenty years since I have stepped into a river or a bath, and I am no worse off for it. He never fails thereafter to pass a wet sponge over all the floor tiles and to wipe them with a rag. After that he gets dressed and kneels beside his bed in order to recite in a low voice, his hands joined and his nose in the air, with a hypocritical fervor capable of deceiving the Devil: "Our Father, who art in heaven, etc."

Having done that, he sits down at his table and starts to write with a sort of fever. I would swear that they are incendiary writings. It is sufficient, to be convinced of that, to see his excessive mental contention, the furrowing of his brow, his haggard and malevolent eyes, the convulsive movements of his pen scratching the paper, and the kind of rage with which he sometimes crosses out what he has written. In those moments, the veins of his forehead swell up to make one think they are about to burst.

A ten o'clock he opens his cupboard and takes out a loaf of black bread, carefully wrapped in a piece of white cloth. He cuts a slice, then pours a glass of water, and eats breakfast. I have, however, seen him counting and recounting several five-franc coins. Finally, after that strange meal, he picks up a book and remains bent over it until midday, the time at which he is accustomed to go out. What he plots in the most distant quarters, in the company of a number of journalists who are rightly suspect, I do not know yet; but at least it can be presumed that things are not going as he would wish, for I observe that his expression gets darker by the day. If he succeeds, moreover, in composing a less lugubrious exterior, the tunes he plays on his big violin suffice to betray the despair that grips him. I confess to you, Monsieur, that I have never heard such lamentable whining; one would sob voluntarily. I prefer something livelier; but a more agreeable music probably cannot emerge from such a funereal soul.

Although it is scarcely credible, Monsieur, he dines as meagerly as he breakfasts, on a slice of back bread and a glass of water. Finally, at night, after a further excursion, and after having said his morning prayer with the same ridiculous unction, he goes to bed and goes to sleep.

That is, once and for all, save for rare exceptions, how this bizarre individual's days are divided up. In his somewhat savage habits you will see, as I do, a muted revolt against social customs. The life of this man, his solitude, his melancholy, his mutism and his owl-like eyes hide, I am convinced of it, the most sinister projects. So I have no doubt that before long, thanks to my observatory, I shall have many important things to reveal to you. I shall transcribe here the letter that I mentioned, which is addressed to a certain Eugène Vachelot, presently resident in a small town in the vicinity of Liège.

> *I am sorry to have no good news to write to you. Since my return here, in spite of an enormous expenditure of courage, no change has yet occurred in my situation. I am tempted to say, like Schiller's Spiegelberg: "Courage augments with danger, vigor with constraint. Destiny doubtless wants to make me a great man, since it bars my route in this way."[1] But I am struggling in vain against the force of presentiments that are obstinate in troubling my soul. There are mysterious and seemingly fateful accidents in the life of men that would disturb the most solid head. Recently, I was traversing the boulevard, plunged in my reveries, interrogating the darkness of the future, when this phrase*

---

1 Spiegelberg is a character in the play *Die Räuber* (1782; tr. as *The Robbers*).

 Destined always to vegetate. I raised my eyes and considered with stupor a man who was walking with a pensive expression and paying no attention to me. I was almost frightened by it. One would be, at least. Is it not extraordinary that in Paris, where perhaps two million people are agitating, I should encounter a stranger just at the moment when a phrase slips through his teeth whose propriety forms such a clear oracle to my address? Reason, of course, cries to me "Chance! Prejudice!" but my intimate sentiment, in spite of my will power, is stubborn in forging instruments of torture against me. Let's talk about something else.

You must remember that while we were happily following the bank of the Meuse, chatting, several times, as if by chance, a name came to my lips—that of Louise. I only waited for the slightest evidence of a legitimate curiosity to tell you the details of a story that I hasten to accord to your discretion. So, to tell no lie, it is my consolation to speak about I child that I love—and it is precisely because if that that I must abstain from seeing her again.

Her father and mother occupy the lodge of a house of which they might once have been tenants. Note that well. Aubin took me there one day, under the pretext of several paintings that the good folk conserved as souvenirs of their former ease. A heart-rending spectacle immediately caught all my attention. A poor girl, lying on a chaise longue, half-hidden under the folds of an old shawl, seemed prey to slow death-throes. Save for red patches of woeful augury, her face had a deathlike lividity. Her hollow eyes, ringed in black, were scintillating—or, rather, flamboyant—with fever. She coughed periodically as if to rip her breast. Those ravages were the result of rigors to which she had suddenly been subjected without any known cause. Far from taking care of herself, as soon as she felt better, she sought for preference coarse and fatiguing labor and did not eat properly. In winter, in the most intense cold, she was to be found in her room without a fire, walking barefoot on the tiles. The father and mother, whose only child she was, lived in despair. Louise, mute to their questions and their caresses, without taking any account of their pleas or their tears, was obstinate in a way of life that was killing her, surely and rapidly.

Drawn by an invincible interest, I returned to that house and applied myself to studying the character of the malady that was devouring the poor girl. In my passion to know her secret, I studied her tirelessly. She soon had for me the transparency of crystal. It required reiterated proofs for me not to believe in an error. An immeasurable pride had suddenly surged forth in Louise's soul, to cause disorders there analogous to those of a poison. To say everything in brief, she blushed as if it were a crime to be the daughter of concierges, and the shame and disgust of her estate had developed in her to the point that she had resolved to let herself die in order to escape the despair of living in a porter's lodge. It is our endemic disease of today.

I set out to cure her—or, more accurately, to resuscitate her. We had immediately sensed a sympathy for one another. Without appearing to suspect the false ideas that were eating away at her, I guided our conversations on to the terrain of her incessant preoccupations. I perceived that the majority of commonplaces on that subject were new to her. I combined them with everything that my own conviction could suggest. I succeeded in convincing her that there is dignity in all estates and that it is always possible, if one wishes, to force the respect of others. Inexorably, I made her sense the ridiculous aspect of her despair and the enormity of the wrong that she was doing her father and her mother.

From the day when I convinced her to obey me, I regarded her as saved. In fact, under the influence of a good diet, calm of mind and, above all, will power, the alarming symptoms disappeared and she regained strength visibly. Today, she is unrecognizable. I wish that you could see her. She is a beautiful young woman, svelte and elegant, endowed with an expressive physiognomy in which soft dark eyes shine, which stream with chaste tenderness for me. The musical timbre of her voice produces the effect of a caress on my ears and stirs me to the depths of my soul. In sum, I do not know of any feminine charms that she lacks. I shall not talk about what she knows, for, compared with what is inherent in her, I regard what she has acquired as very little. The enthusiasm with which I talk about her reveals to you clearly enough how much I love her.

But to deliver oneself benevolently to a passion that, no matter how hard one searches, does not offer the prospect of any fortunate outcome, seems to me to be the action of a madman or a dishonest man. That poor girl would fade away and perish in a wretched environment. I would reproach myself for an unworthy laxity in taking her for a wife with the certainty of making her unfortunate. I therefore made the decision to run away. I intend that she will gradually cease to see in me a person necessary to her existence, and that she will only love me, so to speak, under the benefit of inventory. If my horizon deigns to improve somewhat; if, impossibly, I cease to break my head against the obstacles that grow under my feet as if by enchantment; if I can finally attain the goal of the ambition, so reasonable, of earning my living by the sweat of my brow, we shall have time then to think of giving you a sister who will love you almost as much as me.

Unfortunately, my future is presently limited to thirty days of assured life, and the time is approaching when it will be necessary to make a firm decision. Provided that nothing shameful is demanded—for then, it would be better to die—I am at least determined to do anything, to the extent of giving half my blood, to ward off the fatality that seems to follow me with its eyes as crows follow a funeral procession.

While I think of it, Monsieur, I should not omit that Vannier lives in society with a cat of surprising beauty; I mean an angora cat as white as snow. It has large red eyes, a pink muzzle rounded in the fashion of a lion's muzzle, enormous whiskers, and, in sum, a very pleasant manner. Its mores are almost as singular as its master's. I cannot recall ever having heard it mewl. It sleeps curled up, seems perfectly content while Vannier keeps to his room, and takes advantage of his departure to wander around the house, through the corridors and over the roofs. At the most, it comes from time to time to brush its master's legs in order to obtain a few caresses from him.

Nor ought I to forget that I give frequent tips to the concierge, in order that I am well in with him and that he is entirely at my discretion. See the attached note.

III

Paris, 20 November 1843.

In the annihilation into which the despair of having alienated you plunges me, I throw myself to my knees, Monsieur, and beg you to grant me a favor, that of appealing to my chief's tribunal and perhaps sparing him the commission of an injustice. Oh, proud of my marvelous observatory, it might be that I have been momentarily infatuated with my merit and that my impetuosity has trapped me like a fool. But God is my witness that not for a second have I ceased to have the passion for obedience and to be relative to you what a candle is to the breath that blows it out. I have so much regret for having displeased you that I would gladly pluck out one of my eyes to exorcise my cacodemonic forgetfulness. A smile from you is sweeter to my soul than a ray of sunlight on a rainy day, and lightning is less redoubtable to me than one of your angry gazes. Have no doubt that I will not abandon myself henceforth to personal reflections, that I will scrupulously monitor my errors of pride, and that I will succeed in becoming a model of humility and abnegation. I make the solemn promise only to think about the future when it pleases you to permit me to do so.

I have noted exceptions in the regime that sieur Vannier follows, and this is one that I have cleverly exploited, although it has not produced all that I expected of it.

Once or twice a week, my man goes to take his meal in a tavern situated on the exterior boulevards, well known under the name of the Maison Verte. Usually, he sits in a booth overlooking the courtyard at the back of the establishment. A few young people, doubtless too proud to mingle with the common run of mortals who drink in the entrance hall, frequent that place. Those habitués, employees or artists for the most part, profess opinions subversive to the point that I thought it wise, in an earlier epoch, to slip a sub-agent in amongst them, charged with keeping a daily journal of their words and actions. Monsieur Hégesippe, in all conscience, could not have fallen better. Hazard favored me once again there.

I gave an order to my agent to accord a special attention to sieur Vannier, and to try, as they say, to extract the words from his belly. The sub-agent in question, saving your respect, is a poor devil whom I have succeeded, not without difficulty, in devulgarizing slightly, so that he understands my instructions well enough today and sometimes carries them out with a measure of success. One thing that you know better than me, Monsieur, is that in our estate, so difficult and so troublesome, even mediocre men are rare, let alone capable subjects.

My agent, a tall, robust and sanguine fellow who lisps slightly and wears green-tinted spectacles, really has a priceless exterior. Unfortunately, he has scarcely anything else. However, at first he maneuvered his boat quite well. With the aid of adroit detours, he led the conversation naturally to politics. Because of a decided penchant for logomachy and a certain facility for talking about everything while knowing nothing, and without even understanding himself, he succeeds with many people in passing for an erudite and profound person. Passing from Campanella to Spinoza, from him to Malthus and from the latter to Saint-Simon,

Pierre Leroux, Louis Blanc and Proudhon,[1] he warmed up gradually and finally rose up violently against the government.

This Vannier, Monsieur, would be suspicious of the good God. In spite of my agent's candid and convinced air, he must have had suspicions, for all provocations to revolt left him as cold as marble, and the hypocrite, without defending the government, found the means to say nothing good or bad about it. It tested my patience. My agent was redder than a cooked lobster, to the point that his eyes were bleeding; he agitated like one possessed and made a noise in breathing like the bellows of a forge. At a new observation from Vannier he pretended that he could not be more content. Suddenly turning toward Vannier and thumping the table, he cried "Ta ta!" in a furious tune. "You're an obscurantist!"

Would you believe it, Monsieur? To that furious expression and that insult, atrocious according to my agent, the reptile limited himself to shrugging his shoulders

---

1 Henri de Rouvroy, Comte de Saint-Simon (1760-1825) was a radical political and economic theorist nowadays considered to be the great pioneer of "utopian socialism"; the movement named after him thrived long after his death. Pierre Leroux (1797-1871) was a disciple of Saint-Simon who seceded in order to promote his own philosophy of Humanitarianism, embraced by several members of the Romantic Movement, most conspicuously George Sand. A vocal opponent of Louis-Napoléon, he went into exile in 1851. Louis Blanc (1811-1882) was a prominent socialist who became a member of the provisional government formed after the 1848 Revolution socialist and was exiled thereafter. Pierre-Joseph Proudhon (1809-1865) initially promoted his own political philosophy if "mutualism" before declaring himself an Anarchist. He was imprisoned from 1849-52 for insulting Louis-Napoléon, and then exiled.

and maintaining an absolute silence. Shortly thereafter, he left, very calmly, saluting everyone politely.

So far, so good. It wasn't bad, either.

One of those present, a newcomer to the place, asked who Vannier was. My agent, still utterly furious, cut off the speech of the man who replied, and cried, with a perfect naturalness that he owes to me: "Pooh! My opinion is that he might well be an informer."

"Oh! Oh!" hazarded a few voices.

"And if you believe me," my agent continued, without paying any heed to the *Ohs*, "next time, we'll receive him with cudgels."

That last twist doesn't lack merit.

"I believe, Monsieur, that you're mistaken," replied a young man.

The scene couldn't stop there. My imbecile agent seemed to be in haste to belie the first instincts of talent and to complete the measure of his cretinism and cowardice,

A few days later, Vannier came back to that place at a time when my agent hadn't yet arrived. It's presumable that he learned about the insulting hypothesis raised against him. My agent, who arrived shortly afterwards, noticed that he was welcomed with a glacial coolness. He hung his hat on a peg and came boldly to sit down at the table opposite sieur Hégésippe. But at the same moment, the latter leapt to his feet with the vivacity of a tiger, became whiter than a sheet, clenched his fists, and with the cruel expression that you know, cried in a voice stifled by rage: "Informer!"

It is necessary to renounce understanding what followed. That simple demonstration was sufficient to frighten my agent, who told me with his most stupid expression: "I'm, no chicken, Monsieur, certainly, but you see, when I saw those blue eyes turn black and that pallor turning green, and I can still see it, those eyes entered into my flesh like a drill and pushed me against the wall with an irresistible power. In truth, I admit, I couldn't help it, I was diabolically afraid. I picked up my hat and I ran away."

The table separated them! And the agent, in any case, was as strong as Hercules! He could have crushed that serpent with a blow of his fist! No, Monsieur, when the nature isn't there, education can do nothing to remedy it. Nothing good will ever be obtained from a man who amuses himself trembling before owlish eyes. My discontentment is inexpressible. Because of his cowardice that man is burned, in a milieu in which he cannot decently reappear. I have thus lost a superb opportunity to lift one of the corners of the shroud under which Vannier buries his culpable thoughts. Fortunately, I possess in my observatory a miraculous telescope much more reliable, in terms of ferreting in the coverts of his soul, than the best sound and the most solid harpoon.

I ought not to close this report without at least making mention of an incident that occurred yesterday, Sunday. Vannier received a ticket, with which he went to a concert. I took a seat in the stalls and placed myself in such a manner as not to lose sight of my man. Oh, Monsieur, what stupid music they make in that place! They didn't play, to my knowledge, a single quadrille, and I only remember that someone sang what might be called a ballad. I did, however, hear a brouhaha of whirling dervishes, by a Monsieur Beethoven, the program said, which nearly made me spin like a top, or at least make me dizzy. I cannot attribute to anything else the extraordinary agitation in which Vannier left.

With his arms folded over his chest, he paced back and forth in his room. Inarticulate sounds escaped his throat. He hid his face in his hands, and then looked up abruptly at the ceiling, with the air of a man who no longer has his head. I am recording his incoherent phrases without any comprehension:

"What a man!" he cried. "What a genius! And what destiny! To think that atrocious and implacable dolors were the source of his inspirations! Without the long and unspeakable torture of his deafness, he would perhaps have lacked the sublime and consoling melancholy that flows in floods through his imperishable compositions!"

Suddenly he fell to his knees sobbing, his hands pressed to his forehead. "O my God! At the price of those dolors and others a thousand times more cruel, can I not leave works that stir all souls and make tears flow from the eyes?"

After which, his face still moist, he seized his big violin and started playing things that lulled me gently to sleep.

IV

Paris, 25 November 1843.

Embarrassed as I am by the resolution I have made to efface myself absolutely, it is necessary to tell you that stenography is an art to which I am no stranger. Keen to extend my knowledge, my rare leisure time has been employed in the creation and exercise of an entire vocabulary of signs and abbreviations, with such success that I have succeeded in writing almost as rapidly as speech. One can say of my reports that they are true photographs made with the pen.

Today, at the time when Vannier is accustomed to take his big violin between his legs and sweat tears, someone knocked on the door in an evidently agreed fashion. Vannier opened it immediately. A man named Aubin came in. That individual should already have been found at the tip of my pen, for sieur Hégésippe spent the greater part of the day of his arrival with him, and has already received a visit from him; but I have not learned anything compromising on his account. He is small and might be twice as old as Vannier, whom he treats, moreover, in an entirely paternal fashion. I might have mentioned that he is a portrait painter.

Without losing a second, I seized my board, garnished with an inkwell, paper and pens, and with my eye at the hole and my ear to the acoustic tube, I got ready to note down religiously what I was about to see and hear.

"I've seen Louise," said the painter. "Throughout the time of my visit she never ceased to question me about you. She's astonished by your indifference and very anxious. Everything causes me to presume that she'll come here if you don't go to see her."

"Poor girl!" said Vannier, in a pensive tone.

He would doubtless have been even more pensive but for the painter, who went on . . .

My notes have a gap here, which my memory is insufficient to fill in. I shall resume them at the place where my sleeve ceased to drink the fresh ink and make a frightful smear. It's Vannier who is speaking:

"I love life passionately," he said. "What I have done and what I do every day is irrefutable proof of that. I'm not consumptive, I have health and strength, and whatever an undertaker of my acquaintance might think, who, seeing me cheerful, asked me whether I was drunk, sadness is not an integral part of my character."

He paused for breath and resumed: "I once had ambition. At present it is in my eyes less than a dung-heap. I don't care a straw about that intoxicating smoke called glory. To live, to live—my God, I ask no more than that, even at the price of hard work, even that of manual labor."

Sieur Aubin inclined his head and seemed horribly sad.

Watch in hand, they went for a quarter of an hour without saying anything.

"Oh, my friend," said Vannier, finally. "What a strange métier that of letters is!" (what letters?) "From my tribulations alone I could easily extract a long book as frightening as the seven infernal circles of Dante. I could make you laugh and cry at the same time . . .

"Yesterday, again, I had the unappreciable joy of seeing the proprietor of a newspaper that has ten thousand subscribers. I found myself face to face with a monsieur with the appearance of a valet de chambre, who looked me up and down with an insulting expression.

"'Monsieur,' I said to him, politely, "I have come to offer you a small work that, I believe, would not jar too much with the habitual nuance of your excellent newspaper.'

"'Monsieur,' he said, 'I have no need of articles.'

"'I do not have, Monsieur,' I added, 'the insolent pretention is slipping surreptitiously among your ordinary contributors. I am a passer-by. It might be, by chance, that I have done something that you judge susceptible of pleasing your numerous subscribers. Only deign to acquaint yourself with my manuscript . . .'

"'There would be no point, Monsieur.'

"'Look at the title; the title says a great deal.'

"'You're wasting your time, Monsieur; I don't want to read anything.'

"'But in sum, Monsieur,' I said, 'it might be that I'm bringing you something curious, interesting . . .'

"'You could be bringing me a masterpiece, Monsieur, an incomparable masterpiece, and I still wouldn't read it.'

"I remained confounded. Standing up, he added in a sovereignly haughty and disdainful manner: 'In any case, Monsieur, I need NAMES . . .'

"I turned my back on him. In the office that preceded his study, mahogany and velvet, I riffled through an issue of his newspaper, with a view to knowing what that important man meant by *names*. I found articles there signed, and this is the most rigorous exactitude, *Coquerlet, Janicot, Desnoisettes*, etc., etc. Perhaps they're academicians . . ."

The two friends then talked about an individual well known, it appears in the world of the arts, who dedicates his life, according to sieur Hégésippe, to preparing a beautiful funeral for himself.

"Do you know," he said, "the strange trick that old man played on me. Someone recently engaged me to go and see him, telling me that he was facile at first, inexhaustibly generous and truly meriting the name of 'father of artists.' On the keen instances of a third party, I had already received from him, indirectly, an entirely inefficacious, purely negative service. I chose to visit him under the pretext of saluting him and expressing my gratitude.

"'Good, good,' he said, cutting short my speech. 'I love to see you in these good sentiments. Confess your chagrins to me. I have ears to hear and a heart to sympathize.'

"Innocent I have been, I am and I will be. Moved to the depths of my soul I replied: 'I am firmly resolved not to recoil before any labor, however difficult it might be, but I am literally dying of hunger.'

"'Poor fellow!' he said, with an expression of profound pity. 'You interest me. I want to do something for you.'

"'May I be miserable all my life,' I cried, with increasing emotion, 'if I ever forget it!'

'Good, good,' he said again. 'I too am moved. Now, sit down here. Here are paper, pens and ink. While I go to reflect, put down there, with your heart, the expression of that gratitude.'

"I looked at him in stupefaction.

"'Yes, yes,' he added. 'anything you wish, *currente calamo* . . .'[1] And he went into another room."

"In your place," said the painter, "I wouldn't have written anything."

"I was taken by surprise," Vannier replied. "Besides which, the idea of what it is good to say or to do only comes to me when it is no longer the time. I wrote mechanically what came into my head, a series of banalities.

"My protector returned. I presented him with my scribble. He took it, powdered it with white sand, folded

---

1 *Currente calamo* [flowing from the pen] is a fancy equivalent of the English phrase "off the cuff."

148

it carefully in four without reading it and put it no less preciously into a file. Then he turned to me and said: 'I have your affair. I'll give you a letter. I have no doubt that, on my plea, someone will procure you some work.'

"I was annihilated. The case was so extraordinary that I did not know what to think or what to say. I took the letter that he offered me and withdrew with death in my soul. I have not yet been able to understand that insulting precaution. The idea had never occurred to me of speaking ill of that monsieur. If he had simply replied to me: 'I can do nothing,' I certainly would not have thought of complaining. Was he afraid that I would cry one day over his tomb: 'He has done nothing for me!'"

"And the letter?" asked Aubin.

"I shall make a trial of it in a few days," Vannier replied. "If I obtain something from it, well, I shall limit myself to saying that my protector wanted to take a down payment on my gratitude."

To speak frankly, Monsieur, I fear that the man might have a somewhat deranged mind. I believe that he is all the more dangerous in consequence. Items that I have found, having been forgotten—I don't know how—to add to my latest report, confirm me increasingly in that opinion. Although Vannier has pipes he does not smoke, or at least does not smoke any longer. To the painter, who asked him the reason, he responded with divagations that caused me an astonishment from which I have not recovered at the time of writing.

"No," he said, "I don't smoke and don't want to smoke any longer, because I have come to believe the pipe an immoral habit."

"Oh!" exclaimed the painter.

"One ought, in my opinion," Vannier continued, "to blush at smoking as one blushes at a shameful action."

"You're going too far," said Aubin, inhaling and blowing out the smoke of a cigar.

"Listen to me," said Hégésippe. "Let's leave aside the physical action of tobacco on the body—that, according to some physiologists, it spoils the teeth, weakens the eyes and the memory, draws the blood to the head and disposes one in consequence to headaches and chest infections, and can occasion spitting blood and phthisis in people who have predispositions to those maladies, is of little consequence. I only want to talk from the point of view of habits and ideas. Now, my conviction—an imperturbable conviction—is that tobacco smoke acts in a deadly manner on the brain, that it wears away and destroys, at length, all the faculties, even sentiment . . .

"You only know a part of my miseries. There are incurable wounds in me. I loved my mother with all the force of my soul. Fifty years of unspeakable dolors filled her life. I hoped passionately to live for her, to create supportable days, a little happiness, for so many chagrins. She is dead, dead without even suspecting how much I loved her. I know an old man, devotion incarnate. I would like to render him a little of the love with which he enveloped my youth. He loved, he loves, my mother; his only excursion is to go to visit her tomb. That old man is suffering. Well, perhaps he will die too without knowing my soul, my love. Are they dolors? I shall pass on . . . a pipe! And from those sources of torture will spring consoling dreams, and my sick soul will float in a sort of poetic half-light, and my solitude will be transformed into paradise, and my uncertain and somber future into a cheerful perspective . . . No, I shall not smoke; that satisfaction would be infamous. It would be to admit that the people I love, I love with a sterile amour, an egotistical amour that pours out in words and projects . . .

"The evidence leaps to the eyes; the pipe tends increasingly to isolate men, to render them slack, inert, indifferent, to lessen the faculties of their soul, and because of all that, to loosen and break the interests that bind us, to dissolve society entire.

"I shall summarize thus: If tobacco had prompt effects, if it attacked ostentatiously the organism and the brain, people would mistrust it. It does not proceed in that way. For a long time, neither the body nor the mind appears to suffer from it; one can even say that at times it aids the elucubration of ideas. It is only by degrees, so gradual that they escape the most penetrating observation, that it enervates, wears away, withers and demoralizes the body and the soul—which is to say, the whole man—and renders him fatally, in a more or less long time, to a state of complete insensibility."

What do you say, Monsieur, to that tissue of extravagances? If it were only extravagant, no matter, but I will make the observation to you that at the pace it is going, it will soon arrive, if it is allowed to continue, and the ruination of the most solid of governments. Am I wrong or right to call such a madman dangerous?

V

Paris, 5 December, 1843.

My reports succeed one another, Monsieur, and I do not always receive new orders. I have been assured that the encumberment of various services has momentarily hindered the one of which I am a part. I expect, at least that I shall not be reprimanded later for having omitted to declare how the urgency of my work appears to me to be decidedly contestable. Slender as my merit might be, I believe myself to be worthy of a task superior to that of observing a sort of skinflint who darns his socks and will do laundry on some days. A lost sentinel, so to speak, a slave to my duty, I shall nevertheless remain at my post until the day when it is judged appropriate for me to be relieved of it.

In the middle of last week, sieur Vannier received a visit from the Louise of whom mention has been made. She is, in truth, a very appetizing young woman, with a lily-white skin, pink cheeks and sparkling eyes that might send a soul to perdition. As she came in she lifted up the dark veil that hid her face in part. In Hégésippe's surprised expression she apparently deciphered a criticism.

"Since you don't come to see us," she said resolutely, "it was necessary that I come to you."

I perceived that sieur Vannier closed his door, the key to which was inside, and I was slightly alarmed. I am married and the father of a family, and, I can say, the model of fathers, for, although my little one is crippled and innocent, I love him as much as if he were hale and clever. I have always enjoyed consideration because of my irreproachable mores. Alas, to what are we not exposed? Fortunately, things passed with more decency than I expected.

Sitting facing one another, they looked at one another for a long time like porcelain dogs, except that they seemed to be saying a heap of things with their eyes.

"Would you like to know," Vannier said, all of a sudden, "the idea that you awaken in me, with your black dress and your melancholy face?"

"Go on, speak . . ."

"I seem to be seeing a genteel widow coming to a cemetery to weep over a tomb."

"What a funereal thought!"

"Of the abundance of the heart, the mouth speaks."

"Have you no hope?"

"I have been crushed under a press, so that the hopes have streamed away to fill casks. My friend, precious nourishment and warm clothes for a wife, what hopes! Sweet consolation, for a man of soul, to respond to his family who are complaining of hunger and cold: 'My beloveds, take the blood of my flesh, the marrow of my bones, sate yourselves, here are hopes!' Believe me, Louise, never pronounce that word. It is bread that deceives the soul without nourishing the body. It has only been for me a perpetual excitement to the labor of a squirrel. If I still had the folly of taking account of it, and, under its influence, being obstinate in pursuit of a dream once caressed with passion, to my personal suffering would be joined the tortures far more atrocious of being tormented in my wife and children."

"Is it me, then, who inspires that in you?" said Louise, in a tender voice.

"And the extent of my despair gives you the measure of my tenderness. My ambition to live for my mother was succeeded by that of living for you, in you. I would forget all my bad days if God accorded me the supreme happiness of calling you my wife and going through life at your side, however painfully."

"Why not?" said Louise, with tears in her eyes.

"In my impotence to create a suitable environment for you, what would the word love signify between us? Where there is cold and hunger, amour is one misery more, and one ridicule more into the bargain. A Werther in rags would sicken the heart. Amour is one of the thousand manifestations of the soul. The first condition, the essential condition, for the soul to exist and be manifest in all its forms is that the body should live. A poor man is only a fraction of a man. In a famished and poorly-clad body, the soul becomes an inconvenient superfluity. It is necessary to wait, to subordinate our sentiments inflexibly to necessity, under pain of seeing them turn to bitterness, perhaps to hatred, and perhaps even, horrible thought, to indifference! Then too, poverty in isolation can still be worthy. In the bosom of the family it is ignoble, it impels to all indignities, all basenesses; it defiles and degrades a man under an avalanche of sterile pity . . ."

"At least come to see us from time to time," the young woman said. "I swear to you that I shall never weary of waiting."

"Dear child," Vanier replied, "within a few days I shall have put an end to all your uncertainties. In one fashion or another, my future will be decided. If it is true, as some claim, that logic governs the world, and that our actions unfold fatally and lead to a fatal result, that we can do nothing about events, any more than we can prevent a river from flowing, unless we are masters of something, of being human beings or rags, of ennobling ourselves or debasing ourselves, of developing in God or descending toward the animals, I shall be worthy even so; no human power is capable of making me debase myself; I shall tame even hunger! A little more patience . . ."

Louise took advantage of a moment when Vannier turned his head away to slide across the table, among the books, a purse that she had hidden in her hand.

"It's necessary not to see me again," Hégésippe soon went on. "I need all my courage. Tears weaken it. I'll write to you."

The young woman had no sooner left than Vannier discovered the purse. With one bound he went to open the door and in a feverish tone he recalled Louise, who was going downstairs. She came back, tremulously. Shutting himself in with her again, Hégésippe obliged her to sit down, and knelt at her feet. You might have thought him a saint transported to the seventh heaven.

"Oh, my love," said Vannier tenderly, "whatever one might say about it, we love one another as much as Romeo and Juliet. Our amour does not participate in any vanity; it is a sympathy of an extreme degree of intensity. I would willingly compare it to the irresistible adherence of two magnets. Everything is so common between us—thoughts, dreams, souls—that I cannot conceive anything of you that is not also mine. But, dear beloved, I consider useless sacrifices to be absurd." He showed her the purse and added: "If this money were necessary to me, I would keep it as my wealth. It cannot serve me; as well bury it in a pit. Take it back . . ."

Louse, very red, said: "I can do nothing but this, and you can take advantage of it." Before a firmer refusal on Vanier's part she continued in a voice faint with emotion: "Hégesippe, accept it for love of me."

Vannier held firm. The young woman became annoyed.

"You won't prevent me from seeing in this," she said, with a vivacity that made her ravishing, "a defiance, wounding for me, and a misplaced pride on your part."

Hégésippe put his arm around her waist.

"If I still have some pride," he said, passionately, imprinting a long kiss on her lips, "it is in being loved by you."

Louise escaped Hégésippe's arms, greatly disturbed. Shortly afterwards she left.

Then, with his head tipped backwards and his forehead in his hands, Vannier cried: "My God, have pity for that poor child! My God, I implore you, give me my daily bread! Accumulate chagrins in my soul, let dolors of an unknown violence tear it, but O my God, enable me to live!"

VI

Paris, 19 December 1843.

Monsieur, I have learned recently that mutations have taken place in the personnel of the bureaux on which I depend, so that I am under a new chief, and that the majority of my previous reports have not yet been opened. In the hope that you will read this one imminently, I will dare to congratulate myself on being under the orders of a man compared with whom Rabelais would not have done anything, and who is rightly reputed to have no less wit than Monsieur de Voltaire.

Your predecessor, on the eve of his retirement, must have left you plenty of work in hand. In view of saving you time, I can, with the rough draft that I possess, make you a succinct summary of my labor. In that regard, it will perhaps be sufficient for you to know that it is a matter of an eccentric rogue who has a mania for ablutions, prayers, black bread steeped in water, excursions, visits, and a rage for blackening paper or whining on a large violin. Outside of that, I surprise him for entire hours as motionless as a block of marble. The Devil alone knows what is passing then through that resolute and sinister head. If he moves his lips, he always speaks as if he thought that I am there to overhear him. For a few days only, a new task has occupied him. He has passed in review, with scrupulous care, all the objects that encumber his room: books, papers, letters, etc. He arranges things in a certain order and makes lots of them.

He has a friend who is a painter with whom he had a marvelous understanding to belie all my anticipations. That friend came yesterday at the moment when Hégésippe was finishing getting dressed.

"Louise has come," said the latter. (See my previous report.)

"I know," sad the other. "She told me everything. Do you take pleasure in breaking that poor girl's heart?"

"It would doubtless be better, would it not, to hollow out a void in her heart that I could never fill, to nourish in her the hope of a happiness whose realization seems to get further away every day . . . ?"

I shall pass over her a series of incomprehensible lamentations, which testify that Vannier has a very sick brain. I ought not to omit, however, no matter what disgust I experience, the details and results of a visit that my man announced several days ago. His volubility of language constrains me, however, only to offer you a summary of his conversation with sieur Aubin.

"I therefore went to see the personage," he said, "for he is one, by virtue of his position, his influence and his fortune. I owe him the justice of saying that he received me in an amiable manner. He invited me to sit down. After an attentive reading of the letter and a special examination of the signature, he said to me with an expression of surprise: 'What is this monsieur doing? I know several individuals of that name … is he not … ? Oh yes, I have it; I recall having seen him once. In any case, no matter! What do you want of me, Monsieur?"

"Overwhelmed by confusion at first, I took courage from the benevolent expression of my interlocutor. I explained to him in a few words that I had been laboring for ten years, that, without believing myself to be an eagle, I thought I had some talent; and that, in any case, he could appreciate that better than I could myself, if he deigned to confide some work to me. I added everything that I judged capable of giving him a good opinion of me and touching him.

"He interrupted me to ask me if I was married and whether I had children. He seemed to be thinking: *Otherwise, how can I be interested in you?* Thus, for having lacked the sad courage of linking the fate of a wife with my horrible fate, and seeing in my wake half a dozen wretched starvelings, my poverty did not merit any interest! Diderot said very justly: *Either have no family, or have talent.* However, I am pleased to repeat, he treated me with excessive politeness. For an hour, he did not cease to hold me under the charm of his eloquence. My ears are still ringing with it. He weighed his words and listened to himself speaking, as happens to men whose thoughts are the reflection of those of others. Literature, to which he owes what he is, and which is for rhetors of his force an excellent vehicle to the land of Cockayne, was the sieve though which he filtered commonplaces sufficient to drive the most pacific man to distraction. The phrase: 'It's an estate that cannot nourish a man' was like the obligatory *tutti* of his tirades, longer than crescendos but certainly less brilliant. Finally, having exhausted himself in variations on that theme, he collected himself in a pause analogous to the one that, in a firework display, separates the bouquet from the other pieces, told me with the manner and tone that presages something sublime: 'Recently, our great national poet said before me to a person of note: *Literature can never be anything more than a swagger-stick, never a cane to support one.*'

"I could only curb my head before such grave authorities. 'Besides which,' he added, 'when one holds a pen, it's necessary to have something to say.' Agreed. But how does he know me? Is he a disciple of Gall or Lavater? I confess that, in the mouth of such a well brought-up man, such a statement astonishes me—unless he said it to prove to me that he borrows far more from his memory than from his intelligence.

"I broached the subject of places. The bureaucracy enabled him to talk about money. The expression *bureau* replaced the word *letters*; he repeated an argument identical to the one with which he had just overwhelmed me. I foresaw the moment when he was about to say to me: *Such and such a person said to me: 'The bureau can never be anything but, at the most, a biscuit to deceive the appetite, never a brioche to satisfy it*. Finally, he was kind enough to give me the judicious advice to set aside the métier of letters, no longer to think about the bureau, and to try to earn my living some other way. With what?

"Thus, you see, with the spontaneous decision not to do anything for me, he still wanted to prove to me and to himself that he was the best of men, entitled to my gratitude. I did not make any response. He would not even have listened to me. He would have reproached me harshly for my stubbornness, if not my ingratitude, and would have thrown me out. And I would have been deprived of the joy of shaking the hand of that honest man and the pleasure of hearing him offer good wishes for my prosperity, which certainly did me no harm."

Vannier then talked about a voyage that he was about to undertake. The singular manner in which he said it leads me to believe, that he is finally about to carry out the evil coup that he has been meditating for so long. I am watching!

VII

Paris, 20 December 1843.

Monsieur, I am writing to you under the influence of a frightful impression. When I consider the simplicity of the cause, I do not understand how it has produced such surprising effects.

I only ever have one ear asleep, the other always alert. I was therefore not astonished to have been woken up by a sound as soft as a gust of wind. On lifting my eyelids, however, my eyes were drawn to the middle of my room, at head height, by two red gazes that were radiating in the obscurity like two candles in the depths of a lantern. To give an idea of the shock I felt is the most impossible thing in the world. Those two demonic eyes, ardent, immobile and fixed on me, were hanging on to my flesh like two hooks red-hot from a forge. The sensation of atrocious pain that ran all the way to the depths of my bones made my body the wall of a damp cellar, chilled my blood and paralyzed me. Even my brain seemed to be made of stone. Although I was incapable of action, I was nevertheless capable of thought and will.

I followed, without even trying to defend myself, the circular movement, exceedingly dolorous by virtue of its slowness, of those little blazing globes, which were obstinately searching my breast and my entrails. I would not be able to calculate how long I remained prey to that mad terror. I have been subjected to many proofs: I have had a leg broken by the kick of a horse; I have been obliged to have a finger amputated that was broken by a blow of a stick; but in all my life I had never suffered as cruelly as during that hour, which seemed to me to be longer than a century. One moment more and I would have fainted.

Fortunately, a faint *miaow* suddenly rid me of that horrible nightmare. I understood that I was dealing with a cat, and my satisfaction was so profound that I did not even think of getting angry. In any case, I would have feared attracting the attention of my neighbor, who, as I saw when I applied my eye to the hole, was not asleep and was still working. I opened my door with precaution and the cat hastened to escape in order to go and scratch at Hégésippe's door. I don't know how the beast had got into my room. Let it never fall under my hand in a sure place!

At daybreak, Vannier was still slumped over his table, pen in hand. He was very pale and had violet rings around his eyes. If an example were necessary of what detestable passions and idleness can do to a man, and to the extent to which they are capable of changing and disfiguring him, it would be sufficient to display sieur Hégésippe. I have seen that man, his heart swollen with desire and rage, get thinner and more stooped every day. At present, his face no longer has any flesh; the sinister gleam of his eyes is shining in the depths of profound cavities; the weight of his head is making his fleshless body buckle. People who would have recognized him a month ago would certainly not recognize him now. With his arms folded over his chest and his head bowed, he sometimes prowls around his room like a wild beast in its café. At other times, he puts his hands together and raises his eyes to the sky, the hypocrite! He is despair personified.

He had asked sieur Aubin to come back in a few days. The painter was unable to get a word out of him for some time.

"I'm finally going to quit this room," he said suddenly, in a lugubrious tone, "and I'm not sorry. Everything here disquiets me and makes me feel ill. No doubt the chagrin is reacting on my mind and troubling it, for I'm prey to the strangest visions. It seems to me that someone is spying on me. I'm obsessed by an individual that I find in my path wherever I go. I don't know who that man

is, with a flat face in which the eyes resemble two slash-
es, a brutal manner and a livid complexion, who seems
somehow venomous. His beard is etiolated, like a mangy
fleece. I sense him continually in my head, my back and
my breast. Even here I can't escape the weight of his gaze,
which seems to hold me on a leash. It's the fascination
of the electric eel. Doubtless the imagination has a great
deal to do with that impression, but still, it overwhelms
me and numbs me . . ."

While he said that he was looking in my direction.
Involuntarily, I took my eye away from the hole. One
might have thought that his infernal gaze was passing
through the wall and staring at me. I don't think, however, that he could have been talking about me. The mirror
I consult sends back an image that bears no resemblance
to his description.

The painter asked him where he was going and when
he was leaving.

"I'll write to you," Hégésippe replied. He added after
a long silence, as his friend was getting ready to leave: "I
expect a service from you that demands a great punctu-
ality. I owe a month's rent here. I have no money and I
don't want to argue with the proprietor. I'll abandon to
him what there is here. I'll inform him of my departure
by means of a letter." Then, taking out of his writing-desk
a letter written and sealed yesterday, and handing it to
the painter, he said: "This is the letter. Keep it until the
twenty-fifth. On that day, neither sooner nor later, please
give it to the concierge yourself."

He insisted on those details and made the painter say
ten times over that he would conform to them rigorously.

He retained his friend again in order to talk to him about Louise. "Go to see her often and make her understand that despair is a sterile weakness. I am no more master of myself than a man in the custody of four gendarmes. I am leaving because it is necessary that I go. I am separating myself from her with the conviction of seeing her again one day."

Aubin got up again. Vannier had become more somber.

"Perhaps we shall never see one another again," he stammered, in an altered voice. "The journey I'm undertaking is long and perilous. My old friend, you knew me when I was very young. You know the house where my mother brought me into the world, the yard where I played, the fields, the vines and the river, the memory of which is so sweet for me, the cemetery where I would like to have a small place beside the mother I loved and whom I love eternally. You have been a witness to my efforts; you know my life and my dolors better than anyone else. Before we separate, my friend, may I shake your hand and embrace you . . ."

Tears were flowing from his eyes. I foresaw the moment when the painter was about to weep too. He hastened to depart.

"My God," Vannier cried, in a dejected and profoundly melancholy fashion, "take this chalice away from me!" Then, with sobs in his throat: "My God, may Thy will be accomplished, until the end!"

The next day, after a short absence, Hégésippe came back with a rather voluminous object wrapped in thick paper. It was an earthenware stove. *That*, I thought, *is a singular utensil for traveling.* I supposed that my man, weary of dry bread, was going to do a little cooking in order to give him strength. To my great surprise, that same day, he went out three times and returned, each time bringing back, with the same precautions, a similar instrument. I racked my brains fruitlessly with a view to discovering the usage that he reserved for those three stoves, which he hid carefully in his cupboard. His sadness increased further. He employed a part of the evening setting fire to papers and letters, repeating incessantly: "My God, may Thy will be done ..."

On the eighteenth he proceeded with a considerable acquisition of coal. He filled the three stoves to the brim. Less than ever can I understand the purpose of those preparations. I confess that three stoves for a man who habitually does no cooking, on the eve of his departure seems to me to be very surprising. I awaited in vain the arrival of comestibles. Hégésippe continued to eat his dry bread and drink his glass of water. The matter of burning his papers seemed to trouble him considerably; his face sometimes had the pallor of a dead man. I quivered with rage myself, for those papers doubtless contained many secrets. And still he raised his eyes to the heavens and implored God to have compassion on him. If there is a God, can he occupy himself with such a Tartuffe?

At the moment when I am writing, his fireplace is half-full of black ash, and his fury of burning has not yet weakened. I shall doubtless soon know what all these maneuvers signify. It is presumable that my next report will satisfy your curiosity on this subject fully.

I shall not lose sight of my man. I am horribly fatigued. I have intolerable neuralgic pains in my head. I would not be astonished if I were to fall ill.

VIII

Paris, 25 December 1843.

Monsieur, I am sending you my last report on sieur Hégésippe Vanier. A letter, to the same address as the first, and that I have discovered in a fashion that you will know in due course, will inform you how I have completed my task decidedly. This is the letter:

> *As I write this letter, I have made my preparations; everything will be finished irrevocably. People will say that "driven mad by impotence," I have had recourse to suicide. Perhaps they will be telling the truth, for I believe that a man cannot die unless he has produced everything that he had to produce, when he is no more, so to speak, than an empty bag. However, I have never had more health and energy, never saner faculties; never have I felt closer to the goal than at this moment. It would be a case of crying "Fatality!" It would be bad manners; I shall not commit that stupidity. Scratched out by need, having reached a decision of belated maturity, I have failed. I might as well have been mature on the day when poverty came to sit down at my door, and to stay, and fatality became destiny. Hence, with reason, a German has said: "Destiny, conscience, two words for one idea." Fatality is a deadly prejudice against which a man ought to rage. The*

individual unfortunate enough to believe in it does not take long to be struck by vertigo; he twists his own entrails when he is convinced that he is succumbing under the power of an inexorable destiny.

In any case, I am not free of reproaches. It was necessary to be less absorbed in my work and less stubbornly preoccupied with the goal, to devote time to the study of life. Solitary, I made myself the center of a circle of absolute ideas, when only relative ideas are possible in practice, Only the man assured against hunger, and the rest, can follow a straight line inexorably, dispensing with lies, only obeying, in the expression of what he feels and thinks, the influence of his conviction. To the necessitous, Machiavellianism is no less necessary than talent. To establish oneself in this world it is necessary to appear to be established. One does not fall under the impact of an article of the Code for a little intrigue, a little lying, or a little begging, not to say a little thieving. For want of flexibility, I have broken. I do not proffer imprecations against anyone. I have encountered a number of generous men. I know one of them, among others, of a firm and loyal character, an elevated mind and a great talent, a rare judgment, to whom I have opened my heart gladly. But precisely because he is thus, for having been well treated by him, for esteeming him profoundly, in his eyes less than those of any other, I would never have consented to lack dignity, to become a beggar . . .

God alone knows how profound my passion for life has been. That I shall not regret life bitterly is impossible. If it were only you, with whom I counted on living one day, and Louise, the poor girl who created for us an interior full of charms; if I were only thinking of the dazzling paintings that intoxicated me, the sublime symphonies that caused me ineffable joys, how could I not sink without affliction?

If only it had been possible for me to hide in this world, to bury myself somewhere as if in a tomb! I could have been a simple loving machine on some farm or at some corner offering the service of my arm. That cannot be. Suppose that I were in the depths of Siberia, or in China, or in America, among the savages—well, I know not by what hazard, at a given moment, a man would pass by who knew me and would go to say where and how I was living. And I could never bear that idea. If it is not always true to say that the past obliges, it is at least certain that the man who has lived in an intellectual milieu, who has allowed certain ideas to be credited on his account, cannot consent, in that same place or any other where he might be discovered, to descend to the level of an idiot or a one-eyed horse.

I do not claim to be setting an example by my death. Nor do I think of justifying it.

But I would like the analysis of my life, the awareness of my incalculable labor, the story of the atrocious dolors that have led me to destroy myself, to reach somewhere where there are truly creative men. If one could know once and for all the value of this isolated life, deprived of family joys, immured by hatred or indifference, pregnant with terrors and doubts, and which, most of the time, only ends in poverty and despair! If one could finally be convinced how beautiful that of the peasant or the worker is by comparison, how preferable it is, after all, to breathe the air with full lungs in the fields, or even to etiolate in a narrow space, to guide a plow or to manipulate a plane or a file . . .

But I ought not to leave any trace. I am like a green fruit that a gust of wind plucks from the tree. I have not written a hundred words to this day that I would gladly have signed with my name. I have burned all my papers: projects, outlines, formless manuscripts, incoherent ideas. I am leaving nothing behind, and there will probably be no more mention of me in a week.

At least my ashes will be left in peace, and my shade will not be troubled by one of those generous individuals who take the tombs of the dead for the pedestal of their colossal and indecent vanity.

Adieu, beloved friend; or rather, au revoir. *I am going away melancholy, but*

Now, Monsieur, I am resuming my story at the place where I left it. Sieur Hégésippe did not quit his room on the twenty-second. I do not know that he ate anything on that day, which he employed, like the previous ones, in burning letters, arranging everything in his room and making packets. That task occupied him until dusk. His room, the contents of which, arranged in labeled lots, which were heaped up asymmetrically along the walls, resembled in miniature the hall of an auctioneer. When night fell I thought that he was going to go to sleep. Contrary to that expectation, he commenced to write letters and appeared to me to have decided to stay awake for a long time. I went to bed.

At daybreak I perceived that he had spent the night in his chair, pen in hand. The excess of his fatigue was betrayed by an excessive pallor and a great disorder in

170

his features. It was also visible that he had been weeping. He folded up and sealed three letters, addressed them and went to sleep for about two hours, his head in his hands and his elbows on the table. From time to time he dreamed aloud and proffered halting phrases. Once, he even woke up with a start. His face expressed a profound terror. He recalled his memories, and smiled in a melancholy fashion.

On seeing him take one of the letters and get ready to go out without a hat I had a presentiment of what he was going to do. I got to the concierge's lodge ahead of him, where I sat down in the darkest corner. Vannier soon came in, in fact.

"Will you please put this letter in the post?" he said. "I don't have time to go out." He put the letter and a two-franc coin on the table and went out.

Then I said to the concierge in the most natural tone in the world: "I'm just going to the post office. If you don't want to be inconvenienced, I'll gladly carry out your commission."

The man liked nothing better. I ran to my other domicile; I unsealed the letter with precaution and copied it in haste. I returned to my post promptly.

Here, minute by minute, are the last hours of Sieur Hégésippe.

I was very surprised, suspecting the denouement, to see Vannier take the trouble once again to wash the floor of his room carefully, unmake his bed, turn his mattress over, fold his coverlet in four, and finally to put on clean sheets. Not content with that, which is even more incomprehensible, he sprinkled himself with fresh water, in accordance with his custom, perfumed his hair and beard, and put on his best shirt. Then I saw him turn the key twice in his lock, block the opening of his chimney hermetically and introduce rags into the interstices of his window. After that he took the three stoves out of the cupboard successively and started setting fire to the coal.

His pallor was livid; his hands were trembling; cries of "My God! My God!" escaped from his lips continually. His passion for order only let him rest when he had folded his clothes neatly and knotted his dirty linen in a napkin. In the meantime, the stoves were ablaze and filled the room with carbon vapor. The cat was asleep, curled up on one of the chairs. Vannier knelt down and prayed mentally with an extraordinary fervor.

Oh, Monsieur, my profession has often summoned me to churches, but I confess that I have never seen such a marvelous pantomime. Many devotees could have come to my observatory to take lessons.

Sieur Hégésippe put an end to his prayer in these terms: "My God, I place my soul in your hands! My God, Lord of all things, you know that soul better than I do. Forgive me, O my God. I am departing in order to remain worthy of you."

I was breathless, Monsieur, and you will understand that. Attention trapped my eyes. He was enveloped in his sheets as if in a shroud. The stoves were already almost ardent. White and blue flames were floating over the red coals. Those coals were crackling in the manner of people using their elbows to make room, and launching sparks, true spangles of inflamed gold. It was very enjoyable to watch. Involuntarily, I thought about the pretty flames of a punch. Vannier passed from red to white, and vice versa; his eyes were rolling mechanically in their orbits.

The cat woke up completely. It opened wide eyes full of fear. It made a tour of the room, evidently with a view to finding a way out. Its fur was bristling and it made leaps and bounds. At its plaintive mewling, Hégésippe was re-animated. "Poor beast," he said, "I forgot about you."

He got up, not without an effort, and, staggering like a drunken man, went to open the door. The cat shot out like an arrow, uttering plaintive cries, to make one believe that it was crying for help or wanted to sound the alarm. It ran all over the house like that; its lamentable voice was gradually lost in the distance. It has not been seen since.

The stoves were red. A thick fog obscured the atmosphere. Vannier coughed frequently. His respiration became curt. He was choking. His skin did not stop changing color, alternately taking on red, black, white and violet tints . . .

At that moment, someone knocked lightly on the door. Vanier doubtless heard it, for he made a movement. The knocking was renewed and a voice was heard, a voice as soft as music: "Hégésippe! Hégésippe!"

It was Louise.

Vannier lifted his head slightly and directed his eyes toward the door. A regret contracted his face horribly. He opened his mouth and tried to speak, but the voice expired on his parted lips. He gathered all his strength in order to stand up, but his limbs, already stiff, refused to obey. It was so horrible that I, whom no one could accuse of sensitivity, almost softened.

His head fell heavily back on to the pillow. He was prey to death throes. Like funereal shadows, clouds of black blood passed back and forth over his face; already one could only see the whites of his eyes, the pupils having stopped agitating madly in order to disappear under the upper eyelid. His death-rattle beat a measure that was increasingly precipitate. He opened his mouth wide; a pink foam came to his lips and emerged from his nostrils in little trickles.

Then, all those symptoms of internal convulsions gradually faded away and the contracted muscles of the face gradually resumed a calm expression. Finally, after a few sighs analogous to those of a punctured bellows, I no longer saw any movement . . .

I heard the young woman's footsteps going away. I could not compromise myself by calling her back. Besides which, in my view, Vannier's death was a good thing, not a bad one. It was a case of never acting in favor of those at odds with the law. What is the point of intervening if they cut one another's throats? It is one task less for us, for the judges and the jury. I do not think that a man of that sort warrants pity. He has done justice to himself. I will add that my instructions simply gave me the duty of keeping him under surveillance, not of saving his life.

As I was closing this report I received a formal order to quit my post and to be ready for a new mission. It only remains to me, Monsieur, to recommend myself to you. I hope that the intelligence that I have deployed in this fine work will be taken into account. The patience that it required of me, and the fatigues I have endured, are inappreciable, not no mention interminable excursions through Paris, which last entire days. I have sometimes been obliged to remain in my chair for twenty-four hours without budging any more than a milestone, and having no other nourishment to sustain me but a plug of tobacco in my mouth. My eyesight has been weakened by it and my stomach is completely disturbed. I have also made Herculean economies. I would wager that, during the seven weeks or so that it lasted, I have only spent seven hundred francs in total.

All these considerations being weighed, I am confident that the desire I have dared to express for advancement will be found to be legitimate. I count honorable services, and I doubt that a man fonder of his estate than I am could be found anywhere in the world, or one who exercises it with such a profound conscience. In sum, I have never failed to honor it, and I count on living perpetually in those good sentiments.

A Street Singer

I

"I found myself with two of my friends," commenced Philippe, "at the Fête of Vincennes..."

Philippe, because it is important to know who is speaking, was a third-year medical student, which indicates his age approximately. He was walking in the environs of the city, in magnificent weather, with one of his friends, by the name of Jean, and apparently exercising the métier of story-teller. Philippe claimed to have twenty subjects for novels in his head, and Jean was all ears.

So, Philippe was saying...

I found myself with two friends at the Fête of Vincennes. It was last year, in the same epoch. We had gone to dine at twenty places without getting anyone to serve us something to eat, so great was the influx of consumers. On the other hand, we slaked our thirst more than was reasonable. Bad as it was, the wine inspired me to gaiety, audacity and the brutal conviction that it was sufficient for me to address speech to a woman immediately to make her a victim. So, I looked at the young women whose paths we crossed in a passably insolent fashion. Already I had nearly picked a quarrel several times with local market gardeners, who found my Don Juan manners teasing and irritating to the highest degree.

In that disposition I encountered, suspended amorously from the arm of a worker in his Sunday clothes, a young woman I had once known, I shall tell you in what circumstances in due course. My conceit did not fall silent at the sight of that woman, who could only, however, remind me of sweet and honest memories. I comported myself in her regard with a conquering impropriety, and treated her with a haughty familiarity that was utterly unbefitting.

"Why, there you are, my little Louise!" I cried, without paying any heed to the man whose arm she was holding. "What's become of you? Where are you living? Are you still in Paris?"

I took the blush that rose to her face for the effect of the profound impression that I made on her.

"Yes, Monsieur Philippe." she stammered, with a nonplussed expression. "May I introduce to you my husband?"

I believed myself to be a person of importance. "Aha!" I said, looking the worker up and down "That's true, I didn't remember . . ." Addressing the husband, whose eyes were bulging with anger, I continued: "You have a very nice little wife there, my lad." Them turning to Louise, I asked her in a protective tone: "Are you happy, at least?"

"Oh, yes," the poor child replied, huddling against her husband tenderly.

"So much the better, so much the better," I said, in the same tone. "Anyway," I added, "if you have need of me, you know my address . . ."

And, making her a little sign with my hand, I drew away, very proud of my importance.

In my manner and my speech I had been so indiscreet that my two friends did not doubt for an instant that the young woman had been my mistress, and, although it was not the case, I had the cowardice to let them believe it. I slept peacefully on one or other ear, without even suspecting that I had tarnished my day by virtue of an enormous fault, as I was to learn a few months later, in a truly surprising fashion.

You know that my father, before coming here, was a wholesale wine merchant in Auxerre. We lived outside the town in a suburb. The mother of that Louise, who was commonly known as Mère Leclerc, lived in the neighborhood. She came to the house every day, where a single maid was not always sufficient for the work. The memory of her still causes me joy, she was so neat, becoming and joyful. It is not possible that I shall ever forget her blue smock, striped with black, her red blouse, the short sleeves of which left robust sun-tanned arms bare, her white headscarf with a quincunx of flowers, and her little white peasant bonnet, beneath which her honest ruddy face blossomed. She was often charged with watching over me and taking me for walks.

Louise was the same age as me; never quitting her mother, she was naturally the inseparable companion of all my amusements. We scarcely quit one another except to sleep. I was not romantic; reality has had little to do to stifle the seed of poetry that might have gone astray in my brain. However, I cannot tell you how profoundly that epoch of my life is engraved within me. I could describe to you in the smallest detail the paths where we ran, and count the number of trees in the shadow of which we reposed.

I can see from here the favorite spot of our recreations, a road with profound ruts, which was known as the green street because of a little grass spared by the hooves of horses and the wheels of carriages. It was bordered with ditches in which frogs croaked, and exuberant hedges of eglantines, plum trees and wild mulberries, in which birds built their nests in spring. Entirely given to the pleasure of movement, we scarcely thought of complaining about the warmth of the sun that radiated over our heads, even less of enjoying the delightful silence in which the buzz of flies dissolves so harmoniously, or the little cries of insects in the grass.

Searching the hedges with an implacable curiosity, without fear of scratching our fingers or tearing our clothes on thorns, if we found a nest or merely thought about discovering one, what joy! It suffocated me. "Maman Leclerc, a nest, come quickly!" I had the custom of shouting, in a voice stifled by emotion. Alas, most of the time, it was only a clod of earth caught in the bifurcation of two or three branches.

At other times, weary of not finding anything, I limited myself to picking mulberries or plums, some of which I offered to my little friend, only, naughty child that I was, to tease her and make her cry a moment later. "Maman!" she cried then, "Philippe is making me angry!"

And the good woman, trying to make her voice harsh without succeeding, did not take long to reply: "Wait, wait, Philippe, I'll see to you!"

I will add that all that is sometimes mingled in my thought, I don't know why, with the sound of bells, the sight of the temporary altars of Corpus Christi, houses decked with flags, curtains or multicolored rags, streets strewn with verdure, poppies, cornflowers, and on top of that, the intoxicating odors of leaves and the earth after a shower of rain.

It was also in the green street that, much later, I was to make my clandestine apprenticeship as a smoker. My head spins merely in thinking about it. Oh, let it be said in passing that one endures tortures and expends courage in order to contract a deadly habit that will one day cause sensate people such painful repentance!

When I was sent to college Louise was placed in a workshop. For years, I only saw her at rare intervals. Her mother died. I scarcely paid any heed to it—not, I believed, by virtue of insensitivity but for want of comprehension of death. In the memory of the dead woman, and also by inclination, my mother gladly took charge of Louise. The orphan did not take long to become an integral part of the household, where her intelligence, her activity and her perpetual good humor soon rendered her indispensable. She might have been fifteen; whether she was ugly or pretty I had not yet noticed.

College life had singularly corroded my natural goodness; a little monster of pride swelled out my school uniform. I was perfectly able to measure the distance that separated me from the young woman, and I began to find her addressing me as *tu* an intolerable impertinence. I applied myself to making her sense it. I tried to give myself a cold and haughty manner in her presence; I affected to address her as *vous* and to call her Mademoiselle. She did not seem to perceive it. Far from it; the more the *tu* wounded me, the more easily the accursed pronoun seem to emerge from her lips. For a long time I was desolate in consequence, and almost ill.

Condemned to encounter her every Sunday, I went as far as to deprive myself of going out in order to see her less frequently. I flattered myself that I would intimidate her at length and lead her gradually to respect me more. To my great chagrin, I was deceived in my hope. Patience escaped me and I became annoyed.

"Why are you tutoying me?" I said to her one day, brutally.

She looked at me in amazement. "Oh, the proud monsieur!" she said. And she tutoyed me more than ever.

Scarcely credible as it is, I racked my brain and turned my intelligence upside down, never ceasing to form stratagems uniquely with a view to sparing myself that insolent familiarity. Nothing worked. Pride finally prevailed in the end over all other sentiments, even over a vague dread of being ridiculous. I went to find my mother and said to her in a single breath: "I don't know why Mademoiselle Louise permits herself to tutoy me. I'm no longer a child. What would people say if they knew that at college?"

My mother uttered a loud burst of laughter and I was the talk of the whole house. I would have liked to be a giant with the thousand arms in order to annihilate the whole world, and me with it.

The vacation arrived.

I had for a comrade and confidant a cousin whose baptismal name of Jacques had been changed into that of Jacquot. Precisely in imitation of parrots, he had some memory but was entirely lacking in judgment. His head, moreover, was not without analogy with that of the disagreeable bird. Deep down, he had the genius of patience; he was a man to saw through iron bars with a watch-spring and pierce a wall twenty feet thick with a toothpick. He was envious, like any poor relative. When I saw the fresh colors of that chubby boy, and his large enamel eyes, I scarcely suspected that he was sly, and more perfidious than the traitor Simon. Insinuating, flattering, endowed in addition with an excessively stupid expression, he was much liked by my mother, and possessed all her confidence. He was destined for commerce.

Jacques, or Jacquot, as I called him for preference, applauded my pride and found that I was admirably right not to want to be tutoyed—me, a collegian—by a little girl who, in sum, according to him, was only our domestic. "In your place," he said to me once, among others, "I know what I'd do."

"What would you do?" I exclaimed.

"Firstly, I'd pay no more attention to her than if she didn't exist, and when she spoke to me I'd turn my back on her."

"Alas, my friend, I've used that means and many others, and I've failed."

"Well, I'd shut myself in my room and I'd die of hunger rather than go down to table with her."

That advice, in the species of despair that I was in, did not displease me. I reflected on it maturely, and—would you believe it?—I decided to follow it; but an unexpected discovery occasioned a complete revolution in my sentiments.

I was wandering from room to room looking for my cousin, who thought that I was in town. To the right of a door behind which Louise was working, bursts of laughter made me prick up my ears. Holding my breath, I drew nearer. What I heard froze the blood in my veins, Jacques was there. He was being amiable with Louise and, while sniggering, was telling her in a falsetto clarinet voice, about my torments and my despair, not forgetting my resolution no longer to eat in order to escape the shame of sitting down beside her. Imagine my amazement! What a sledgehammer blow was the abrupt certainty of being the victim and the dupe of a rogue that I thought to be a frank imbecile! In the blink of an eye, I was at least a year older.

I had the strength to contain myself and to resist the desire to make a fuss. I withdrew quietly, as I had approached. My cousin's conduct gave me much to think about. Evidently, he had views with regard to Louise and planned to keep me incessantly aside, doubtless for fear of finding a rival in me. The result of that was that, for the first time in many years, I thought about looking at Louise. Why was I not a painter or poet? In all my life, I had never seen a young woman so fresh, so pretty, so well made, so gracious, so coquettishly dressed—in a word, so essentially attractive.

Where had my eyes been, then? What folly was mine? Of pride, as you might imagine, there was no longer any question. On the contrary, I was suddenly assailed by the dread of not being preferred to Jacquot. It seemed to me presently that I had a right anterior to that of anyone else to the young woman's affection, and that someone would be stealing from me by infringing that right. I did not, however, make honorable amends immediately. In doing that I was thinking less about sparing my self-esteem than of putting one over on the cousin, whom I now held in great aversion. I persisted in ignoring Louise ostentatiously while, in private, while showing a little ill humor, I gradually showed her a better countenance. I succeeded in deceiving everyone, except her.

My first confession escaped me, in a sense, inadvertently. One Sunday evening my father and my mother were playing cards; I was sitting beside my father; Louise was sitting opposite; Jacquot was leafing through a book nearby. By chance, Louise's foot bumped into mine under the table. I felt a commotion, which caused me so much pleasure that I wanted to renew it instantly. Pretending to be keenly interested in my father's game, and scarcely breathing, I moved in the shadow, with the slowness of a tortoise, to encounter the daintiest foot in the world.

At my contact, it recoiled upon itself, as a snail, when touched, draws in its horns. I was not discouraged. After a few minutes of blind man's buff, I finally seized the sensitive slipper and held it passionately embraced or a long time. A sort of magnetism invaded my being and filled me with an indescribable happiness. In the meantime, the young woman and I avoided looking at one another with great care, and appeared to be complete strangers.

How short that evening, when I was praised for good behavior, seemed to me, and what difficulty I had going to sleep! All night long I dreamed about Louise, and when I woke up, my first thought was of her. Presently, the *tu* in her mouth produced on me the effect of an ineffable caress. I soon seized the privilege of using the magic syllable again, in addressing her. I do not know what I had to do in order to stifle in her the memory of my ridiculous pride. I could no longer sate myself with the sight and sound of her. I watched out, with a savage cunning, for opportunities to be alone with her.

I must hasten to say, though, that her conduct was precisely the inverse of mine. To my cruel disappointment, she became more reserved every day and gradually discontinued addressing me as *tu*. I was horribly afflicted by that. In matters of badinage between us she developed an excessive intolerance. Scarcely did I make the appearance of provoking her or teasing her than she told me with an annoyed expression to go and play with my equals. I cannot tell you how much I suffered. My imagination, magnifying my errors, added to my torture. I would have given half my life to reconquer her good graces.

However, her coldness increased; now she used the respectful *vous* with a pitiless firmness. The better-welcomed assiduities of my cousin finished exasperating me. One might have thought that she was taking pleasure in irritating my jealousy, and wanted to inflict the pain of talion upon me. She chatted willingly with Jacques, but affected, on the contrary, to avoid me as I had once done with her. I could no longer live like that.

I succeeded in surprising her alone one morning in the kitchen. Her hair was untidy, her bonnet and head-scarf disordered, her skirt tucked up in one corner; her feet were lost in clogs large enough to contain her entirely; the strings of a blue apron circled her waist; her arms were bare to the elbows. Thus accoutered, she was standing by the sink soaping her lace. I approached her on tiptoe; I passed my head quietly over her shoulder; then I stammered in a barely-intelligible voice, so rapidly was my heart beating: "Louise!"

Without astonishment, as if she had sensed me coming, but also without looking at me, she said to me, in an ill-assured voice: "What do you want with me?"

"Why do you no longer tutoy me?" I continued.

"Because it causes you pain," she replied.

"At present," I said, "I want you to tutoy me."

"But I don't want to."

"Why not?"

"Because . . ."

"You don't love me, then?"

"No."

What, no! I became bold enough to pose my lips on her neck. Then I ran away.

Not to tell a lie, I don't know whether my inclination would have conserved that character of innocence for very long. Seen through that adventure, at any rate, the future only offered unfortunate perspectives. Whatever happened, I could only trouble Louise's existence profoundly, even supposing that reason remained mistress of sentiment on the poor girl's part. But my honored mother was a woman of notable perspicacity. I believe, too, that Jacquot had already put her on the alert. At any rate, she perceived the danger that her ward was running and put a stop to it immediately. Before I had had time to recognize it myself, within twenty-four hours I was interned in a college in Paris . . .

Philippe and his friend walked for an hour without thinking about fatigue. At that moment the sun was shining directly overhead and warming the atmosphere to the temperature of a stream-bath. At a bend in the road a pretty guinguette suddenly offered the shelter of its arbors to their eyes. They sat down under the shadiest one before a jug and glasses. Philippe stuffed his wooden pipe, applied a flame to it, and resumed his story after slaking his thirst.

Five or six years later, my father retired from commerce and came with my mother to live here, close to me. Louise was naturally part of the emigration. Let's take care not to omit that my cousin had come ahead of them in order to be apprenticed to a druggist. It resulted from that that we frequently found ourselves all around the same table, as before in the province. But how time had already modified us all! The graces that had formerly been only buds, so to speak, in Louise, had now developed into beautiful flowers, which enveloped her in irresistible charms. While Jacques, having become a tall and robust fellow, was overtly aspiring, with maternal consent, to marry her, I felt my old pretentions to her reborn in myself, with a less juvenile emotion.

I confess, to my shame, that I was animated by a thought of vulgar seduction; I meditated nothing less than taking her to live with me in the Latin Quarter. In the example of many men more vicious in boastfulness than deeply corrupt, I would have been glad to put one over on my cousin by stealing a woman who might have become his, and proud of showing my friends such a beautiful and decent mistress. In the meantime, because I feared that the prospect of a marriage might tip the balance in Louise's soul in favor of Jacques, I made every effort to mortify and ridicule him in front of her every time an opportunity presented itself.

In the number of pleasantries that I renewed incessantly, there was one that rarely missed its effect. In the most serious tone, every Sunday morning, on perceiving him, I said: "Bonjour, Jacques, have you had breakfast?" In their argot, students call that a *scie*.[1] Jacques could not get used to it. He made every effort not to get annoyed; in his rather pale face the blood, the blood went for preference to his beak-like nose, as to the crest of an angry turkey, and gave him an appearance twenty times as grotesque. With a little more penetration I would have spared him the worry of being alarmed by it. Louise had never loved him, but since he had begun talking to her about marriage, about his work, and had confided his hopes to her, she had almost come to hate him.

However, it did not get me any further forward. Louise's intelligence and character had developed sin-

---

1 Literally, a *scie* is a saw, and the English word is still used metaphorically to refer to a cliché, or a catch-phrase, as in the antiquated French argot. The reason that it qualifies as an insulting joke is that "As-tu déjeuné?" [have you had breakfast?] was one of the stock phrases that owners taught pet parrots to repeat, and, as previously referenced, French parrots were called "Jacquot" in much the same spirit that English ones were called "Polly."

gularly since our first and innocent amours. The poor girl, who was honesty itself, and knew perfectly well that I did not want to be her husband, only succeeded by means of indulgence in not seeing my propositions as so many insults. She limited herself to taking precautions in order not to be alone with me. If hazard contrived a tête-à-tête with her for me, in spite of that, I found myself confronted by a little dragon, who stood up to me and reckoned with me to the point of disconcerting me and reducing me to silence. I was offended, irritated and exasperated—I dare not say unhappy, for throughout that adventure I was much less the victim of passion than of my vanity.

Between my mother, on the one hand, who, increasingly sensible to Jacques' hypocrisy, had decided that he would marry Louise, and on the other, the competitive courtship between my cousin and me, with essentially different objectives, the young woman's position was intolerable. Because it did not suit her either to marry Jacques or to be my mistress, the house became for her a sort of purgatory in which she was expiating the pretentions and stupidities of others. Covertly—and it was her right—she was thinking of escaping by means of an impulsive action that accorded with the enthusiasms of her loving nature. While my cousin and I were disputing her favors, a third lover, lurking in the wings, made us play, unawares, the ridiculous role of the two thieves of the fable. You can imagine the stupefaction of all of us on the day when Louise, speaking to my mother in private, confessed to her with a blush that she was in love with someone and desired to have her consent to marry.

I renounce depicting for you the state of my mother at that news. It was more than disappointment, almost despair. At length, Louise had become necessary to her; without her ward, she felt like the leading role in a tragedy without a confidant. In addition, the young woman, who was cheerful, who had a good memory, and an accurate voice of an agreeable timbre, sang Christmas carols or old ballads while she worked, and rendered the interior of the house less monotonous and sad in consequence. A personal consideration, although, I believe, purely instinctive, pleaded in my mother in favor of Jacques. The latter's marriage was naturally subordinate to his position; now, his position was far from being solid enough for the weight of a household; there was every reason to believe, therefore, that Louise would still remain in the house for some years.

In sum, my mother, who was otherwise an excellent woman, as you will see in due course, nevertheless had her little faults. Her character was entirely stubborn. Not to mention the rights that she believed she had to Louise's gratitude, she considered her almost as her daughter, and by that title, as a fief, a property, a negro in slavery, of whom she flattered herself that she was able to dispose at her whim. My cousin and the rest apart, nothing could offend her more cruelly than seeing the young woman choose a husband without consulting her.

In the house of which we occupied one floor, in the Rue de Marais, a young workman, a manufacturer of pianos, had been living for nearly six years, a German from Vienna named Georges Moser. Picture a fellow of twenty-five or twenty-six years, of medium height, with blond hair, blue eyes, an aquiline nose, a white and pink complexion and a little tuft of wooly side-whiskers to either side of his cheeks. Everything in his face, to a greater extent than that of any other, respired honesty, candor and serenity. He worked in the Érard workshops in the Cour de Bretagne in the Faubourg du Temple.

Something to note, perhaps, is that without my mother, he would never even have suspected the existence of Louise. My mother was bored and wanted to return to playing the piano. Her instrument, not having been tuned for at least fifteen years, was in need of considerable repair. It was only natural that she thought of Moser, who had been mentioned to her as a very skillful worker. The young German was smitten with Louise at first sight, and Louise immediately divined without displeasure the sentiment that she inspired in him. He was young, endowed with a charming face, earned his living well, was reputed to be a serious fellow, and had, in brief, everything necessary to please a reasonable young woman. Louise encouraged him at first with her gaze. They met frequently thereafter on the stairs or while out walking. Gradually, they began to have furtive conversations; finally, they agreed to marry.

My mother flattered herself to begin with that she would discover, by enquiring into Moser's life, pretexts for a reasonable opposition to the marriage, but after obtaining information from authentic sources, she was constrained to admit that the young woman's choice was excellent. Her objections to the marriage, therefore, could no longer obtain purchase except from sentiment. This is very nearly what she said to her ward:

"I have never ceased to have for you the tenderness of a mother, and by virtue of that title I have some rights to your obedience. I flattered myself that you would not leave the family, and that you would marry Jacques. He's a worthy fellow, who loves you and would make you happy. You would wound me mortally be disappointing my hope. Reflect."

What impression could that make on the heart of an amorous young woman? Louise limited herself to replying that she loved Moser and that she would never love my cousin, which was decisive. My mother persisted nevertheless, obstinately, in trying to change her mind. Our house was divided into two camps. If my father and I came out in favor of the young woman, there is no need to say which party Jacques adopted.

In any case, the virile firmness that Louise drew from amour rendered her capable of standing up to the entire household. Her inflexible resistance occasioned a profound irritation in my mother. A few days before the marriage, in one last scene, under the empire of resentment, she said to her: "I declare, Louise, that if you cross the threshold of this house to marry Moser, I shall never see you again, and for me, it will be absolutely as if you were dead."

"You put me in despair, Madame," the poor girl replied, with tears in her eyes. "If I obey you, I shall be unhappy; if I resist you, you will withdraw your tenderness from me. You cannot doubt my respect and my devotion, but I will tell you sadly that I have given my word and I cannot break it. I still hope, Madame, that you will end up rendering me justice and that your anger against me will not last forever."

She married, and I did not see her again.

Our intimacy, I affirm, did not surpass the limits that I have indicated. Perhaps you will think that I have emphasized those details too heavily; nevertheless, I have not done so needlessly, if you are presently convinced that there never existed a more honest young woman, more imperturbable in her rectitude. After that, it is permissible to you to appreciate whether I had the right to treat her as I did at Vincennes, and the point to which, in that encounter, my conduct was gratuitously brutal.

I belonged then to the category of young men who imagine that money substitutes for all things. I was literally another man on the day that I was able to measure the extent of the harm that had resulted from my stupid excessive vanity ...

III

At this point in his story, Philippe, who felt his eyelids becoming heavy, observed that Jean was making heroic efforts not to fall asleep. Under the influence of the coolness of the arbor, the two friends were gradually delivering themselves to slumber. After about an hour of that siesta, they woke up to look at one another, laughing. Then, entirely reposed and refreshed, they quit the guinguette and continued their stroll. The sun was already sinking visibly toward the west; the elms by the roadside projected large oblique shadows; a slight wind rose in the north and caressed the face agreeably. At Jean's request, Philippe went on.

In order to reconnect the day of the fête at Vincennes to the day when I saw Louise again, it is necessary to make a leap of at least seven or eight months. I was going to the Charité every morning, as I still do today, where I had an active service, under Doctor Maison, in two wards: one of women, the Sainte-Anne Ward, as a clinical aide; the other of men, the Saint-Charles Ward, as a hospital extern.

With the stoical indifference that the spectacle of the most intense suffering soon produces, I went into the Sainte-Anne Ward one day at the customary hour, where I had various dressings to change. It was a little before the visit of the chief of the clinic and the professor's lesson. While hanging my hat on a peg and putting on an apron I said to the young woman in service: "Well, Madame Elisabeth, what's new this morning?"

"There's someone in number twenty-two," she replied.

"What is it?" I added.

"I don't know," Madame Elisabeth replied. "She seems to me to be very ill. Since yesterday evening, when she came in, delirium hasn't quit her. The numbers to either side complain of not having been able to sleep because of the racket that she made last night."

Those details were for me a banality incapable of striking my attention. I prepared my plasters with no less phlegm.

Nevertheless, to the right of number twenty-two, dominated by a purely mechanical curiosity, I turned my head toward the new patient. What a shock! I do not know that one can be unexpectedly stirred by a more powerful and more dolorous commotion. In the pale and distressed face of the patient I rediscovered all the features of Louise!

After all, perhaps I was mistaken. I drew closer. For my torture, no error was possible. The physiognomy that I had before my eyes, although ravaged by the malady, was engraved in my memory in characters so neat and profound that I could not be mistaken. Louise!

Stupor nailed me to the spot, while anguish tore my breast. What dolorous imaginations flooded my brain simultaneously! What series of misfortunes had thrown her, whom I had quit so happy, into a hospital bed? Could her presence here signify anything less than a horrible drama? What was that drama?

I took her by the hand; I questioned her; I called her by her name. She did not see me and did not hear me. Her skin was moist and hot, her respiration halting and painful; her haggard eyes were rolling madly in their orbits.

If I did my work in haste, if the patients had to lament my abruptness and my inattention, I scarcely paid any attention to it. I was at grips with the sharpest anxieties; I waited with a mortal impatience for the chief of the clinic to arrive. Scarcely, in his round, had he approached number twenty-two than I came running. Louise's mental state rendered extremely difficult, if not impossible, the exact appreciation of her physical condition; it was necessary, to begin with, to try to extinguish the intense fever to which she was prey. The chief of the clinic, who, at my request, conducted a long examination, was only able in the end to prescribe a calming potion. I made the poor woman take it personally. I only drew away from her bed regretfully; I was affected pitifully. Before leaving I recommended her warmly to Madame Elisabeth.

Not content with that, I came to ask for news of her in the evening. I would gladly have watched over her all night. For the first time, in a long time, my slumber was full of trouble. All that agitation, so scantly in harmony with the insouciance you know me to possess, might surprise you, and, in fact, I have witnessed many other miseries without being moved; but as you can also conceive without difficulty, Louise was for me a being apart; she reminded me of a thousand sweet memories: my homeland; my childhood; my excursions; Mère Leclerc, who had held me in her arms so many times; and finally, the first indelible sensations of amour—and, in truth, all of that warmed my blood and elevated the cold temperature of my soul.

The next day, when I went into the Sainte-Anne Ward, I was greeted with the most reassuring words. Louise had spent a calm night, and reason had returned to her entirely. In the fear that my unexpected presence might cause her too vivid an emotion, I did not go to her right away, however much I desired to do so. I charged Madame Elisabeth with going to tell her that there was someone asking to see her, a friend Philippe, a medical student in service on the ward.

Madame Elisabeth soon came to tell me that the patient was waiting for me.

As soon as she saw me, Louise tried to get up; I made her a sign not to do anything. I had rapid heartbeats to suppress, and I even recall that my legs were not very steady. And in voice faint with emotion, taking her by the hand I said: "You here, my poor Louise! What does this mean? What has happened to you?"

She attached to me a gaze full of melancholy, in which I also read that I merited reproach, and that she forgave me.

"Oh, without meaning to," she said, "you've done me a great deal of harm, Monsieur Philippe."

I took a step back and looked at her with amazement. "Me!" I said.

"I said without meaning to," she went on, "for I know that you're incapable of ever having had the intention to make me unhappy."

My interest was excited to the highest point. I drew nearer.

"I don't understand, my good Louise," I said, in a low voice. "Apart from an evil thought that I nurtured against your honesty, a thought that you thwarted by your conduct, I don't know that I have any other fault for which to reproach myself in my relations with you."

"Have you forgotten our encounter at Vincennes, then?" she asked.

"Certainly not," I said. "I even remember having behaved in a rather vulgar manner. But I must say, in my defense, that I didn't have a very clear head."

"I don't hold it against you," said Louise, "but know that from that encounter all the evils have flowed that brought me here."

I was confused. In fact, I confess that, for me, no more impenetrable problem had ever been posed to the sagacity of a human intelligence. I immediately renounced the honor of discovering the solution, and begged Louise to spare me, by means of a rapid explanation the trouble of searching for it.

Fragment by fragment, in part before the visit and in part afterwards, she told me as best she could what I was in haste to know. With your imagination, you can fill in at your leisure the lacunae in a story that is necessarily very incomplete. I'm certain, in addition, that the resources of an ingenious psychology will not fail to explain and fathom facts whose perfect exactitude I cannot guarantee ...

IV

Philippe paused momentarily, and then continued.

You know Louise, and I have little to add to the portrait of Moser that I have made for you. It would be difficult to encounter two natures better matched—that is the word, for, without resembling one another, they completed one another. In the inverse of what households ought to be, the wife, in the one in question, represented reason, and the man sentiment. Moser had not taken long to recognize his wife's superiority in matters of interest, and soon relied entirely on her for everything relative to domestic economy. He limited himself to trying to attain every day the maximum of a wage, of which he brought back the integral sum every Saturday. He had, in exchange, a neat and joyful interior, varied and solid nourishment, linen that was always white, and garments that were always in good condition and well brushed.

Their life, if it was deprived of great joys, was also exempt from great troubles. From time to time, the sun and the solitude of their quarter drew them outdoors; they passed the barrière, wandered through the countryside, and dined in the shadow of trees to the sound of tavern quadrilles. When the uniformity of that life threatened to become burdensome, a child was born to them, who, in realizing their dearest hopes, rejuvenated, in a way, the charms of their association.

Everything, in brief, smiled upon them. Louise's childbirth was accomplished without even the appearance of an accident; she was soon back on her feet, as fresh, as cheerful and as beautiful as before. After some six months, they resumed their tranquil excursions. Confiding the slumber of their son to the care of an aged neighbor, they profited from one fine day to set forth for Vincennes, where my unlucky star, as I have told you, threw me into their path.

Can you already foresee the consequences of that fatal encounter? Was it possible that what appeared clearly evident to my indifferent friends would not appear so to a husband of umbrageous character and the most limited judgment? Add that Moser, since his marriage, had not discontinued living in clover—which is to say, comfortably, without trouble and without chagrin, and that he had, in a sense, to expiate that long serenity, of which he had yet to know the price. By the avidity, so to speak, with which he seized the suspicion and implanted it within him, one might have sworn that he was weary of the benefits of a profound peace and hoped to be subject to proofs.

Louise exhausted in vain the treasures of persuasion and tenderness; she explained to him who I was and entered into all the details capable of justifying, up to a certain point, the familiarity of my manners and my language. He did not even seem to hear her. Nevertheless, he did hear, but only to find in all the things she said so many testimonies of a liaison that was to take on, in his eyes, an increasingly criminal character. An iniquitous suspicion gained him increasingly and invaded him like a gangrene.

His slumber, normally so peaceful, gave way to dolorous insomnia. His forehead was perpetually charged with clouds, and he only spoke any longer in monosyllables; he rejected his wife's caresses rudely and even affected no longer to care about his child. His interior became odious to him; he gradually lost the habit of taking his meals at home, got up in the morning earlier and earlier and returned later every evening. Louise could no longer address a word to him without irritating him further; she therefore fell silent and contained her tears in the hope that time, might reckon better than her with a despair founded on chimeras.

Far from that, time, instead of attenuating the energy of the poison that I had poured into the unfortunate fellow, seemed to increase its violence. He came to suffer from it to the extent of seeking in debauchery an alleviation of his torture.

To complete the misfortune, he did not escape the need for communication that we all experience in sadness, as in joy. I say to complete the misfortune, since he also chose, it appears, the one of his comrades who was least appropriate to the role, a cheerful and skeptical

Parisian who, beneath an appearance of frankness and bonhomie, hid an excessive mockery. He called Moser "Sauerkrautman," and did not like him, firstly because he was not from Paris and then because he was married, laborious and economical. If, after having provoked them he listened willingly to Moser's confidences and appeared to share his chagrins keenly, it was to encourage him in his jealousy, to make a victim of him and turn him to ridicule.

Among the laborers in the workshop, all were soon informed as a proven thing of Moser's misadventure; to the burden of his tortures, some of them found it amusing to shake his hand in their turn and to bring him their mocking condolences—not to mention that not a day passed when the Parisian did not drag him to the barrière and cause him to make a number of stations at wine-merchants' shops. Between two bottles, remarking his incurable melancholy, he said to him:

"You're rather stupid to be afflicted for so little. As if no greater misfortune ever happens! Know, my old Sauerkrautman, for your guidance, that we are all before or after it. Go on, empty your glass, and we'll go drink a liter further away."

Monsieur drank, but in the midst of his drunkenness, the memory of Louise, suddenly crossing his mind, filled his eyes with tears and his throat with sobs.

That was not all. If the poor devil was not the object of a keen sympathy, his wife was detested by three or four old crones who did not admit that someone should be exclusively occupied with her household and refuse to associate with them. Needless to say, they seized the opportunity to satisfy their rancor. In accord with overly complaisant husbands they drew Moser into their society and applied themselves to envenoming his wounds, under the pretext of bandaging them.

One of them said to him: "All these hoity-toity women resemble one another. With their Saint-Touch-Me-Not airs they're worse than the others. You wouldn't believe it if you didn't know where hypocrisy leads."

Another added: "God, how good you are! In your place, I wouldn't amuse myself dissolving in tears. I'd do the same as her, and we'd be quits."

He could not turn around without feeling the sharp point of some similar remark. One might have thought him an unfortunate individual covered in wounds and plunged into an acid bath. By dint of only seeing people so firmly convinced of his misfortune, he ended up having the certainty of it. Prey to dolors, the subject of which was perpetually put before his eyes, he no longer went to the workshop except with disgust and only went home with a sort of horror. So he accepted more and more frequently the half of the bed that the Parisian offered him. Under the guidance of that worthy friend he soon only worked at rare intervals and gradually took root in guinguettes and taverns. To meet the demands of those disorders, he gradually withdrew his savings from the money-box. Already, for some time, he no longer gave his weekly wages to his wife. He gradually imposed the harshest privations on her, until the day when he was obliged to do violence to himself in order to bring her the barest necessity.

I was less astonished than you might think by the imbecility of that Moser. To begin with, undoubtedly, even admitting that his conviction was founded, he could not fail to appear inexcusable. He owed so much to Louise that an amnesty for the past would have been not so much generosity as justice and prudence. But Moser did not participate either in our education or our ideas.

The opportunity has often been given to me since to see him and study him. I found myself confronted by a tender, passionate man of the narrowest mind, completely submissive to the contractions of his diaphragm, and as easily capable of an absolute confidence as an excessive mistrust. By virtue of the fogs that troubled his German head, he had forged an ideal that he thought he had found in his wife. I had suddenly ruined his illusion. Louise had soon no longer been anything but the soiled realization of the dream of his life. He had imagined that his wife, of whom he was proud and for whom he had an amour mingled with veneration, far from meriting that worship, was no longer worthy of anything but scorn.

Under the veil of aversion, an atrocious retrospective jealousy had invaded him and had stifled within him even the appearances of free will. Benevolent words and sage advice would infallibly have brought him back to more human sentiments. His brutalities were only the consequence of a lovesickness that was devouring him, and it would have been easy to inspire forgiveness, at least, in a soul so weak and so forcefully smitten. But his pretended physicians were only torturers who turned the knife in his wounds and poured vinegar into them instead of balm. His suffering did not leave him an instant of relief, and maintained him perpetually in a distress close to frenzy.

Meanwhile, Louise's situation was becoming more precarious by the day. Because of the cares that her child required, it was forbidden for her to undertake any coherent labor. Without counting the needs to which she found herself prey, she was harassed daily by creditors at the end of their patience. Until then she had endured everything without complaint. After having tried persuasion and tenderness, she had embraced the only course of action that remained to her, that of keeping silent and waiting, but her deprivation had reached a degree that no longer suffered any delay. She armed herself with resolution and waited for her husband.

With tears in her voice she exposed to him the extremity to which she had been reduced, and the impossibility she was in of living like that any longer. The poor insensate was drunk; he listened to her with a scornful expression. As soon as she had finished, he exploded in ignoble insults and forgot himself to the extent of raising his hand to her. Nevertheless, he stopped abruptly and fled, as if ashamed of his own fury.

Counting the hours, the minutes and the seconds, Louise waited for a day, two days, a week; her husband did not reappear. The people who she asked for news of him replied that he was no longer working in the Cour de Bretagne, and had changed quarter. Presently, she ought no longer hope for anything from him. In order to struggle against an immeasurable poverty, only her strength remained to her. She withdrew into herself and measured the depths of the abyss boldly.

Without credit, with debts of the worst species, she had already pawned or sold everything in her home that had any value. She was feeling the first effects of hunger. There was no family, relative or friend to whom she could legitimately address herself. The last words of my mother still resounded in her ears like a malediction: "May I never see you again! From this day forth you are dead to me!" It was not that she lacked the courage to implore her pity, or that she despaired of obtaining it; she would have gladly, for the sake of her child, trampled her pride underfoot; but it would also have been necessary to let her glimpse the unqualifiable conduct of Moser, to admit at least tacitly that she had been wrong to marry him, and all her strength vanished at the mere idea of accusing her husband. If she thought about me, it was to renounce immediately a step that might give an appearance of justice to the insulting suspicions of which she was the victim.

She did not escape any of the affronts of poverty. In her distress, two phantoms never ceased to pass back and forth before her: death and mendicity. Fainting with terror, she clutched her child convulsively in her arms and begged Heaven to send her an inspiration.

At that moment, her door was ajar. Someone was going downstairs. The appearance of a young woman who occupied one of the corners of the attic caused to spring forth in Louise's soul the flash for which she was waiting. That girl was nothing less than one of those sickly warblers who, in order to live, scrape the strings of a guitar and draw a few shrill false notes from their throats. Because of her bronzed skin, the flames of her big black eyes and her savage expression, you might have taken her for another Mignon regretting the homeland where the golden apples were ripening.[1]

---

1 "Mignon Regretting Her Homeland," an 1838 print of a painting by Ary Scheffer illustrating a scene from Goethe's *Wilhelm Meisters lehrjahre*, was a huge best-seller, long found on the walls of many Parisian households,

Louise called out to the child and plied her with questions. The information that she obtained determined a resolution that one can qualify loudly as admirable, not to say heroic. By dint of prayers and tears, she succeeded in moving two of her most ferocious creditors and making benevolent protectors of them. They consented to accompany her to the police commissaire, where they attested willingly to the verity of the story that she told him.

Her face colored by the shame of lying, in a voice that she tried in vain to render firm, she said that Moser, her husband, had gone to Austria to see his parents, and that since his departure, which dated back three months, she had had no news of him. She added that she could only attribute his silence to a malady, and that if he did not arrive, he would certainly write some day. In the meantime, she had exhausted her resources and found herself without means of existence. Resolved to profit from the songs she knew in order to live, she had come to beg the commissaire to give her the necessary certificates.

On the testimony of the patented witnesses, the public official gave Louise the paper that she needed. In possession of that paper, in which it was declared that "he saw no inconvenience on permission to sing being granted to the said Madame Moser," Louise ran to the prefecture of police, where she obtained without great effort the right to exercise her new profession in the taverns and courtyards of certain quarters . . .

V

As Philippe entered into these details, Jean redoubled his attention, which he manifested by opening his eyes wide and, so to speak, enlarging his ears. He was reminiscent, in his attitude and his expression, of a man in whom dormant memories are reawakening, or of whom two or three notes are putting on the track of a musical remembrance.

When Philippe depicted Louise's new existence for him, and represented her wandering, or rather dragging herself, with her child, from courtyard to courtyard and from café to café, incessantly at grips with the dread of encountering scorn, and—what was a thousand times more dolorous—that of being recognized by one of her old acquaintances, Jean could not retain a cry of surprise.

At the same time he turned his head abruptly toward his friend and looked at him with a sort of stupor.

"What's the matter?" Philippe asked.

"You ask that!" cried Jean. "But I believe that I know your story."

"I would be surprised."

"When I say your story, I mean an episode that certainly relates to it."

"You're making me curious."

Jean collected himself and appeared to be recalling his memories.

"I'm sure," he said suddenly, with multiple gestures. "Evidently, it can only be a matter of your Louise."

"Go on, I'm listening," Philippe replied.

After a pause, Jean continued, initially in a slow voice, but soon with increasing rapidity: "It was in the Rue

Saint-Antoine, if my memory serves me right, in some tavern, one afternoon, that the scene must have unfolded. Wait. I can only remember the impression as yet, but the details will come back to me . . . I have it . . . a young woman, holding a sleeping child in her arms, slips all the way to the counter of the establishment and asks the demoiselle sitting there for authorization to sing. Her pretty face and her air of honesty, disposed immediately in her favor, at the same time as her eyes reddened by tears and her thin features give evidence of intense chagrins and great privations. Her attire, although very neat, is miserable.

"I'll try not to forget anything essential.

"Standing amid the tables, her eyelids obstinately lowered, she tries to make audible the accents of a voice that emotion stifles in her throat. It's difficult to comprehend that she's singing; you might liken her to a worn-out piano in which half of the keys no longer work. The benevolent attention that is lent to her multiplies her embarrassment tenfold, and her voice is weakening by virtue of the silence that falls around her when a heart-rending exclamation suddenly makes all heads turn toward the darkest corner of the tavern.

"A strange tableau was floating, so to speak, in the penumbra.

"Three young men, at table before bottles and glasses, were playing cards noisily. In the midst of the increasing silence, the voice of the singer soon reached their ears. At that voice, one of them shuddered, as if a bullet had touched his heart. Almost simultaneously, he raised his head, uttered a cry, dropped his cards, leapt to his feet, overturning glasses and bottles, putting his hand over his eyes, and, in sum giving signs of the most violent despair.

"However, from that young man, whose pantomime excites surprise, the eyes of the spectators have soon returned to the singer, who, for her part, falling silent and examining with stupefaction the man at whom everyone is looking, utters a dull cry and falls in a faint. People get up and form a circle around her; they hasten to help her.

"She only emerges from her faint to search with her eyes for the unknown man; but he has taken advantage of the disorder to escape from the tavern. His features, it is said, were distraught, his eyes haggard; he seemed to be in a state neighboring dementia. His two friends, stupefied and nailed to their places, had not even tried to retain him.

"Can you understand my amazement now?" Jean asked his friend. And without waiting for an answer, he added: "Is it possible that the young man was not Moser? And the young woman who, pressed with questions, only gave evasive answers and only thought of escaping the solicitude of which she was the object, could she be anyone but your Louise?"

Philippe had not ceased to nod his head as a sign of approval.

"Beyond a doubt, he said, "your characters are mine. I will add that the scene did indeed unfold thus. From whom did you get that? Perhaps you read it in the small print of a newspaper. After all, there's nothing miraculous about it. Some reporter might well have been among the eye witnesses of the scene. But your reporter could not have had any presentiment, what no one could know except for Louise, is what the poor woman suffered in her new estate, before and until that final crisis. I was moved to weep like a woman myself when she told me about the cruel struggle she had sustained before deciding to implore the pity of men and hold out her hand to them.

"During the few days that she exercised that horrible métier, the horrible torture that martyrized her was perpetual. She went back and forth twenty times before a public place before going into it. Scarcely was she there than she had to make superhuman efforts to open her mouth. Her forehead reddened with shame, her legs trembled beneath her and her heart beat as if to break her breast. Most of the time, having run out of courage, she went away without even daring to make a collection.

"Already weakened by months of anxiety, insomnia and privations, her strength abandoned her on the day when, having gone into a tavern, she recognized her own husband among those whose compassion and alms she had come to solicit. After her faint she was shivering with fever. She left the establishment gripped by an immeasurable dolor and buckling under the weight of her child. Increasingly incapable of sustaining herself, marching at random, she found herself without knowing how in the heart of a quarter that was unknown to her. It might have been four o'clock in the afternoon. Her uncertain step began to awaken the curiosity of passers-by. She sensed her reason becoming troubled and saw objects dancing around her.

"Courage finally failed her. Without ceasing to clasp her child in her arms, she collapsed alongside a wall and lost consciousness. From that moment on she had no more memories. It was impossible for her to recall what had happened since her fall until the moment when she woke up in the hospital ward . . ."

VI

The two friends' walk was approaching its end. Apart from the numerous pauses they had made, they had only measured the route slowly, and had not thought of counting the hours. The day, for them, had gone by with the rapidity of an arrow. Philippe, fatigued by such a long narration, scarcely gave himself the time to draw breath.

In telling me her misfortunes, Louise, forgetting herself, had interrupted me twenty times to ask me what had become of her child, whether he was being cared for, and then to worry about her Moser and feel sorry for him. As to the former, I was in a position to reassure her immediately. In accordance with what happens in such cases, when a mother is taken to hospital, the child had been sent to the hospitals' depot. He would be returned to Louise's caresses as soon as she had recovered. As for Moser, I could only promise to occupy myself with him ardently without delay.

Before anything else, it was a matter of attending to Louise's illness. Not trusting my knowledge alone, I begged our professor to be kind enough, by exception, to examine a patient in whom I had a particular interest, Doctor Maison, an excellent man, granted my request willingly. He had an opinion diametrically opposed to that of his clinic chief, and disapproved of all his prescriptions. Fundamentally, his conclusion was the same. Mental dolors, even more than privations, had determined in Louis a commencement of pneumonia—pardon the word. The consequences were already not to be feared; all the symptoms permitted the assurance that she would not be long delayed in entering into convalescence.

Tranquil in that regard, I resolved seriously to set out in search of Moser. I soon drew up my plan. I went directly to the workshop in the Faubourg du Temple. Moser had not been seen there for some three months, and none of his comrades knew what had become of him. Then I obtained a commercial almanac and made a scrupulous note of the addresses of all the piano-makers in Paris. Consecrating a few hours every day to enquiries, in less than a week I had visited the majority of the workshops. To my great chagrin, I wasted my time and my steps. Poor Louise, who was aware of my journeys, waited for me in the morning with the keenest anxiety, and as soon as I appeared she devoured me with her eyes. She divined promptly by my expression that I had nothing fortunate to tell her.

In spite of her husband's wrongdoing, she still loved him as profoundly; she knew very well that he was only guilty by virtue of an excess of sensitivity and amour. Her anxieties increased by the hour, and, by depriving her of the calm of which she had need, slowed down the progress of her cure in proportion. I was striving to give her hope when one day, I was discouraged. One last resource remained to me: that of going to the prefecture of police, to the bureau of lodgings. Provided that Moser had not left Paris, I might perhaps succeed in obtaining an indication of his domicile there. I admit, of course, that the step in question caused me the most profound repugnance. I recoiled before the necessity of making it, and always put it off until the next day.

The annoyance in which I found myself cannot be measured. My patients could not help but feel it. It is certain that the moment would have been poorly chosen to put my patience to the proof. Meanwhile, every time I went into the Saint-Charles Ward—the men's ward, as I believe I have said—a singular event did not fail to occur. A patient, who had entered the hospice offering the symptoms of a species of gastroenteritis—another big word for which it is necessary to pardon me—delivered himself as soon as I passed his bed to a pantomime that commenced to intrigue me and irritate me. The patient was young. Blond curly hair, a pale beard, even more blond, and a complexion as white as milk, gave his head something of the appearance of that of a sheep. He propped himself up to his elbow when I approached and stared at me with blue eyes that were bursting with fury. In the depths of my memory there was an image analogous to that face, but an image so confused and so faint that I was impotent to recall its origin.

I did not remark the behavior of the patient immediately. When I perceived it, I was not troubled by it to begin with. Gradually, I began to pay attention to it, and I judged it increasingly strange. Finally, the invalid seemed to me impertinent and occasioned a feverish impatience in me that I had ever more difficulty in suppressing. The result was that one day, when I was in a mental disposition even worse than usual, I felt sharply wounded by the young man's gaze. I approached him abruptly and said: "Do you have something against me?"

His nostrils flared and his teeth clenched, he plunged his eyes into mine with an expression of frightening hatred.

"Do you know me?" I added, increasingly surprised.

He nodded his head affirmatively and continued to fix me with his eyes, from which flames sprang.

"You're doubtless mistaken," I said, after a moment's reflection. "I don't know you."

He tried to speak, but emotion stifled his voice in his throat.

I was confounded. Today, I can't be astonished enough that I didn't divine immediately who I was dealing with. That encounter, to tell the truth, was so far from my mind!

"What is your name? Where have you seen me?" I said, then.

Fury paralyzed his tongue; the muscles of his face agitated under the skin like snakes under a cloth; his fists clenched with rage.

The threats of that paltry fellow seemed to me to be more ridiculous than redoubtable. In any case, I did not understand at all. The idea that I was perhaps the object of scorn, or that I found myself in the presence of a madman, crossed my mind and recalled me to myself. I turned my back and passed on, privately making the resolution no longer to occupy myself with the poor devil.

Instinct was stronger than my will; my trouble persisted. An ardent curiosity gradually invaded me, and stopped me as I was about to leave the ward. Perhaps, after all, it was a matter of an adventure that had slipped my memory. At any rate, I wanted to know the man's name. Nothing was simpler. I retraced my steps with a certain precipitation.

Aided by the most energetic images, I could not depict for you the fear by which I was struck when I read on the label attached to the foot of his bed: *Georges Moser, piano-maker.*

What an encounter! Could any more stupefying be made?

Louise's husband, for whom I had searched fruitlessly throughout Paris, was before me, on a bed in the hospice, in a room situated directly underneath the one in which his wife lay. I received such a shock that I was stunned, or to put it better, petrified.

For a long time, I could not take my eyes off Moser. In addition to the stupor caused to me by that encounter, I sensed movements in me comparable to those of despair. This, then, was my work! For having obeyed slavishly a fit of vanity, I had disunited two excellent beings and made their misfortune. How could I remain indifferent in the very presence of the consequences of my fault? How could I not be stirred to the depths of my entrails? I did not lack heart at that point. The torments of my conscience drove me to the utmost limits of repentance. I swore mentally not to take any rest until I had restored to its initial state a household in which I had so maladroitly sown discord and chagrin . . .

Jean seemed delighted. He took advantage of a pause on his friend's part to state his opinion of that new incident.

"I'm wonderstruck," he said. "However, I expected it. I must even admit a culpable thought that occurred to me. At the very moment, while listening to you, I was saying to myself *in petto* that if Moser were not found in the hospice, I would permit myself to be put there. The event proves me right, and I'm very glad. Once more I acquire proof that reality can sometimes be in accord with the desires of the imagination. As for the denouement, it costs me to anticipate it. I'd like it to be happy, but in truth, I don't see how it would be possible for you to act efficaciously on the mind of that unfortunate fellow and erode a conviction that seems so firmly rooted there."

"I shared your fears at first," Philippe replied. "In thinking about the umbrageous character of the man, the nature of his prejudices and the tenacity of his rancor, I expected, in fact, to besiege an impregnable fortress. Well, it was quite otherwise. In spite of the hatred that I inspired in him, I was able to acquire enough empire over him to make him listen to me. If I collided in the beginning with a sort of rock, one might truly have thought that the rock in question was made of snow, so rapidly did it melt in the end, under the heat of my protestations. The fellow was weary of hatred, he was at the end of his strength and dolor; his passion, moreover, multiplied tenfold by a separation of some five months, possessed him with more violence than ever. And don't believe that I handled him with kid gloves. On the contrary, intentionally, I talked to him with an arrogant disdain; I abused without reserve all the advantages that education and fortune gave me.

"I reminded him that his wife was an orphan taken in by my mother, and that she had never had any but a subaltern condition in our household. Without taking into account that I was too proud to link myself with a girl who, entirely honest as she was, had nevertheless to be classified in the rank of domestics, it was to insult my mother to suppose, even for an instant, that in her house, under her eyes, any culpable relations could exist between Louise and me. I had been wrong, undoubtedly, to treat her as a servant when she was married and on her husband's arm; nevertheless, it was no less ridiculous to make a crime of a familiarity for which my pride and conceit were responsible. I added that, for my part, I did not know any woman in the world purer than Louise, and that if she had ever committed a fault, it was that of marrying, against my mother's advice, a man who was not worthy of her.

"Gradually, the poor fellow opened his eyes to the light. I can't describe to you the energy of his regrets and his chagrin. It was a heart-rending spectacle to see him drowning in tears and writhing in his bed under the effort of intolerable dolors. At other times, he remained plunged in a profound prostration from which nothing could extract him. He tried to attenuate in my eyes the brutality of his conduct by admitting that he had temporarily ceased to be master of himself. Jealousy had inflicted atrocious tortures on him, an incessant agony, under the empire of which, afflicted by a sort of dementia, he had abandoned his wife and child. Perfidious counsel had completed driving him to despair and dooming him. Soon incapable of struggling against his suffering, he had sought forgetfulness in disorders that had gradually caused his health to deteriorate and had brought him, half-dead, to the hospital bed.

"For many days I was impotent to console him. He did not think that he could ever expiate a past by which he was horrified, and he only succeeded imperfectly, in spite of my affirmative language, in believing in Louise's forgiveness and hoping for happier days. He gave me much more cause for alarm than his wife, who drew an ever firmer confidence from my reiterated assertions, and was now in full convalescence."

VII

Philippe and his friend no longer had more than a few moments to remain together. It was getting late. In the east, shadow was gradually invading the sky, while on the opposite horizon, large clouds were tinted with the bright colors of the setting sun. It was marvelous to see the long horizontal zones that, from pale blue, passed through tender green, and then violet, and then blood red, and then molten gold. You might have thought it a splendid Indian scarf bordered with a golden fringe. It was the hour when the idle sparrow, on the edge of its hole, chirps like a sleepy child; when the bat opens its blinking eyes and stretches its palmate arms; when the swallows, jealous of presaging, by their flight, a fine tomorrow, cross one another's paths in the air and design great curves there analogous to those of a skater on ice. At the same time as the lighter of candelabra, armed with his lamp, longer than a Cossack's lance, set light successively to the gas of the lanterns, a few stars, comparable in the dusk to iron points heated white-hot, emerged here and there in space.

Jean, who did not want to wait until the following day for the end of the story, pressed his friend to tell him the denouement rapidly.

I only have two or three more facts to mention, in any case. As you have doubtless divined, I carefully refrained from informing the husband and the wife of their respective fates. I experienced the most profound repugnance at the idea of seeing them reunited and reconciled in the hospital ward. I limited myself to assuring them that all would be well and asking them for a little patience. Internally, I meditated means of causing as many tears of joy to flow from their eyes as I had caused tears of chagrin to flow, and to acquit with interest what I considered to be a debt toward them.

I chose a day when my cousin was dining in the house. My silence and my sadness had not failed to surprise my father and mother for some time. Until then, in my family, no one had done me the honor of attributing serious sentiments to me, and I passed there, with sufficient reason, for being more inclined to pleasure than to work. I had even endured merited reproaches on several occasions. An accident had suddenly matured me and made me a man. I no longer thought that it was shameful to have sensibility and to let it be seen.

When evening came, contrary to my habit, I did not go out. Interrogated visually by my mother and verbally by my father, I floored both of them abruptly by this enigmatic admission: "In fact," I said in an ill-humored tone, "such as you see me, I am very unhappy. Thoughtlessly, stupidly, with an inexcusable lightness, I have caused unhappiness to the two best people in the world. I will not hide from you that I intend, at any cost, to repair my stupidity and that I need your collaboration to do that."

At that declaration, my father, my mother and my cousin looked at one another with the most profound surprise. I presume that they feared for a moment that I might have gone mad. I removed them very rapidly from error.

Resuming speaking immediately, I recounted my encounter at Vincennes with Louise and all the miseries that had resulted from it for her. If I slid willingly enough over the deplorable motive that had inspired me on that occasion, I emphasized nevertheless the consequences that my fault had had. I told the story in minute detail of Louise's misfortunes and presented her in the most touching light. I was truly eloquent. At first my story only extracted syllables of amazement. At the scene in the café, I saw my mother's eyes fill with tears. She could not retain her sobs when I described Louise, after that scene, wandering the streets like a madwoman, succumbing under the weight of her child, and finally falling unconscious, to be picked up and transported to the hospital.

My father too was moved to tears; he never ceased repeating: "Oh, the poor child! The poor child!"

Only the cousin could not find a tear in the corner of his eye or a word of compassion in the depths of his heart. Under his contrite expression, I even recognized the indications of a malign joy. Rancor prospered in the depths of his evil nature; the memory of Louise's disdain was as vivid as on the first day. I could not doubt that he rejoiced in seeing her unhappy; so I sensed a dull anger against him accumulating and stirring within me.

My mother, in her emotion, did not yet extract the sentiments that I expected from her. In her soul, Louise's misfortune was partly stifled by an old leaven of resentment. Scarcely had I let her glimpse what I counted on her to do than she spoiled her tenderness with a cruel reflection:

"She doubtless had much to lament, but it's also a little her fault; why did she leave me?"

That seemed barbaric to me.

Jacques, who had not yet breathed a word, was sufficiently emboldened to add: "My aunt is right."

I was no longer master of myself. My eyebrows furrowed, my eyes glittering, my nostrils flared, scarcely breathing, I turned toward him with a bound and launched at him like a poised arrow: "What does it have to do with Monsieur Jacques? Who asked for his opinion? People of heart and he have nothing in common."

After that sortie, which rendered him as mute as a fish and caused him to retreat, as it were, underground, I turned to my mother and addressed her. Without departing from the respect that I owed her, I remarked to her forcefully that she could not, without the most blatant injustice, criticize the conduct of Louise and accuse her of ingratitude.

"I sustain," I went on, "that by her work, her cares, her patience and her devotion, she had rendered you, and beyond, the benefits that you claim to have lavished on her, and, that, on the contrary, with regard to her, you might well have forgotten momentarily to be good and generous.

"She challenged my authority," said my mother. "She failed in all her duties toward me."

"In what way?" I replied. "For having refused to link her fate to a ridiculous man who only inspired aversion in her, and for having obeyed her penchant, she is not, after all, so criminal."

"In any case," said my mother, "we owe her nothing."

"But for my part," I cried, "I have caused her an almost irreparable prejudice. Under pain of being a dishonest man, under pain of committing a cowardice that would poison my entire life, it is forbidden to me to envelop myself in my egotism and to witness with folded arms a misfortune of which I am the unique source."

My mother indicated by the shake of her head and her expression that she found my opinion exaggerated.

"Yes," I went on, with increasing warmth, "in my conviction, in order for my honor to be saved, in order for my conscience to be tranquil, in order that my entire future should not be stained, a reparation is necessary, a striking reparation that surpasses, if that is possible, the importance of my error."

I followed on my mother's face the oscillations of her unsteady will. I was approaching the goal. I hastened to add:

"Have you lost your memory, then? But that child, you have seen her born, she developed under your eyes, she was the companion of my childhood; her gracious face, her pretty voice, her entirely filial attachment for you have not ceased to charm your eyes, your ears and your heart. Is it necessary for me to remind you also of her mother, that worthy woman who was the providence of my young years, whose cares and vigilance have saved my life? And you hesitate! Your heart does not break in thinking that Louise, almost your daughter, has been reduced to wandering the streets like a beggar, singing in cafés and holding out her hand! You only have sterile tears when you know that she is lying in a hospital bed, that she is on the eve of being put outside, without resources, with her child, and all because of my fault, the fault of your son!"

My mother sobbed again and seemed to be asking me for mercy. Doubtless I was harsh, but it was necessary. Otherwise, I might not have succeeded in vanquishing her resentment. I concluded by looking at my father. I knew that he was the best man in the world, but also a little too economical, if not parsimonious.

"Finally," I said, with a firmness that must have made him shudder, "I warn you that I am ready to sacrifice a part of the dowry that you destine for me, to engage my signature, to encumber my heritage, and to ruin myself, in order to have the money I need."

I would like to believe that my mother was not sorry to hear me speak with that warmth. The fact is that I succeeded in making her share all my intentions. In reality, her tenderness for Louise was only dormant; it woke up in her heart with a new intensity. For his part, my father, aided that fortunate revolution by agreeing that it was necessary to occupy himself with Louise and reestablish her in the situation she had had before the accident. I soon saw my good mother as ardent as she had previously been lukewarm, and I was glad to hear her declare that she intended to take care of everything. I gave her *carte blanche* gladly, knowing that she was liberal and more capable than anyone else of arranging things well.

As for Jacques, he no longer knew what face to put on. In the little war that had just taken place he had maladroitly embraced the side of injustice. His found himself in regard to us in the most false position. He understood that perfectly. His nose swelled and became red, as always happened when he found himself prey to any emotion.

VIII

Philippe, who, without thinking about it, had continued to take pleasure in his story, seemed decidedly reluctant to be brief. He resumed precipitately.

The day arrived when Louise's *exeat* was signed. I had lavished her with hopes, but had not made her any formal promise. In the morning, when it was time to get dressed, she found beside her, on a chair, one of the dresses that poverty had obliged her to pawn. At eleven o'clock I came to find her and conducted her myself to the reception room. My mother was waiting for her there; she was holding the little Moser in her arms.

At that sight, Louise was gripped by an emotion that almost choked her. I felt her entire body tremble and saw that she was about to lose consciousness, which caused me to regret momentarily not having warned her. But the joy of seeing and embracing her child gave her the strength to overcome that weakness. She quit me abruptly and ran to her little boy, whom she lifted in her arms and devoured with kisses. Then she took one of my mother's hands and inundated it with tears. My good mother was weeping too, and she embraced her ward effusively.

I was troubled in the satisfaction that pathetic scene gave me by the presence of two or three witnesses. The pleasure I felt did not absorb me, like Louise, to the point of rendering me indifferent to what was happening around me. I urged my mother to depart. We climbed into a carriage and took the road to the Rue de Marais.

On the way, Louise, incapable of sitting still, shifted like a madwoman; she could not get enough of contemplating her child, kissing him and hugging him; her gratitude for us burst forth in her eyes and in exclamations of joy. She suddenly interrupted herself in the midst of those expressions to interrogate me sadly with her gaze. I had no difficulty in understanding.

The turn of my mind is far from romantic, and, unlike my mother, I only have a mediocre liking for surprises. I therefore judged it appropriate to prepare Louise for the excess of happiness that awaited her. I told her that I had finally had news of Moser.

"Have you seen him?" she cried.

"Yes."

She looked at me anxiously. "Well?" she said.

"He has been ill too," I replied, laconically. "I succeeded in making him listen to reason; you'll doubtless see him soon, penetrated by repentance and fonder of you than ever."

As a gesture of thanks, Louise took possession of my hand and pressed it to her heart. New tears flowed from her eyes and moistened her pale cheeks. We arrived.

My father welcomed the poor girl with an entirely paternal generosity and told her obligingly that the time of ordeals was over and that she only had happy days to hope for. She was fêted, pampered and caressed as much as a cherished invalid who had reappeared, against all expectation, full of health. People who had known her before wanted to see her, embrace her and compliment her. Although profoundly touched by those marks of affection, a painful memory came and went in her heart and moderated its delight.

Moser's *exeat* had been signed at the same time as his wife's. I had given him a rendezvous at the house, and I was already impatient at not seeing him arrive. In the meantime, my mother said to Louise: "Now, my girl, let's go up to your apartment."

Louise and I looked at her with a profoundly surprised expression. While extracting my intentions with regard to the husband and the wife, my mother had constantly refused to tell me her own. Having gone up to the third floor, we stopped in front of a door whose key was in the lock. In order to spare Louise's strength, my mother had taken the little Moser in her arms.

"Ring, my daughter," she said to her.

Footsteps were heard within; Louise recognized them; without waiting any longer she turned the key, pushed the door and fell in a faint in Moser's arms.

I shall renounce, for lack of time, describing that scene. I gladly abandon that care to you. With my help, Moser transported his wife to an armchair and knelt down before her. He wept, kissed her hands and looked at her with tenderness while waiting for her to come round. Scarcely had she opened her eyes that she leaned over him passionately and mingled her tears with his. For a long time, sobs stifled the words in their throats.

My mother and I watched the spectacle in silence, both transported by a limitless contentment. For my part, I believe I experienced, on that occasion, the purest and most vivid enjoyment that I had felt, and doubtless will feel, in all my life. I cannot tell you how happy I was to have contributed to a scene that, "in the species," as a man of law would say, was one of the most touching that can be imagined.

Nevertheless, the transports of their delight calmed down by degrees; a little order was introduced into the chaos of their sensations, and they finally found voices and speech to heap one another with questions. In the midst of their intersecting stories, they never ceased to interrupt themselves to caress their child and turn eyes full of tears toward us. One might have thought that they were waking up from a long dream and enjoying a new union in a better world than ours.

The room in which we were was the principal one in small lodgings of an exquisite neatness and the most cheerful appearance. Without informing me, my mother had rented it and had it furnished in an entirely comfortable manner. Curtains of cheerful perse garnished the windows; a mirror and an alabaster clock ornamented the mantelpiece; the drawers of a chest and the shelves of a large cupboard had been filled with linen and objects of toilette. A gleaming array of copper saucepans and a collection of faience plates and pots decorated the walls and the dresser of a small, very clean and very bright kitchen. In her generous foresight, my mother had gone as far as decorating the walls of the apartment with a series of colored prints, and the window sills with the most beautiful flowers of the season. It was more like the apartment of petty rentiers than that of poor workers.

My mother showed the husband and wife around and enabled them to appreciate all its facilities. Although the intelligent anticipation of a housekeeper was visible even in the slightest details, my mother said to Louise: "See if you have everything you need; I might have forgotten some things. In any case, I believe I've put a little money in the middle drawer of the chest, in order to provide the most urgent. Besides which, between now and when your husband has found work, there are some small funds downstairs at your disposal."

So much liberality and so many delicate attentions filled Louise and her husband with gratitude; they searched the depths of their hearts, in order to express it, for words that did not come to their lips. I confess that I was no less content than them.

What more can I tell you? Moser became again, as before, the most laborious and the most economical of workers, as well as the most tender of husbands and the best of fathers. He rendered to his wife an exclusive confidence that even the most compromising of appearances would not have been capable of damaging. His amity for me almost made Louise jealous. I saw them at least once a week in the house, where they dined with us *en famille*. As I speak, they have two children, whom they are bringing up very well and on whose subject they have the most beautiful dreams.

You will perhaps not be sorry to learn that their presence has put my cousin Jacques to flight; we no longer see him. I am deprived of the pleasure of contemplating his sly face and hearing him remind me of Vaucanson's duck.

That is my story; make of it what you will. It is, at least, a canvas easy to extend, embroider and embellish.

"God preserve me from that!" Jacques exclaimed, shaking his friend's hand. "The thing is complete as it is. I will add that, without suspecting it, you have told me a story that is the image of the three ordinary phases of life: in the beginning, amour; in the middle, struggle; in the decline, repose. I shall limit myself to reproducing your story as faithfully as possible, and will deem myself fortunate if I can cause others the pleasure that I have had in listening to you."

Héloïse

THOSE who remain make the history of those who have gone; that is the order of things. They are the memory that perpetuates funereal remembrance, the eyes that translate into tears the dolors of extinct existences. In vain they try to distance themselves from the sadness of that task; thought brings them back via a road that is lined with tombs. Is the part of the absent individual not preferable? Is it so pleasant to see the people one loves agonizing and a void forming around oneself?

I found in a notebook yellowed by age this thought, which I have collected because of the approval that I already gave it there a long time ago: *For myself, I swear, if God were to give me the power to return to my mother's womb and to return to earth to enjoy there what is known as a happy fate, I would not want it.*

Yorick's epitaph, if you remember it, would suit me well enough—"Alas, poor Yorick!"

I have often been accused of harshness, for want of a little hypocrisy. I have never been able to feel pity for imaginary or artificial dolors. In all things, but especially in matters of sentiment, the conventional and the false have always been odious to me. If a man gesticulates, utters loud cries, and proclaims himself the most unfortu-nate among those who are suffering because a laundress has forgotten to bring him a false collar or an excessively hot iron has imprinted a bad crease in his waistcoat, I confess that it scarcely moves me, except to pity. I know that the man would find me heartless . . .

Exposed to the caprices of hazard, against which the efforts of a powerful will so frequently fail, I had been obliged to quit Paris in order to reside temporarily else-where. The incident was vulgar; I would not talk about it and would scarcely remember it but for a touching episode, the impression of which left me with a durable memory.

From my lodgings, through the geraniums and the long cineraria that partly masked my window, I could see, extending in an oblique plane, the poor and irreg-ular façades of one entire side of a street. I had a grocer opposite, at the corner of a lateral street. The chocolate-colored decoration of his shop front was visible. There were clusters of sponges, balls of string, bunches of feath-ers, houndstooth brushes, rackets, shuttlecocks, bundles of brooms, a few baskets full of cork, barrels filled with plums or wallpaper paste, veritable water closets for the local dogs. Behind the windows, on glass shelves, mer-chandise was heaped, the garish wrappings of which seemed cut from a Harlequin's costumes. Outside the door, early in the morning, a boy only half awake would burn coffee-beans in a blackened cylinder that he rotat-ed slowly over a fire of woodchips. The environs filled with an odorous smoke, about which no one thought of complaining.

Alongside there was a haberdashery. The narrow façade of the house was half-timbered. On the ground floor, in the display-window of the green shop, the petty mercery could be seen of tulle bonnets, the pink or blue ribbons of which attracted the eyes of young women in passing.

Then came a silversmith with his apparatus of chandeliers and copper censers sweating verdigris; then a locksmith's shop, the interior of which, in the evening, resounded with the rhythmic sounds of the anvil and was resplendent with the glare of the forge; then a butcher; then a chocolatier; and then a dealer in second-hand clothes and old furniture. I will admit that the butcher's meat stall was very agreeable to me. The rows of cutlets and quarters of mutton suspended and lined up like soldiers, the disemboweled calves with their aprons of grease, the rumps and other cuts of beef, ornamented as if for sacrifice: all those shades of pink and red, so fresh and so vivid, rejoiced my eyes no less than the fat cheeks of the butcher, who scarcely found room at his counter for his exuberant form, and seemed, with the odor of meat, to respire health.

From the place where I was accustomed to sit I could not see any more.

There was a market at the end of the street and, in consequence, in the morning, there was a procession of housewives who passed by empty and came back with their bodies bent double, losing their balance, their baskets full of vegetables, fruits, butter, cheese, eggs, meat or fish.

At numerous windows in the part of the street that comprised my view, I could also often see the heads of women of all ages.

All of that was very lively and very cheerful.

One Sunday in February, on opening my window to warm myself in the sunlight, I perceived in the second house, occupied by the haberdashery, a young woman. I did not know then whether she was married or not, and from my position I could only judge that she had a pretty face. I saw brown hair, soft eyes, a pale and slightly elongated face—a melancholy ensemble. She seemed to me to be quite tall and well made. She looked to the right and the left, and seemed to be resting from the fatigues of the week.

I was interested in her right away, although I don't know exactly why. I know, at least, that it was not by virtue of any sentiment of covetousness. Not all hearts catch fire like gunpowder at the mere sight of a woman. Having said that, my isolation perhaps entered considerably into the interest the young woman caused me. I presumed that she kept the shop on the ground floor. I would have liked very much to know whether she was married . . .

I often saw a deformed little old woman coming and going, in whom I soon recognized her mother. Her fashions of acting, and a vague family resemblance, left me no doubt as to that. Analogous observations enabled me to divine the father in a man in a blue blouse, about fifty years old. He smoked his pipe with great phlegm and had the air of a man who is bored by having nothing to do, but who is nevertheless not in haste to procure work.

Young men who, I think, were workers, frequented the house. There was one among them who came more regularly and who spent entire hours at the window where I had seen the young woman for the first time. I did not doubt at first that it was her husband. After less superficial observations I was less certain. The young man's manners were reserved, even a little cold. I explained that by supposing that they were not married, but that they would be some day, although they only loved one another moderately. I soon left that opinion to return to the first, and then that one to return to the second, and thus passed back and forth for some time without succeeding in retaining the same one for twenty-four hours. It is difficult to comprehend how I suffered from being tossed between the two alternatives, when it would have been so easy for me to emerge from uncertainty.

I had for a landlady the most excellent woman in the world, not too self-interested—which is rare—and who had maternal attentions for me. She always found a pretext for coming into my room when I was there. She only wanted to chat. Unfortunately, I dared not interrogate her on the subject in question, and I lacked the talent to lead her to talk about it herself.

It is here that it is necessary to analyze myself, as if I were an enigma to myself. I read the other day in a very serious writer: "If a woman is well-known for being timid, one can say that she has a natural tendency to avarice and pettiness; that she is crafty and secretive; that fear makes for speak softly and submissively; that she is suspicious, mistrustful, incredulous, a bad friend etc., because all these vices are effects of timidity, which is itself an effect of weakness."[1] There is a little of my case in that.

---

1 Author's note: "This is badly expressed. I do not know to what extent mistrust and incredulity are vices. Bentham has already said that envy and jealousy are not vices but difficulties."

I say "a little," for those who have rejuvenated that opinion, as old as the first physiognomic observation, have not perceived that there are two sorts of timidity, one innate and invincible, which gives rise to the aforesaid result, the other accidental, which stems uniquely from education, and which only occasions a profound mistrust of oneself. Have the misfortune to have a despotic and brutal father, who will not suffer that you open your mouth before him, who never ceases to treat you as an idiot and to embed his opinions, true or false, in your mind, and you will end up being afraid of your own voice, forming a prodigious idea of other men, and you will be humble and timid before them, but if you are fortunate, experience and observation having aided you later to appreciate what they are worth, you will succeed in vanquishing that mental infirmity and recovering your aplomb.

I admit that, in that regard, whatever I have been able to do, I have never obtained a radical cure. I will add that, with regard to women and the sentiments they cause, I had, by virtue of my humor, a reserve that would surely have made the most awkward schoolgirl smile.

It would have been very simple to question my landlady: "Who is that young woman? Is she married?" Or even: "Is the young man I see going into the house her husband?" But, good God, how would she have translated my curiosity? *Ah, so he's interested? Ah, doubtless she pleases him. Perhaps he wants to make her his mistress. Truly, the monsieur has no shame.* And the mere idea of those hypotheses frightened me, and stifled any whim of expression. If she had even suspected my preoccupations, I would no longer have dared to look her in the face.

I had not been in my new situation for three weeks when I was already lamenting it keenly. My story is that of many others. For half of the day and a part of the night I was riveted to labor that did not suit me. All my thoughts turned to bitterness; hypochondria invaded me like gangrene. I no longer knew what a calm night devoid of nightmares was. I woke up with a start, my heart swollen, with tears in my eyes, stifling. At those moments my mind had a marvelous lucidity. I only glimpsed desolating things in the future. In the morning, when I opened my eyes, it was very rare that a half-comical and half funereal gibe did not come to my mind: "Get up, wretch and plane a plank for your coffin . . ."

In that state of mind it was not astonishing that I would occupy myself so much with my neighbor. Spying on her, perceiving her, and studying her entourage, and by that means, getting to know her life and discovering the details about which I dared not ask, was my entire joy. Without the help of anyone else, I had become certain that the young man who had disquieted me so much was her brother. That certainty caused me a great joy, although I did not love the young woman and had no plans in her regard. From that day on, the interest I had in her had gained sensibly in vivacity and depth. The life she led, in its ensemble, resembled mine considerably. She did not budge from her counter all day long, and often spent a part of the night there as well. I never came back before three or four o'clock in the morning, and it was rare that I did not perceive light through the crescent cut out in the shutters of the shop. She scarcely rested except on Sunday, in the afternoon. If she went for a walk, it was by chance; she owed it to a sacrifice on her brother's part. Most of the time, she leaned on her window-sill or chatted on the doorstep with the people of the neighborhood, who seemed to like her a great deal and to have a particular consideration for her.

What I would have liked would have been less indifference on her part; she only looked in my direction in a manner that was too vague and too distracted for my liking. One does not always desire to be loved by a woman, but what one does not support gladly, what always causes chagrin, is her indifference. To tell the truth, indifference has degrees. Between looking at a person, even mechanically, and taking no more account of them than if they did not exist, there are infinite nuances. I was reduced to weighing those delicacies. Her gaze gave me joy or pain, according to whether or not it was charged with a hint of sympathy.

Happiness is manifest in me by means of strange desires. I aspire to plunge myself in music and colors—which is to say, to sate my ears and my eyes with the nourishment that they love passionately. Either by virtue of abuse of those two organs or vicious organization, bizarrely, it is my ear that perceives colors and my eye that hears sounds, so that symphonies are dazzling paintings for me, and paintings admirable symphonies. In the lines of a statue and a church I see music, and I am sometimes convinced that a certain cathedral is the solidified hymn of a great subterranean organ. I cannot cure myself of it. Every song, for me, has the blue of the air and the green of the trees, and the changing reflections of water, and flowers, and the contours of a woman . . .

On the other hand, what sepulchral thoughts, what a desire for the coffin I had, when I only discovered in her eyes the vagueness of idleness, without the slightest hint of interest.

I had one fine day. Not far from the town there is a little river, very limited in its course, which gives its name to the département. The banks, without being picturesque, are pretty and cheerful. In the deep water, as blue as the sky, the tall trees, bushes, gardens and more-or-less bourgeois constructions of every sort are reflected, which are on the slopes of the banks. In summer, especially on Sunday, the water is furrowed by a multitude of boats going back and forth, with people chatting, laughing or singing.

One Sunday morning, someone came to find me to go for a walk in that place. The sky had a perfect purity; the keen air was softened by sunlight that was already warm; everything presaged a beautiful day, rare in the month in which we were. That invitation clashed with my intentions. For a few moments I was indecisive. I feared exchanging the pleasure of seeing my neighbor for a boring excursion. Nevertheless, the idea of escaping the enervating embrace of the walls of a town, of respiring the open air, of seeing horizons, and also I know not what annihilation of my will before the sincere insistence of my friend, persuaded me to accept.

Contrary to my anticipations, I found in the country the good fortune for which I would have waited in vain had I stayed at home. Scarcely was I in the fields than I felt an inexpressible wellbeing. When I was gliding over the water, that wellbeing only increased. The landscape had a very particular charm. The trees, although as yet devoid of leaves, were already less sad than in winter; the black trunks were taking on a green tint in places. A multitude of buds, dripping sap, already enormous and ready to burst under the development of new leaves, were shining in the sunlight. The thorny hedges were going green in places because of the precocious shrubs with which they were mingled. The pale green meadows, soaked by a mist that the sun had drunk as it rose, developed dazzling perspectives of freshness and light to the right and the left. The vegetation had already reached the active point at which one could, so to speak, follow the labor that it undertook in spring with the eyes. Above that was an entirely blue sky, an atmosphere simultaneously keen and mild, a penetrating calm—the calm of things that one feels but cannot express. Finally, I had for a guide a silent man who rowed gently and seemed to be under the influence of the same impressions.

A part of our day was spent on the river. We went at hazard, taking turns to row, saying very little, but dreaming on our own. We went as far as possible, in order to avoid the noisy boats that always emerge in sunny weather. In fact, when we returned, the closer we came to our departure point, we crossed paths with boats whose number increased with every thrust of the oars. Almost all of them moored at a tavern on the bank kept by a fisherman. The terrace of the guinguette, which was bathed by the river on one side and which supported the slope of the hill on the other, was covered with customers, some sitting and drinking, others standing and watching the movement on the water.

We were passing the foot of the terrace, without paying any heed to the people crowded there, when I heard someone call out to me. I perceived my landlady in the crowd, in the company of her husband, her little child and my neighbor.

My amazement occasioned a long pause.

"I wasn't expecting to encounter you here, Madame," I said.

"In truth, we were scarcely thinking of coming this morning," the excellent woman replied.

"The sunshine will doubtless have persuaded you."

"And then, it's a long time since we've gone out!"

"The walk will do you good. For myself, I don't feel at ease."

"You live so enclosed . . ."

We were unable to chat any longer. Although the movement of the boat had slowed down, the oars had nevertheless not ceased to work. We were already drawing away from the terrace. I sent my landlady an adieu that was also addressed to the young woman.

My contentment was profound. It would be necessary to have had oneself one of those funereal melancholies that flow in the flesh like blood and envelop ideas in crepe to appreciate my happiness. Convinced that I would not see my young neighbor, I had perceived her at the very moment when I was most saddened by that certainty. I took a good augury from that. To complete my joy, I thought I had read in her eyes less indifference than I had supposed her to have. She had looked at me as curiously as I had examined her. I had had the time necessary to study her exterior well. She was pretty; her features gained from being seen at close range. I doubt that a regular face has ever had as much physiognomy. Her dark eyes, partly veiled by long lashes, hr pale cheeks, and her sadly smiling lips, indicated not only fatigue but also a habitude of suffering.

She was well made, although slightly curbed. She was clad in a brown merino dress and a green shawl, and coiffed by a bonnet with violet ribbons. Those colors suited her marvelously. One could not see any trace of affectation in her. What is called coquetry in women ought to be no more perceptible than artistry in a well-written book.

The thought of her, after that encounter, was to leave me less tranquil than ever.

I wanted ardently to know the cause of her dolors, and yet, still the same with my landlady, I contented myself with interrogating my own observations. In the external appearance of the mother I ended up detecting heartlessness and avarice, in the bored features of the father an incurable apathy, in the habits of the brother the banal indifference that stops short of sacrifice. I was certain that the poor young woman, who poured out floods of tenderness from her eyes, was stifling between that trinity of egotists, and allowing herself to be overtaken by the unhealthy sadness that is caused by lack of affection.

I said to myself: *What has she done to be cloistered in that mortal milieu. What is the good of having given her a sensibility that, for want of having any opportunity to expand, is concentrated within her and is killing her?*

And I felt my sympathy for her increasing every day. Gradually, I recognized so many charms in her, and so many qualities, that I esteemed the man who would have her for a wife very fortunate. Within myself, I formulated a particular theory regarding that marriage. I thought that it would not be bad if passion were excluded from it; that submission on one side, justice on the other, and a certain conformity of tastes, were sufficient to make a happy marriage. It was thus that, without feeling amour for my neighbor, I came to dream complaisantly about marriage, whereas until then I had only thought about it with repugnance. But I limited myself to speculation. My lack of audacity, and my suspicion of myself, forbade me to take a step or to pronounce a word toward a denouement that, in my conviction, would have made my happiness.

I was very satisfied in not seeing her, in her misfortune, with a dog or a sparrow. I can see nothing unnatural in the attachment one can have for a cat or a parrot, but that the attachment takes on the proportions of a veritable passion, that one finds therein consolations for a great dolor, is what I can no longer explain. Sentiment is too precious to squander on beings incapable of sensing its value.

My hours of liberty were entirely devoted to my neighbor, and that, I repeat, without my having what is called amour. I grasped of her life what it was possible for me to grasp of it. For some time I had seen her much less. A change had taken place in her everyday habits. She scarcely stayed up late one night per week, that of Saturday and Sunday. A nightlight never ceased burning by night behind the curtain of a second-floor window. Then another young woman, whom I had not seen before, came to the house in the morning and did not leave until late in the evening.

It seemed to me that the young haberdasher only quit her room very rarely. I discovered her two or three times, in the middle of the day, leaning on her window-sill. She was wrapped up in a huge shawl. Her cheeks seemed to me to have paled considerably, and her eyes had become shinier.

I noted those details with scrupulous care. Another would have been alarming. In spite of my suspicion I collected those symptoms tranquilly. I thought: *She's temporarily indisposed. Working by night exhausts her. Nor is it rare to be ill in spring. It's probable that she'll be well again before long.* And the idea of marriage crossed my mind once again, but more seriously. I was convinced that I could not find a better wife. I was anxious about routes to follow; I went as far as to specify the epoch. My habitual timidity gave way to an extraordinary boldness; I no longer recognized myself. But alas, it was still a pure fiction that I allowed to develop in my mind, and of which I willingly made myself the dupe, because I found an intense pleasure in it.

There was nothing more. I no longer saw my neighbor. Physicians came to the house and left incessantly. There was an unusual flux of neighbors through the house, who went in and out with anxious expressions. It was impossible for facts to speak in a clearer language. However, I was not alarmed; I was convinced that I would see the young haberdasher again imminently, in better health and more beautiful than ever. I awaited that day with impatience, but without anxiety. I was so beautifully infatuated by my dream; I had lodged it so firmly in every corner of my mind, and I was so completely derived of any other joy, that I did not doubt for a moment that reality would, so to speak, mold itself to it precisely.

And truly, I would have been wrong to despair. One day, my neighbor, whom I had not seen for at least three months, reappeared in the frame of her window. The resurrection of a beloved absentee could not have caused me a more energetic joy.

I knew that she would recover her health! A chaste young woman who has those limpid eyes, those broad shoulders and that appearance of strength cannot languish in maladies for long. Youth, full of sap has easily reckoned even with a cruel illness. Her suffering must doubtless have been intense, for it has left such profound traces on the face and body of the beautiful child that I scarcely recognize her, she is so much paler and has become so thin. But in sum, she is better, since she has got up; she is evidently entering into convalescence. The fine weather will also help her cure. As happens at that age, when maladies are often only transformations, she will revive prettier and more seductive than she has ever been.

That official declaration of my soul was as precise as a tracing; I wrote it under the influence of the most vivid memories. At present, I wonder how I could have lacked sagacity to that point. I must have had a great need to lie to myself. It required the brutal fact to arrive to lift my eyelids and force itself into my head. My observations contained warnings that did not even succeed in diminishing my confidence.

The young woman, who seemed to be nailed to her bed, was no longer seen, but I told myself that convalescence requires excessive protection, and that a relapse is more dangerous than a malady. My landlady spent nights with her, but in my eyes that was uniquely to make her recovery seem less protracted. If the physician only came at rare intervals, I saw nothing in that but grounds for reassurance: his presence was becoming increasingly unnecessary.

Strangely enough, I caressed the idea of marriage with more passion every day. I was already searching with my eyes for the friend who would receive my confidences and spare me the ennui of preliminaries. My heart was sometimes constricted, because I thought about the possibility of a refusal. I wondered what I would do once married. I would leave behind, then, all the tinsel of youthful dreams, finally to live the positive life. About the arithmetical sort of life that I led, I could not help saying to myself: *It is claimed that marriage puts lead in the head; it seems to me, more truly, that it puts it in the feet.*

Under the influence of those ideas, which, in spite of the precision with which I adapted them, were only pure reveries, I read the *Lieder* of Wolfgang Goethe, the German colossus who always conserves a free eye to observe even in the frenetic throes of passion. I recall—and this proves once again how scantly solid my positivism was—the extent to which I was shocked by this passage:

I cannot forget it and yet I can dine tranquilly.

On the other hand, I only admired more the fall of the final strophe:

Free of all dread, too great to be jealous, I love, and I love eternally.

A fluid sympathy results, the effects of which have been observed many times. Two persons who love one another, who live a hundred leagues or more from one another, will be affected at the same moment with the same dolor or the same joy.

A foreigner afflicted with nostalgia told me:

"I have a brother far from who I am constrained to live. Our mutual amity is never belied. Choking sensations once extracted me abruptly from slumber. I was in tears. I perceived with stupor that what was making them flow was the memory of my brother. Anxiously, I wrote to tell him immediately what had happened to me. I marked the night, the time and other details. He replied to me: *On the same night, at the same time, in the same circumstances, I experienced exactly the same impressions.*"

Now on the night of the day when I read Goethe's *Lieder*, my slumber was troubled by dolorous presentiments. I woke up in tears several times. As soon as I opened my eyes, the memory of what had frightened me went away, but not the fear. I recall confusedly that I heard heart-rending cries and sobs. At daybreak I went back to sleep, due to lassitude, and I only woke up again at ten o'clock in the morning.

I opened my window, and I was very astonished to see the haberdasher's shop closed, as if it were Sunday. People from the neighborhood were going in and out of the house continually. I still cannot conceive how I did not deduce anything disquieting. I was still so full of my romance, it held me so forcefully by the heart, that my understanding was blocked by it and the truth could not reach the light for want of the slightest fissure. But what is most strange is the manner in which I explained the closure of the shop. I thought that she had recovered completely and was celebrating her recovery by means of a walk in the country.

Who knows, I added, *whether she has not gone to some wedding?* And I went out in a spirit of perfect calm.

When I returned at about four o'clock in the afternoon I saw the physician commissioned by the municipality to certify the deaths of the poor going into the mercer's shop. Does it not seem that the odor spread around that mortuary individual should have dissolved the scales over my eyes and that reality should have seized me in its cruel pincers? Nothing of the sort. A ridiculous tale was intruded into my mind with the rapidity of an electric spark. Without probable elements, I persuaded myself that an old woman, whom I had never seen, who lived on the first floor—which appeared to be vacant—had died during the night, and that the physician who had arrived had come to certify her death.

I would not have advanced such an event, however, if it had not had its source in a very common sentiment. Many people are similar in that regard. They cling to dreams with the desperation of a drowning man and convince themselves so fully of their imminent realization that their faculties and their senses are troubled accidentally, and they do not have hypotheses in their imagination mad enough to round out that conviction, which they sometimes push beyond the absurd, and they play the role that I am playing here more often than they think.

The next day, I began to be moved. In the young haberdasher's window something happened that was very simple, and also very sinister. A woman of whom I could see nothing but the bare arms hung out of the window in the sunlight, mattresses, sheets and blankets—in sum, a whole bed. I watched that with amazement.

This time, I lent myself to the most cruel hypotheses.

Is it possible? Could I have duped myself to the point . . . no, no! However . . . ah! I have it . . . they are profiting from her absence to air her mattresses.

I sought yet again to lie to myself; but I did not succeed in reassuring myself; a leaven of uncertainty swelled, inflating in my mind. I had a painful slumber, during which I was pursued by fears analogous to those that tormented me awake. I got up well before the usual time, so impatient was I . . .

I could no longer stand it. Funereal presentiments eroded hopes within me as my will gave birth to them. I commenced to glimpse as possible what I had previously relegated to the most implausible and most ridiculous conjectures. My imagination, having run out of lies, delivered me bound hand and foot to atrocious anxieties. It was necessary for me to emerge from that anxiety and know the entire truth.

I knew the time at which my landlady came up to my room. I waited As soon as she appeared, I said, forcing myself to remain calm: "Madame, can you tell me what is happening there?"! I indicated the haberdasher's shop. "That young woman . . . ?"

"Oh, Monsieur," said the good woman, raising her eyes to the sky, "she's dead."

"Dead!" I lowered my head and opened my eyes immeasurably wide, and I searched for the meaning of that word.

A woman, even a woman who is indifferent to us, does not pass suddenly from life to death without our being moved at least by a profound astonishment. In order for death not to surprise us, it is necessary, in a sense, to follow the progress of the disease, to witness the depletion of the invalid and her agony.

"Dead!" I said, again, and I felt something like a hand reaching for my heart and crushing it with an omnipotent clench, and what multiplied my torture a hundredfold was the effort I made in order not to let it show. A grim modesty prevented the tears from rising to my eyes.

"Yes Monsieur, dead," said my landlady, wiping away a tear.

There was a rather long pause. She added: "She was buried yesterday morning. You were probably still asleep."

"But," I said, after a further pause, "it was only three days ago that I saw her."

"Oh, Monsieur, she had struggled for a long time; it was not for lack of a desire to live."

"Dead!" I said, again, so difficult was it to adapt myself to that idea. "But how? Of what?"

"Does one know, Monsieur?"

"But one does not die of nothing . . ."

"Oh," said the good woman, shaking her head, "I can't get it out of my mind that with care and affection she might have been saved."

"What about her mother?"

"Pooh! I don't know a more avaricious woman. It was necessary that her daughter earned money . . ."

"Her father?"

"He never said a word to her. He smokes his pipe all blessed day long."

"But finally, her brother . . ."

"Well, he's a good lad, but a brother, you know, would rather be with his friends than his sister."

"So she was unhappy . . ."

"Oh, it's as I tell you, Monsieur. That girl had a chagrin that killed her. If she had been my daughter, I swear to you that she wouldn't be dead."

We remained silent for some time. My landlady, supposing that the conversation did not interest me much, started to make my bed.

"Poor child," I said, in a low voice.

The excellent woman stopped. "Yes, Monsieur, you're right," she said. She parted the curtains and embraced the mattress. Then, turning her head in my direction she said: "Well, I assure you that I don't know whether she isn't better off dead . . ."

I looked at the good woman with a gaze that requested an explanation of her thought. She stood up and leaned on the bed-head. For my part, I leaned back against an item of furniture. She talked for I don't know how long. If I don't recall all her expressions exactly, at least I've conserved the memory of the sentiment that she put into it. It seems to me that I'm still witnessing her sincere dolor and can hear her tearful voice.

"She got through the work," she said, "of two seamstresses. To see her, you would have thought that her minutes were counted; it ruined her; she changed visibly, but her mother, who saw it clearly, didn't have the heart to prevent her spending her nights. 'You're wrong, Madame,' I said to her twenty times, 'to let your daughter work as much; you can see that she'll come to harm.' 'Well, yes,' she growled, turning her back on me in a fashion that signified that it wasn't my business. Now we'll see what she does without her daughter; that's all she's thinking about now . . .'"

My landlady consulted my face to see whether I was listening; she met my eyes, which begged her to continue.

"I did what I could to distract the poor child, but I couldn't always be there; I have my house . . . In summer we took her to the country. Oh, Monsieur, what a good girl! How cheerful she was! And loving! I can tell you that, me, having known her when she was very small, and I didn't take my eyes off her for an hour. It's also true that she loved me more than her mother . . . Never any complaint. How much trouble to make her admit the chagrins that were undermining her! You see, what worried her the most was having reached a certain age and not being married. I said to her: 'But my dear girl, you can't think so; you're not yet twenty. When one has your age and your looks, one's spoiled for choice.' Nothing worked; she was convinced that no man would want her, because she had nothing. Oh, Monsieur, she would have made a man happy! God, how stupid men are! Not counting you, Monsieur. Instead of taking . . ."

I uttered an *alas*, which interrupted the good woman momentarily.

"What's certain," she went on, "is that it's that malady that carried her off. It always preoccupied her, although she never talked about it. And I perceived it again the day when we met you. The joy of others, reminding her of her sad life, added to her trouble. And then, as I told you, she spent too many nights working. Even a stronger girl wouldn't have resisted it. Would you believe it, only a fortnight ago, although she could hardly stand up, she wanted absolutely to spend Saturday night working so that she wouldn't get behind. And to think that her mother didn't oppose it! She was perishing visibly and becoming fearfully thin. When I changed her she showed me her ribs, which were about to pierce the skin. Her back was nothing but a wound for having remained lying down. I didn't know what to say. I had difficulty not weeping . . .

"In the last days I never ceased to watch beside her, for I knew it gave her pleasure. She didn't lose her head for a moment. We talked—or rather, I talked and she listened. As she didn't think about death at all, and always had marriage in her head, I did my best to nurse those ideas in her and avoid her seeing herself dying. I said to her: 'A little patience, my dear Héloïse, the good days will come; you'll get your strength back and we'll go to the country. And then, something—I don't know what—tells me that you'll find a worthy worker who'll marry you and love you very much. Believe me, don't despair.'

"She shook her head. 'That's not very sure,' she said. 'You know I have nothing. All the same, how I'd love him!'

"There was so much passion in her voice that it made me feel horribly ill. But she went to sleep with that and died without suffering too much. I wept at the time . . .

"Last Wednesday, the doctor took me aside and said that it wasn't necessary for him to come back, since she wouldn't last the night. Oh, Monsieur, I knew that she wouldn't get better, and yet . . . ! I wanted to watch over her until the end. A priest came in the evening. She no longer knew where she was. She couldn't see or hear anything. She was writhing to make one think that the death-throes were already beginning. In the morning, she became calm again. She called to me in order to kiss me. Then she wanted to go to sleep. For my part, I was dropping from fatigue and drowsiness. I sat down in an armchair. At the same time I heard a *glug-glug-glug*. I turned my head, and moved closer. She was dead."

The good woman choked. She rested for a moment, after which she concluded the young woman's story thus:

252

"Oh, Monsieur, it's necessary that there's a paradise. Where else could that dear child be paid for her troubles?"

That naïve belief, which did not permit the conception of a crime without punishment or an unmerited dolor without remuneration, was not for me, as it seemed to be for the good woman, an efficacious source of consolation.

I was sobbing internally. My entire body was weeping. It seemed to me that my blood became drops of water, flowing toward my heart, too small to contain so many tears. What I suffered I can't describe. Well, I still reproach myself for not having had a large enough capacity for the suffering, and I would have liked to magnify myself in order to suffer more. I thought that I could never expiate cruelly enough the crime of having played with that young woman and having made her the heroine of a fantasy that I would doubtless never have dared to realize.

I ought to have pierced the walls, divined the drama that was unfolding in that bedroom and saved that child from death. Had I not just heard: "With cares and affection she would have been saved." I had preferred to go to sleep in an egotistical nonchalance, to lose myself in the twists and turns of a dream in which I was seeking my happiness rather than hers.

And perhaps, at this moment, I'm weeping more for my vanished youth than her death, and even finding a bitter pleasure in recounting my torture. Oh, let me at least not profane her tomb with my declarations. I scarcely glimpsed her. I don't even know to what extent I ever awoke her sympathy. However, the fact that that child perished under the weight of dolors that make no sense takes its place in my memory alongside those that I love and respect the most. Until the hour when I am no longer breathing in my turn, my most tender regrets will never cease to form a cortege around her shade.

The Dolors of a Name

TO say everything once, the heroine of these few pages was a young and beautiful person full of grace and good taste, of a rare modesty. She only had one fault, if one can qualify thus, for example, the breath that tarnishes the corner of a splendid mirror; it was rather a misfortune, and, in that sense, a grave error for the common run of humans, that of being called . . .

But what can I do? At the moment of writing it, the fingers refuse to do it, No name, in fact, ever sounded so badly. It does not even seem, given the memory of the gross insult that it awakens in the mind, that one can articulate the two syllables without wounding the least delicate ears. How many dolors and tears that malign impertinence of destiny cost her!

She was the daughter of an honest man who was the steward of the property of the Comtesse de Gournay. When her steward died, that excellent woman willingly took charge of the orphan's interests. Raised with care, the young woman, scarcely eighteen years of age, emerged from boarding school to become the governess of the children of Baron Anatole, the son of the comtesse. Four or five persons at the most knew the secret of her name;

she was only called "Mademoiselle Hélène," as before, in speaking of her father, people had said "Monsieur François." The jealousy of a vindictive woman was not to leave her for long in a situation in which she would have liked nothing so much as to grow old.

The baron, disgusted internally by the cantankerous humor and stormy temper of his wife, suddenly had a whim to take out of its case a violin that had been sleeping there since his marriage, and to play sonatas with the governess of his daughters. That musical relationship determined a very ardent liking on the baron's part for Hélène. But Baronne Stéphanie, in whom the discovery of that passion inspired an implacable hatred for her rival, gradually became excessively demanding with her, until the day when she passed from epigrams to insults.

Hélène, in ignorance of the motives for those persecutions, could only be astonished and weep in secret. Madame de Gournay, as scantly perspicacious as her ward, wasted her time in attempting reconciliations between the husband and the wife, whose relationship became increasingly bitter by the day.

The catastrophe that was easy to foresee happened at the exit from a family dinner in the presence of at least twenty people, and fell upon the young woman like a thunderbolt. Suddenly affecting airs of tenderness, the baronne expressed the desire to go for a ride in a carriage with her husband. Monsieur Anatole looked at his wife with surprise and refused flatly. Madame Stéphanie insisted with all the more ardor because she knew about the measures taken by her husband to spend the evening with Hélène. Gradually reaching the peak of exasperation by virtue of the stubborn refusals that she endured, she lost the strength to contain herself.

Her face was extremely pale; a disdainful hauteur contracted its muscles; her body trembled. The acidic and contained tone of the remark that escaped her lips finally betrayed all her anger.

"Ah! Doubtless Monsieur le Baron would prefer to make music with Mademoiselle ***!"

At grips with an irresistible fit of temper, she did not hesitate to pronounce energetically a name that, even among persons of an inferior rank would have produced the effect of an incongruity. The funereal silence that followed that strange sortie was instantaneously troubled by the sound of a slap. The baron, thrown off balance by his wife's insulting indiscretion, had just committed an act of violence for the first time in his life. A very painful scene followed, Madame Stéphanie felt ill. She only recovered from her faint to declare her intention to formulate a demand for separation the following day. For several days the memory of the insult maintained her in a state of indescribable overexcitement and rendered her unapproachable. Neither her husband's repentance, nor her mother-in-law's tears, nor the sight of her daughters, was sufficient to appease her.

They only succeeded in vanquishing her resentment, finally, on condition of dismissing the young governess and forbidding her entry to the house.

Hélène had not suspected yet that her name could be thrown in her face like a whiplash. That disgrace, however, found her full of resignation. Her paternal heritage, swollen by the liberalities of the comtesse, constituted for her what is known as an honest ease. To judge by appearances, what a happy life hers was! A devoted maidservant had accompanied her in her retreat, and took care of her small, comfortable and elegant interior. Free to study in accordance with her tastes, esteemed by all those who knew her, having the exclusive tenderness of a young heiress she had known at the convent and who could not let a single day pass without seeing her or writing to her, welcomed with favor everywhere that she deigned to appear, it seemed that no chagrin could afflict her. But who does not have a hidden source of bitterness?

It would not have cost her any more to make a reputation for beauty and wit than it costs a diamond to absorb light and dazzle the eyes, but she expended all her prudence in passing unperceived, in being nothing in society but insignificance personified, for, however little eyes were open to her merits, people would not have failed to say immediately: "Where did that young woman come from? What is her name?" And curiosity would not have wearied before having a precise answer.

This passage of a letter to her friend, Estelle Locar, then in the provinces, in the home of a grandmother who, incapable of changing location, requested that her granddaughter spend a few months with her every year, gives the secret of her preoccupations:

> *I have composed a waltz in the German style, and have written verses that I believe to be good, because I have not searched for them and they have come into my head of their own accord. But supposing my waltz to be a masterpiece and my verses as many pearls, write my name beneath and imagine the effect! Sincere friends advise me to use the tolerance that exists with regard to names, and*

to modify mine—to suppress, for instance, the first syllable and to sign myself boldly H. S. Lope.[1] I think that an unworthy pettiness. A deceit is repugnant to me, which might be discovered and attract a merited ridicule.

In any case, frankly, I am not sorry to sense a brake on my vanity as a poet. Female authors, save for rare exceptions, have always seemed to me to be very bad, and I sense that if I were a man I would not like them. I cannot forget that, in thinking of Jean-Paul and Hoffmann, the one, you will recall, called them flamboyant embers, and the other, as soon as he knew that one was beside him, picked up his napkin and plate and ran to find another place.[2]

Outside that circle, in the most ordinary circumstances of life, Hélène was subjected to new proofs every day, and her good grace and distinguished manners did not always preserve her from the harshest humiliations. One

---

1 Contemporary French readers would necessarily have jumped to the conclusion that the syllable whose abridgement was being suggested was "Sa," *salope* being an abusive French term meaning "slut" or "whore." The majority of them would have been well aware that there was a very successful contemporary English novelist who signed herself Mrs. Frances Trollope, and was familiarly known as Fanny Trollope.

2 It is significant that the cited authors are both German, reflecting the reputation that Germans had in France for excessive sexism. In France female writers played an enormously influential role in the Romantic Movement, which obtained its name from Madame de Staël, was nurtured in salons hosted by Juliette Récamier and Sophie Gay, and included Marceline Desbordes-Valmore, considered by Charles Baudelaire to be the leading poet of her generation.

morning, she went with her maidservant to the office of a theatrical newspaper in order to take out a subscription. The same hall, large and profound, served for the administration of several enterprises. When she entered, fifteen or twenty clerks looked at her like schoolboys who see the sister of one of their comrades appearing. That sort of insolent inquisition intimidated the young woman greatly. The cashier, enclosed in his iron wire trellis as if in a cage, took a register and said, in a loud voice: "Your name, Madame?"

At the profound silence that fell, Hélène was convinced that all ears were attentive, and that conviction increased her malaise. She stammered her name. The cashier only heard half of it.

"Hélène . . . ?" he said rolling his pen between his fingers.

The clerks held their breath in order to hear better. The young woman, shaking off her pusillanimity, pronounced her name clearly. The effect was sad, as usual. It seemed that all the clerks, riveted to the same chain, had received a simultaneous electric shock. Their faces expressed the same amazement. They looked at one another, lowered their heads with a mechanical uniformity, and the rumor of suppressed laughter circulated in the room. Hélène, all of whose blood flowed away from her heart, perhaps exaggerated these details. At any rate, she felt a dolor that made her feel ill. The impassive and sarcastic manner of the cashier finished disconcerting her. Imagining that she could see on the latter's lips the commencement of a smile, she was convinced that he was only waiting for her departure to share in the unseemly gaiety of the others.

In spite of her firm determination, Hélène only succeeded imperfectly in extinguishing the gleam of her eyes and effacing from her features the charm of youth, and, above all, in delivering herself from the innate grace that each of her gestures revealed. The increasing number of those who showed her sympathy and attachment began to frighten her.

> *I am*, she wrote, *the object of two effective adorations. Picture, on the one hand, a monsieur of a height that never ends, very amiable although of an obsolete gallantry, explained by his age; he is over forty, as cunning as an examining magistrate, which he is, always dressed negligently, scantly careful of his person, never ceasing to extract enormous pinches of tobacco from a golden snuff-box, with which he stuffs his nose and soils his white waistcoat, and, on top of that, is a widower with two daughters who are said to be very pretty. On the other hand, there is a doctor in law, a very young man, with a charming exterior, irreproachably dressed, with beautiful eyes, soul in his voice, who expresses himself with a reserve that announces merit. The compliments of the former slide over my soul like drops of water over a mirror; as for the other, he interests me and attracts me, and I cannot weary of hearing him; and I believe that I perceive that I cause him a no less vivid impression. Supposing him to be such as I see him, and as seriously smitten as he seems to*

*be, he would certainly overlook the consider-
ations that make me so unhappy. Dear, dear
friend, may Providence finally take pity on
my misery!*

Apart from what sagacity permitted her to grasp,
Hélène knew nothing about the young doctor except
that he was a doctor in law, that he had applied for a position as a magistrate, that he had some fortune and that
his name was Arthur. Arthur what? At the moment of
asking him that, the fear of hearing herself asked a similar
question paralyzed her tongue. She also wrote:

*I do not like the forename Arthur, but I
can remedy that by only calling him by his
family name. I would like to know that name.
You will understand why I do not question
him on that subject. No matter! But what
astonishes me is that he has in that regard
the indifference that I pretend to have, and
is content to know that my name is Hélène.
Given that, who knows? Perhaps he knows
me better than I suspect.*

Hélène's preference for the young doctor did not
escape the examining magistrate, who, either out of conceit or for some other reason, did not seem to experience
either fear or anxiety. Attentive to not troubling the long
conversations of the two lovers, he left to propriety the
care of putting an end to them. His hour sounded then
to come discreetly to sit down next to the young woman
and recite his chaplet of gallantries. No trace of ill humor

or gallantry was visible in his attitude; for from it, he was extremely jovial, and found the means, in spite of his age, not to be too ridiculous a gallant. Pretending to amour no longer suited his age; a little amity sufficed for his ambition. He pushed forbearance and self-abnegation to the point of seeking the amity of his rival and making his eulogy. Because of that, above all, Hélène did not weary of finding some pleasure in his company.

Madame Locar's salon was open to a mixed crowd, into which eccentrics of all sorts slipped. A physician, still young, whose name was Doctor Bidault, was certainly not the least curious. The perfect propriety of his preoccupations with the subject of the present story gave the impression of a figure imagined at pleasure, or at least placed deliberately in that frame, whereas his existence was no less real than that of the milieu in which he shone.

That doctor, with his long bald head, his full pale face, framed by flat light-russet side-whiskers, and cut transversally by gold-rimmed spectacles, with his smooth forehead, his satisfied lips, his austere manner, had applied himself by turns to phrenology, magnetism, and all the theories that were on the fringes of medicine, and pleased some people all more because they were little known and mysterious. His pretentions went as far as divining, in certain cases, the name of a person at first sight. There was some rumor of a pamphlet of his on the subject. The dogmatic and pedantic tone, and the air of serene conviction, with which he developed and defended puerile ideas and strange analogies that he was heard to summon to his aid enabled him to pass in the minds of some people for a profound mind, and in those of others for a simple charlatan.

One of the soirées given by Madame Locar was to feature, by exception, music and dancing. The doctor, whose gravity was ill-adapted to noise and agitation, went to salute the Marquise de Couvry, a young woman of an unbenevolent character who only came to the home of the widow of her former banker in order to aliment her critical and mocking humor. Only seeing in the physician a diverting caricature, she amused herself at his expense and did not hesitate, on occasion, to play tricks on him. He sat down beside her, in a place from which the eye could embrace the entire company, and started explaining his theory to her in a leaden and magisterial fashion. His endless developments, of a pathos whose triviality disputed with its emphasis, could be reduced to this:

"Names, whatever they may be, were, in the beginning, only soubriquets. Those soubriquets depicted, in a brutal or delicate fashion, a salient aspect, moral or material, of the individual. So, one is not astonished, so common is it, to see members of a family perpetuate in multiplying some of the traits of their ancestors. Thus, by virtue of that fact, nothing ought to be less rare than encountering some who, even after a long space of time, justify in some respect the name under which the rootstock of their genealogical tree grew."

The Marquise, in a half-serious and half-ironic tone, objected cautiously that physiognomies, temperament and characters would probably be subject to radical modification in the course of two centuries in consequence of marriages, maladies, accidents, mores, occupations, intellectual development and the reaction of the moral on the physical, etc., etc.; but, perceiving that the doctor's mind, troubled by these objections, was becoming murky, she pretended, out of pity, and also to get rid of him, to agree with him.

The physician did not have the discretion to leave it there. It was truly necessary to know him well to see anything other that badinage in the connections that his theory suggested to him. Adjusting his spectacles, and, with the same gesture, indicating a man of tall stature who was talking volubly not far away from them, and gesticulating abundantly, he said in a low voice, in a delicate manner:

"I'll make you the observation, Madame la Marquise, that that monsieur, not content to be called Moulin, is a public prosecutor, and much the most verbose of public prosecutors."[1]

The question, envisaged in that way, appeared to please the marquise more. She smiled.

That's nothing," the doctor continued. "Do you recall Monsieur Génie, a friend of the household? Perhaps you don't know, Madame, that Monsieur Génie is a remarkable engineer, and in addition, the inventor of the most ingenious machines."

"That's prodigious," said Madame de Couvry, hypocritically.

"And Monsieur Rétif!" cried the physician, with an inspired expression. "You're aware of his liking for paradox, his penchant for contradiction and his rants against common sense."

---

1 *Moulin* signifies "windmill." In the same fashion, *génie* signifies "genius" and *rétif* "restive," or "mulish"—although the author might also have had in mind the eighteenth-century writer Nicolas Rétif, who preferred to sign himself "Restif de la Bretonne," and whose posthumous reputation was suggestive of support for Dr. Bidault's theory.

The doctor took the marquise's new smile for a decisive approval.

"I can multiply proofs," he added, superbly, "if I see that you are not convinced. While I think about it, one more example. I am convinced, Madame, that, like me, you hold Monsieur de Beaufort, the singer more jealous than an artiste to be a *beau fort* man."

The marquise, whose liaison with Monsieur de Beaufort was not unknown to anyone, except perhaps for the physician, took the play on words for an epigram, and wanted to avenge herself with an immediate trick.

"You're a terrible logician, Doctor," she said, in a mocking tone. "There's no means of resisting you. Decidedly, I'm a convert, and I'll prove my zeal to you by furnishing you, without delay, with weapons against your adversaries."

Neither Madame de Couvry nor the physician had noticed that a very young man had come to sit behind their seats and was listening to their conversation, as if it were the most natural thing in the world.

"Look, Doctor," Madame de Couvry continued, "at the two men standing next to the fireplace chatting amicably. Do you know who they are?"

"No, Madame."

"I'll tell you. You'll agree with me that the younger one has a fortunate physiognomy; I even find that he has a certain air of distinction. He's a doctor, I don't know of what. People only reproach him for being a little melancholy. The other, on the contrary, who has grown old in the métier of examining magistrate, is guilty of a deplorable insouciance in matters of attire. He aspires to marry for a second time in order no longer to have the worry of two little girls of whom he takes no more care than he does of himself."

"I didn't know those details," said the doctor, parenthetically.

"Well, Doctor," the marquise went on, in a manner that would have deceived the most cunning diplomat, one of them is named Monsieur Marie, the other, whom one might think had been baptized by some vaudevillian, really has the absurd name of Arthur Cochonnet."[1]

The candid physician had no suspicion of the trap; he fell into it head first with the irreflection of a child, so triumphant were his ideas within his heart. He hastened to apply the name of Cochonnet to the examining magistrate, and that of Marie to the young doctor in law, which nearly brought a burst of laughter from Madame de Couvry. Unfortunately, the marquise, curious to extend and complete her vengeance, repressed a fit of hilarity that might have given the physician warning. She indicated to him two other individuals, two women, one of whom was Hélène and the other an ugly and deformed spinster whose name was Mademoiselle Gabrielle de l'Ange.

"Let's commence with the one who is playing whist," said Madame de Couvry. "Not to mention her gaucherie, observe her red hair, her jaundiced complexion, her extinct eyes, her flat nose, her skewed mouth and her deformed shoulders. It's also necessary that her disagreeable physiognomy should be the perfect image of her character. Her fortune makes her a brilliant catch, and her desire to marry renders her no less difficult in the choice of a husband. She has not yet encountered a man brave

---

1 Among the several significations of *marie*, "bridegroom" is perhaps the most relevant here, whereas *cochonnet* signifies "piglet."

enough to attempt her conquest. Now compare the little monster with that beautiful and well-made young woman doing tapestry-work over there. No appearances were ever less deceptive. She's a simple girl full of sense, and of the best nature. The existence of that summary of perfections is scarcely comprehensible. I'm certain, doctor," the marquise added, after a pause, "that I'm not proposing an enigma to you in telling you that one is named Gabrielle de l'Ange and the other Hélène . . ."

Madame de Couvry, whose thirst for vengeance rendered her unscrupulous, had no hesitation in articulating the name of the young woman clearly.

"Either my theory is profoundly absurd, and in that case, I would be even more so than my theory," replied the physician in a tone of certainty, "or that is Gabrielle de l'Ange"— he pointed at Hélène—"and that is Hélène . . ."—and he indicated the red-haired young woman.

"You're a sorcerer, Doctor!" cried Madame de Couvry, as joyful as a little girl guilty of a cruel malice. "It's unbelievable. Really, I can aid you with all my might in the propagation of your admirable theory . . ."

At that moment, the young man, who had not ceased to lend an ear to what the marquise and the physician were saying, stood up and plunged into the crowd. A collegian scarcely emancipated, he was making his debut in society and yearning to play a role therein. His slightest fault was indiscretion; presumption, conceit and vanity disputed his precious person. Not content with having given proof of an absolute lack of good manners, he tried to put himself forward with the aid of details that his indelicacy allowed him to discover. He circled Hélène a few times and finally decided to ask her for a quadrille.

This is what happened, according to the young woman's own account.

Scarcely was he standing next to her than he said: "Can you, Mademoiselle, help me to recall the name of the doctor who is conversing in a corner of the room with Madame a Marquise?"

"You're doubtless referring to Doctor Bidault," Hélène replied.

"Ah, yes, yes!" said the young man, with the air of someone recovering a memory. "One of the luminaries of science, a universal mind, a man who would have been burned alive in the time when people believed in sorcerers."

"I admit, Monsieur," replied the young woman, "that this is the first time I have heard anyone speak of him with that enthusiasm."

"Ah, if you knew him, Mademoiselle!" exclaimed the fop, whose body was no less mobile than his tongue. "I was conversing just now with him and the marquise. Oh, what a man! He developed a theory for us that will certainly make a noise."

Hélène, who had an instinctive dread of that monsieur's loquacity, did not reply. Unperturbed by that silence, the impertinent fellow went on: "Can you image, Mademoiselle, that that singular doctor, without any other indication than a person's appearance, can divine the person's name."

One could not broach the subject of names before the young woman without making her shudder. She turned her head abruptly toward her dancing partner and looked at him with amazement. The latter, believing in good faith that he interested her, went on: "I understand your surprise, Mademoiselle; I am speaking nothing but the truth, however. I have just been witness to the prodigy. Although your name was unknown to him, the doctor did not hesitate for a second to state it. I give you my compliments, Mademoiselle," he added, bowing, "on an adorable name, which depicts you entirely . . ."

Hélène put her hand to her breast in order to compress her dolor and indignation. To see her immeasurably wide and staring eyes, you would have believed her annihilated. The imperturbable fop was still talking.

"On the other hand, Mademoiselle, you would never suspect how that ugly red-haired woman is named whom you see at that whist table. Ha ha! One would have difficulty in finding a name that suited her better. Will you authorize me to tell you? Otherwise I can do nothing; I would be afraid of displeasing you. I warn you that no one has ever been named thus. A name, Mademoiselle, to have all doors refused to one . . ."

The wretched young man did not cease for a few moments to speak in that tone, with no suspicion of what the young woman was suffering. The latter looked at him with a bewildered expression, and seemed still to be searching for the key to what was for her an atrocious enigma. In the end, importuned and pushed to the end by the verbiage, the circumlocutions and the reticence of her torturer, she looked him in the face and said, dryly: "But in the end, Monsieur, deign to give me the key to your remarks, for I confess that I understand absolutely nothing."

The young man, who was tormented by the desire to be clearer, replied: "Ha ha! Mademoiselle, I have nothing more to object; I am entirely at your service." And, indicating Gabrielle de l'Ange, he applied Hélène's name to her.

The poor young woman took a step backwards, and appeared to be on the point of succumbing under the weight of that gratuitous insult. The truth suddenly burst forth before her eyes. One could not suppose on the part of such a young man so much malevolence and audacity. He was doubtless the dupe of a trick.

Looking him up and down with hauteur and disdain, the young woman said to him: "You're mistaken, Monsieur, for the name you are applying to Mademoiselle Gabrielle de l'Ange is, in fact, mine."

With that, Hélène turned her back on him and returned to her place. The maladroit young man was devastated. He disappeared like darkness at the sudden appearance of the sun. From that day on, he was never seen again in Madame Locar's house. To his awkwardness, however, he added the impudence of telling the story of the adventure, taking care to attribute it to his best friend.

In her letters, Hélène, having related that scene and admitted poignant dolors, deemed herself still fortunate to have a preservative against despair, which was an allusion to her imminent marriage.

She spoke about it with the joyful calm that invalids often have on the very eve of their death, in speaking of days to come. Fever no longer quit her; a sort of disorder full of delights was substituted in her veins for the regular movements of life. She was all fire, all passion and all enthusiasm. Young Arthur was not only a husband in accordance with the most cherished dreams, he was also a liberator, the man who, so to speak, would extract her from limbo and make her a new and splendid life; so she did not hide anything, she confessed in terms inflated by tenderness that she loved him—oh, holy sensuality!—as scarcely anyone had loved before.

One point to establish is that the doctor in law did not yet know Hélène's family name. That is doubtless strange, but it is a fact, an authentic fact. The young woman, of course, supposed it to be an indifferent omission. Far from it; the desire to know the name of his future wife was his incessant preoccupation. However, because everything contributed to put him to sleep, the obstinacy of his research had limits. If Madame Locar and her daughter were not alone in knowing Hélène's name, as the latter believed, the number of those who knew it was really very restricted. What is astonishing, given that, about the fact that the people to whom Monsieur Arthur addressed himself, not without delicate precautions, had not be able to respond in a satisfactory manner?

The examining magistrate, his admitted rival, had not departed, in that occasion, from his habitual amiability. "I know very little," he had said. "Her father was the steward of the Comtesse de Gournay. He was an honest man, the pearl of stewards, highly esteemed by the comtesse. I have no need to tell you that Hélène received a brilliant education. To tell you about her knowledge would be superfluous; you know that she is an excellent muscienne, plays the piano admirably and speaks several languages. As for her beauty, her character and her sensibility, you are a more competent judge of such matters than I am. To sum up, I do not know any woman that I would prefer."

The wily and prudent magistrate, who gave evidence of a profound skill throughout the adventure, was only discreet relative to Hélène's family name. He drowned that detail adroitly in the half-light of circumlocution. The young woman's name "escaped him." What was more reassuring for the young doctor? His rival could no longer remember Hélène's name after having heard it pronounced! Evidently, that name had nothing bizarre about it, nothing shocking; it was a name that, after all, must be a thousand times preferable to his own. The fact is that the first syllable of that name was not known to him when, after having put off until that day a decisive conversation with Hélène because of scruples analogous to those that tormented the latter, he finally decided to speak to her about the grave and important matter of marriage.

His face had a darker hint of melancholy than usual on the evening when, sitting bedside Hélène, he told her that he wanted to talk to her about matters of the utmost gravity. That made the young woman shudder, who divined immediately what that beginning portended.

"Oh, my God, you're frightening me," she said, in a tone that belied her words.

"The weakness I have had in postponing this confidence until today demonstrates that it requires great courage today . . ."

"One would think, by your manner, that you were about to make a speech for the prosecution," said Hélène, mocking a preamble that she thought unnecessary, at least.

"Would you like me to exhibit a mad gaiety, then," replied the doctor, "at the moment when you are about to decide whether I must live or die?"

"I am the jury, then, and you are the tribunal, including the accused?" said Hélène, who was having difficulty containing her joy.

The conversation proceeded smoothly until the moment until the young man, all the sadder as Hélène's humor became more jovial, said: "Your disposition to laugh convinces me that you have no suspicion of what is preoccupying me . . . for myself, as I speak, there is sweat on my brow and I lack strength . . ."

Hélène suddenly became serious. "I'm lost," she said, "in the detours of the road you're taking."

The doctor continued, lowering his head sadly: "I've told you, Hélène, that I've solicited a position as a magistrate. I should have added that I knew that it would be a wasted effort."

"A great misfortune! Is there nothing above the joy of putting one's life to sleep in the armchair of a tribunal? Why don't you try to build a clientele at the Palais, as you put it?"

"The same reasons oppose it. However, the obstacle that bars my path might be evaded. That depends entirely on you, Hélène."

"Why are you hesitating like this, then?" exclaimed the young woman, with vivacity.

"Since our liaison," the doctor continued in a tremulous voice, "I don't know that you have ever thought of asking me my name. Has someone informed you of it?"

Hélène felt the shock that never failed to shake her every time the inconvenient question of proper names was broached before her; but her mind was too far from the truth to have any presentiment of it. She responded negatively with a shake of the head.

"Oh! But at this moment," said the young man, "I sense my wrongdoing profoundly. I ought to have warned you sooner. But I have not ceased, in your company, to be in an intoxication that has closed my eyes to the future . . ."

"Please, Monsieur, explain yourself," said poor Hélène, in a faint voice, her face expressing both surprise and sharp anxiety.

The doctor replied but in a tone so low, so quiet that the young woman had to lean forward in order to hear it: "Alas, I have the misfortune to have a name that is equivalent to the negation of my personality, my labor and my merit . . ."

All images, comparisons and analogies known and imaginable would be impotent to express the dolor of the blow that the young woman received in the heart. She was astonished later to have survived such a shock. It is true that a glimmer of hope had immediately moderated its violence. The idea that the doctor was mistaken, or at least exaggerating the evil, had crossed her mind.

"But again, Monsieur," she said, in the staccato, feverish tone of a person choking, "that name . . . ?"

The young man, in a pitiful state, plunged his hand mechanically into his pocket and pulled out a visiting card, which he handed to Hélène with an expression of shame. The latter took the card swiftly and deciphered it avidly. For a few moments her eyes remained fixed on the name. Then, her nerves, tightened by an excessive curiosity, relaxed under the influence of the dolor that invaded her all the way to the marrow of her bones. Her arms fell on to her knees, her head leaned forward, and her entire body seemed to collapse like a wall without a foundation. The impetuous flow of blood to her temples filled her head with a buzz, through which arrived, like a distant noise, the voice of Monsieur Arthur, which said:

"The misfortune that your dejection presages does not take me by surprise. I cannot say what I have already suffered because of that name, which has caused me disillusionment, cruel humiliations, to the point that my days have been darkened and poisoned by it. I affirm to you that there are dolors that, for being singular, are neither less serious nor less poignant. In a humbler milieu, perhaps I would have been less cruelly persecuted, but I live among people who are much less interested in the fundamental value of something than of appearances and fine speech."

Hélène tried to stiffen herself against the cruel evil that was tearing her apart, and, at moments to raise herself up and speak, but her limbs had lost all elasticity and her lips seemed paralyzed. She struggled against an inertia stronger than her will, as in a nightmare.

Ever sadder, Monsieur Arthur let her understand that the situation, inextricable in appearance, might be sorted out to everyone's satisfaction. Slowly, she raised her pale face, contracted by the anguish of doubt, and attached feverishly ardent eyes to the young man.

The doctor lowered his own and went on: "In marrying me you ought to abandon your name in order to take mine, and I understand your repugnance. But what prevents, unless it is you, the contrary taking place, and that in marrying you, I abandon my name in order to take yours?"

Hélène allowed her head to fall again, heavily.

"If you love me," added the young man, "where is the obstacle? A man who has due credit has promised me formally to obtain for me the faculty of taking my wife's name immediately after my marriage . . ."

Large tears suddenly sprang from Hélène's eyes and trickled on to her knees.

"I swear to you that I wasn't thinking of that when I met you."

"I believe it," stammered the young woman, in a voice stifled by sobs.

"It required nothing less than my profound amour, and the certainty of not being indifferent to you, to make me conceive the plan of which I speak. Furthermore, have no fear that I will complain if you refuse to link your fate with mine. I have measured the extent and depth of the sacrifice that I am asking of you. I will understand if it is beyond your strength . . ."

Hélène continued to weep.

"Don't be afflicted thus, dear Hélène," the doctor went on. "I cannot believe that my memory has very profound roots in you as yet. You'll forget me. As for me, I am ready for that sad denouement . . ." The young man got to his feet. "If my destiny wishes to become less harsh," he continued, "and permits you to render to my reasons, deign to let me know by a gesture of your hand. I desire at least to know that you are convinced that there is not a man in the world who understands you better than me, who loves you more and wishes your happiness more ardently."

Monsieur Marie, who had not quit the two young people with his eyes, and seemed to be watching for his rival's departure, no sooner saw the latter leave the drawing room than he approached. Composing a suitable expression—which is to say, a very sad one—he said to Hélène; "What's the matter, my dear child? Your pretty eyes are all red, and you seem to be very dolorously afflicted."

Hélène made no reply.

"The moment might be poorly chosen," the examining magistrate continued, "to talk to you about my sentiments. Don't forget, however, dear angel, that I am entirely at your service, and that I will never be as happy as on the day when you put my devotion to the proof."

Monsieur Marie apparently knew that when one is suffering, nothing is as irritating as banal phrases and condolences that are not heartfelt. He left it at that.

Hélène spent part of the night sobbing and despairing. Bitterness, in swelling her soul gave birth there to the conviction that no human power could reduce the damage of a wisp of straw, that the disaster was irreparable. Only the slow tortures of resignation remained to her.

"O my heart, my heart!" she cried, indignant at suffering so futilely. "Why can I not reduce you to silence?"

What multiplied her chagrin a hundredfold and completed its accumulation was the ridicule heaped up in the affair. Could one imagine anything more farcical than the scene that had closed her amours with the young doctor? Had it not become a joke for all of society?

Slumber did not close her eyes for an instant. In the morning, a constriction of the heart woke her up. Her tears flowed again and new plaints wandered over her lips. The intensity of her chagrin only allowed her to find charm in violent action. The cloister finally appeared to her as the sole refuge that remained to her henceforth. An imperious need to unburden herself inspired her to write to her friend and describe the previous evening's scene in detail. From beginning to end, her letter respired the resolution to finish with sterile dolors and quit the world. Then Monsieur Arthur occupied her thoughts. After having reflected maturely, she thought she could not do better than to address this laconic note to him, signed by her name and forenames written in capital letters, clearly traced:

> *Monsieur, you will not be surprised if, in response to your declaration of yesterday evening, I limit myself to sending you the signature of your very humble servant, etc.*

But things were not to stop there. Estelle Locar, at that time, returned from the province and hastened to go to embrace her dear Hélène.

It seemed, at the outset, that the latter remained insensible to all consolation. Gradually, however, she renounced her projects of retreat and even decided to reappear in society. Her absence from Madame Locar's soirées had been noticed; people saw her again with pleasure. Although her face was calm, an experienced eye would not have failed to perceive there traces of fatigue and tears.

On learning the name of the young woman, Monsieur Arthur had been surprised, but not desolate. He did not see any serious obstacle to his marriage, and he thought in addition, with satisfaction, that Hélène would not have any sacrifice to make to him.

The young doctor came to meet her with a deliberate and almost joyful expression that surprised her. Monsieur Arthur, whose exterior had previously respired melancholy and embarrassment, now had the alert manner of a man rid of a heavy yoke. Hélène, for want of being forewarned, fell into a strange scorn.

He loved me very little, then, she thought, bitterly. *Here he is, already consoled.*

That painful reflection immediately inspired in her the desire to appear tranquil.

Her reserved air, her cold manner and her ironic tone struck the young doctor dolorously. He interrogated her. Not content to elude his questions. Hélène appeared eager to close his mouth. That singular conduct had the eventual effect of exasperating Monsieur Arthur, who, in his turn, was provoked to feign coldness and indifference. Angrily, the young woman amplified the expression of her disdain. They parted very discontented with one another.

In the days that followed, Estelle Locar, having become a common friend, tried in vain several times to reconcile them. Their mutual resentment persevered, to the point that one might have believed at one time that they had quarreled seriously and that everything was broken off between them.

Privately, the wily examining magistrate rejoiced in the quarrel and flattered himself on seeing it envenomed. Monsieur Marie was not only a subtle man, he was also a cold, methodical one devoid of false pride, who aligned his reasoning as an accountant does his figures. One glance had sufficed for him to understand that Hélène would be a veritable treasure in a household, and he was resolved to attempt everything possible for her to enrich his. Hazard served him as much and more than his skill. Hélène had linked herself precisely with a man who could not become her husband, a man who had preoccupations identical to hers, and who, by virtue of that fact, was bound to break with her some day. The more profound the young woman's amour was, the more Monsieur Marie believed himself to be sure of success, since her need for consolation would doubtless be in direct proportion to the vivacity of her chagrin. He was simply hoping that dolor, solitude and despair would throw Hélène into his arms.

His tactics, until today, had consisted of being patient, discreet, complaisant, and ever ready to smile or to be afflicted, according to the circumstance—in sum, to strive not to displease. His penetrating eye had not lost a single detail of the little intimate drama whose imminent denouement, by virtue of foreseen peripeties, seemed certain to respond to his ambition. Hélène treated him well and listened to him willingly. Monsieur Marie believed that the moment had come to reckon with her, while waiting for that if the radical cure to arrive. His humor bore him to proceed by means of insinuations.

"Our dolors," he said to her, in a crafty tone, "have their source, most of the time, in our ideas, and the mind, if it only wants to, has the marvelous property of curing its own wounds. But let us suspect the imagination, dear Hélène; the imagination is our greatest enemy."

The following day found him bolder. "What is the good of being desolate? Efforts are for us; results are in the hands of another. A fortunate quietude does not take long to recompense resignation. In any case, everything passes: youth, and beauty, and amour even more rapidly than the rest. Only the resources of the mind are inexhaustible." Etc.

By the way in which Hélène listened to these predications, Monsieur Marie imagined in good faith that he was convincing her and winning her over, and the hope of soon having her for a wife gained ground in his mind every day.

Events came brutally to dissipate that beautiful dream. Thanks to the indefatigable cares of Estelle, and perhaps also some other cause, a rapprochement suddenly took place between Hélène and the young doctor. The two lovers gradually resumed their long conversations. Monsieur Marie soon remarked with anxiety that their intimacy had never been more frank or more ardent. As the days went by, the tender spectacle of which he was the unfortunate witness multiplied his perplexities.

That reconciliation evidently hid a secret. One morning, the *Monitor* gave him the key to it. Chancing to cast a glance over the fourth page, he read a short paragraph more redoubtable to his eyes than Belshazzar's *Mene, Tekel, Upharsin*:

> *Monsieur Arthur Cochonnet, doctor in law, having applied to Monsieur le Ministre de la Justice for the authorization to change his name, has been authorized henceforth to name himself Monsieur Arthur Verneuil.*[1]

---

1 The name Verneuil would have had no particular significance when the present story was written except being that of several places, including one where the French lost a battle during the Hundred Years War. Dr. Bidault might have been interested to know, however, that one Auguste Verneuil was subsequently to pioneer a method of

The disappointment and confusion of Monsieur Marie cannot be described. Some pretext or other served for him not to show his face for some time.

New projects extracted him from his retreat. In his resolution to put an end even so to his widowhood, he found the courage to attach himself to Mademoiselle de l'Ange.

That demoiselle had scarcely thought of marriage except as one dreams of wining the lottery. She nearly lost consciousness at the first overtures of the examining magistrate. In the intoxication into which the hope of that marriage threw her, and for fear of seeing it fail, she scarcely took time to reflect. In spite of a promise exchanged and the most positive conventions, the poor young woman had lived until then in such incredulity on the subject of a husband that she really did not believe that she was not having a dream until the day of the signature of the contract.

Among the number of persons who witnessed Hélène's marriage were noted, in addition to Madame Locar and her daughter, Monsieur Génie, Monsieur Moulin, Monsieur Rétif, Monsieur de Beaufort, the Marquise de Couvry and, finally, Doctor Bidault.

The last-named, when Hélène's name was pronounced, leaned toward the marquise's ear and whispered: "What do I hear, Madame? That demoiselle is not Gabrielle de l'Ange?"

"No, doctor."

"But in that case, Madame you were making fun of me!"

---

manufacturing artificial gemstones.

At that naivety, the marquise could not help smiling. The doctor seemed thunderstruck. He went the color of the branches of his spectacles, and remained plunged in a bleak dejection.

From that epoch onwards, no more mention was heard of the *Report on proper names and the united physicality and mentality of individuals*; but he did not take long to embrace another that was doubtless scarcely any better; for, what is a theory, if not, most of the time, to speak graphically, a huge imaginary vat in which some ingenious or absurd mind studiously brews one petty truth with a hundred thousand errors?

The Thousand-Franc Bill

THE night was well advanced; there were no more carriages and no more pedestrians; everything was asleep. I was slowly walking through my quarter, plunged in the saddest reflections. I was at the end of my resources. I had wearied the good will of my friends. I had reached the degree of poverty that one hides like a shame, or only admits by force of humility, unless by force of pride, and I was returning desperate after a day of vain steps. I could no longer hope for anything but a miracle. My head was bowed, my eyes staring at nothing . . .

They were suddenly drawn to the recess between two shop-fronts by a small black object. I bent down. It was a portfolio almost the size of a purse. Only a moment before, I had said to myself: *If only I could find a thousand-franc bill!* And I had spent a few minutes searching the sidewalk carefully, picking up all the pieces of paper I could find. I had soon blushed at my stupidity and abandoned that work in order to return to ideas better adapted to the frame of common sense. Now, it was precisely at the moment that I least expected to find something, because the idea seemed utterly absurd, that my hand touched a portfolio. What I experienced is impossible to describe.

Many a time I had reflected on an analogous situation, but I had only formed a very incomplete idea of the emotion that I felt then. I had a weakness, which was translated into a chill in my bone-marrow, sweat on my brow, a nervous tremor, turbulence in the head and stifling heartbeats.

Reflection suddenly rendered me calm. I had so little faith in fortunate hazard that I was convinced that I would only find insignificant papers in the portfolio. I put it in my pocket and continued on my way, still very preoccupied.

I had only taken a few steps when I saw in the distance, by the gaslight, a man coming in my direction. Agitation troubled my eyes. It seemed to me that the man was looking down and searching for something. I am presently convinced that he was not; but the illusion was so strong that I had an excessive fear. I suddenly imagined that I was dealing with the owner of the portfolio, and that the portfolio contained important securities. I want to be sincere: a very dishonest sentiment sprang spontaneously into my mind. I turned round and started to run as fast as I could, without knowing where I was going.

In my vertigo, my ears were ringing, my respiration was making a noise analogous to the bellows of a forge, which made me think for a moment that someone was pursuing me, and I almost felt sick. Those nightmares in which one tries to run away in spite of the inertia of the limbs certainly do not cause as much suffering.

After running madly through twenty streets, I finally arrived at my house, the bell of which I snatched. I threw myself through the doorway and closed the door after me with a feverish violence. There I stopped for a while to catch my breath.

My legs buckled beneath me. I clung on to the banisters and climbed the stairs one by one. The blood was leaping in my heart like a goat and seemed to be making *plops* in my chest, like a blister bursting. The same reflection that had calmed me before calmed me a second time.

I'm mad, there's nothing in it, I said to myself.

I went into my apartment more tranquil. I sat down at a table and took the portfolio out of my pocket. I noticed that, although I had it, my hands were trembling as if suddenly attacked by paralysis.

It was a small portfolio in shagreen leather, bottle-green in color, without a clasp. Never did reading the finest novel caused me a more intense interest. There were four pockets, one of which was closed by a tongue. I was only breathing with difficulty. I emptied the three open pockets, which simply contained: firstly, a rent receipt; secondly, two letters; thirdly, an IOU for three hundred francs; fourthly, a piece of taffeta for repairs; fifthly, an inch of old lace; sixthly, the receipt for a refreshing tisane; and seventhly, a hairdresser's invoice. There remained the closed pocket. I opened it, singularly chilled by the discovery of the aforementioned items. I was wrong, because I took out of it—and a powerful emotion traversed my flesh like an electric current—a thousand-franc bill folded in four.

Oh, what a sensation! I don't know how long I remained in ecstasy before that silky paper, veined and satiny, on which the letters M,I,L,L,E F,R,A,N,C,S entered my eyes like razor blades. An immense joy invaded me. It scarcely crossed my mind that that bill could not belong to me. I was delirious. "A thousand francs! But that's a fortune! O Providence! It's incredible! A thousand francs! What, I have a thousand francs? Oh la la!" These impulses surprise. But does one know what the unexpected possession of a sum of money can blow over an unfortunate whose brain has been shrunk and whose morals have been soiled by poverty?

I cannot recall all the calculations and all the plans to which I delivered myself, all the dreams and the twenty novels that I composed in a flash. What I do remember is that my joy, so intense that I had a fever in consequence, did not take long to be traversed by atrocious sensations.

A man loves a woman madly. Let him take her in his arms, let him be certain of being loved, and he will die of joy; but if he doubts her, if he supposes her on the heart of another, no torture is comparable to his. I was subject to the same ordeals. "This belongs to me," I said to myself, and there were emotions of an indescribable charm. An instant later, I doubted the legitimacy of my right, and I suffered more than a damned soul. What a night! It would not require many similar ones to kill a man. I only slept at daybreak, by force of necessity.

When I awoke my mind was more lucid; I envisaged the matter from a point of view that diminished my contentment considerably. I was not dead to all honesty, and in spite of myself, it was necessary to listen to what my conscience said. Among the poor there are very few who have not thought of finding something and have not also said in the evening, returning home fatigued and desperate: *If I could only find a thousand-franc bill!* Nothing is as commonplace as discussions of that subject. People who do not have a primary, spontaneous probity, but who, on the contrary, only have a relative, calculated and circumstantial probity all reason in very nearly the same manner. It has been heard twenty times over, in similar terms:

If I found a banknote, what would I do? I'd put it in a safe place, and then I'd wait. I'd obtain precise information about the person who has lost it and the social position of that person. If I were dealing with some poor devil, a man like me, a clerk or a delivery man who would have to bear the loss, a small shopkeeper who would be ruined by it, a rentier for whom that sum represents existence, etc., I'd return it; but if it were a matter of a banker who lights cigars with banknotes—in a manner of speaking—who makes two or three hundred thousand francs with a single cast of the net, oh, then I'd keep it. Rather than return it to such a person, I'd prefer to burn it. By keeping it, what harm would I be doing him? Would he be more or less rich? Would his affairs go less well? Would the economy of his affairs be disturbed even by a wisp? Yes, certainly I'd keep it.

I do not appreciate the morality of that reasoning. What I observe is that out of a hundred people who abandon themselves to such dreams, at least ninety-nine profess that theory; for it is not in order to return it that they want to find something. By the force of an irresistible impulsion, I could at least be classed in that category of finders. I had, therefore, to enquire about the person who had lost the portfolio, and that obligation afflicted me greatly. I feared that my research would end in the discovery of some unfortunate ruined, and perhaps dishonored, by the loss.

I thought, with an interest mingled with a great deal of anxiety, of the means that I had of arriving reliably at the truth. I wanted to do it as promptly as possible and to know immediately whether I had reason to rejoice or to curse my luck—in other terms, whether or not chance had smiled upon me with the sole objective of recalling me to a sentiment of my condition and adding to the impatience that my deprivation caused me.

The papers that were in the portfolio, and at which I had scarcely glanced, would doubtless put me on the track of the owner. I therefore took the portfolio and made a new inventory of its contents. The first thing that came to hand was one of the letters. It bore a Rouen postmark and was addressed to Mademoiselle Turpin, number 4 Passage Verdeau. The writing was poorly formed and the orthography strange. I give it such as it was:

> *my good turpin*
> *how tormented I am not to reseive your*
> *news and I beg you if you are not ill to rite to*
> *me rite away I have so much to tell you my*
> *poor hart is so full that it overflows if you saw*
> *how I am changed you could not recognize*
> *your louise of before*
> *adieu good turpin I embrace you with all*
> *my hart your old friend*
> *louise*
>
> *Madame louise che monsieur Dubois*
> *sider shop in the cort la rene Rouen*
> *I am giving you my address I think you*
> *have lost the other.*

That was truly too surprising. Imagine my amazement! I knew that Louise, for having seen her in Rouen and having spoken to her at that very cider shop, where I had sometimes eaten. She was approaching fifty. Her husband, a colporteur and drunkard, whom she had once married against the wishes of her family, left her without a sou for entire weeks and beat her when he returned from his tour. She lodged in an attic of the cider-seller's house and did housework in order to live. I owed it to her confidence in me that I knew of her poverty and the abandon in which she was left by her relatives, for the most part rich or at least comfortable. Even her son, although well established and earning a good deal of money, was not the person who showed himself least harsh with her. The poor woman did not talk about her wretched situation, into which she swore she had only fallen by virtue of her excessive devotion, without having tears in her eyes.

Was that encounter not extraordinary? I find a portfolio and inside, a letter from that Louise! Hazard often produces analogous events, and yet I can never be astonished enough by those bizarre coincidences.

But who was the Turpin to whom the good woman had written such an affectionate and urgent letter? I picked up the portfolio again and took out another item. It was the rent receipt.

> *I the undersigned, proprietor of a house situated in Paris, no. 4 Passage Verdeau, recognize having received from Mademoiselle Turpin the sum of one hundred and fifty francs for a quarter's rent of the rooms that she occupies in the said house, due on the first of April 1850.*

*Quittance, without prejudice to the cur-
rent term, and under the reserve of all my
rights.*

Paris, 8 April 1850.

E. Renaudot.

That quittance put a little balm in my veins. The portfolio evidently belonged to Mademoiselle Turpin. That demoiselle occupied a six-hundred-franc apartment. I concluded that she was well-to-do, perhaps rich, and that the banknote was not indispensable to her, that in appropriating it, I would only be causing her mediocre harm. I looked at the bill amorously again and recommenced enumerating all the benefits attached to its possession.

The examination of the other papers proved to me that my presumptions regarding the fortune of Mademoiselle Turpin were accurate. The tenor of the IOU and the second letter attested that the demoiselle was even in a situation to lend money to people of whom she had once been the servant.

*I recognize having received from Made-
moiselle Turpin the sum of three hundred
francs, which I promise to repay on 5 April
1850.*

Paris, 4 January 1850.

*Laure de G***.*

The letter, signed by the same name and relative to that note, testified to a grave and entirely decisive fact. It seemed that Mademoiselle Turpin practiced blackmail and usury in uncommon proportions. At least, that is what Madame Laure de G*** thought, since she did not employ any semblance of circumlocution in order to write:

> *Your threats to speak to my husband afflict me greatly, my dear Turpin, and are incomprehensible to me on your part. You have too much common sense not to comprehend that you would do me irreparable harm without profit for yourself. Return my letter; I will give you another of 350 payable on the eighth of next month. I cannot do better. In case that is not sufficient for you I will pledge enough jewelry to cover twice that sum. But for the love of God, don't strike these bogey-man attitudes any more and don't threaten me for such trivia. You have not forgotten how fond I was of you in the time when you were my family's housekeeper. Be sure that I still love you dearly.*
>
> *Laure de G****
> *19 April 1850.*

What need had I to know anything else? In accordance with my theory I had to believe myself well and truly the owner of the bill. And yet, the conviction did not fill my mind to the extent of leaving no room for doubt. There was a struggle, and pangs of conscience that caused me, in flashes, very painful constrictions of the heart. A moment later there was an extravagant, ineffable joy, which can only be understood by a person who has nothing and knows the value of money.

A thousand francs! For a worker who has a family and is out of work for a quarter of the year; a thousand francs! For a dreamer who contents himself with bread and water and who has arrived at his last sou; a thousand francs! For a Bohemian out of friends and expedients; a thousand francs, what a fortune! A thousand francs means no more cold, no more hunger, no more shame, but on the contrary, ease, comfort, work, dignity, lack of worry about the future. A thousand francs! It is enough to make one lose one's head.

With what passion I divided up that sum, how cleverly I distributed its employment. *I'll pay here, I'll pay there; I'll buy this and that, this item of furniture, these books of which I have so much need, etc. How tranquil I'll be, how hard I'll work! Oh, it's too much happiness all at once.*

That is assuredly very wretched; but I repeat that one does not know sufficiently how much perpetual hindrance, poverty and sometimes even education shrink the mind and disturb the morality of an individual.

In order to enjoy my fortune in peace, I had to plan the intrigue of an entire long comedy. I might awaken suspicions by an excessive expenditure, since I was known to be poor. It was necessary that in the eyes of my friends I lived as in the past, with the appearances of poverty.

Changing the bill was not the least of my embarrassments. It was possible that Turpin had been to make a declaration at the prefecture of police, and that warnings had been issued to all the money-changers. My exterior was far from announcing wealth. Would not the person to whom I offered the bill for exchange ask me my name? Might he not have me followed? Might he not raise the alarm in my regard? My legal knowledge was paltry, but

I suspected that the Code had foreseen crimes of this sort. What to do, then? I resolved to hide the bill for some time and to act with a consummate discretion and prudence.

I had recently frequented the establishments of merchants who lived in one of the lateral streets of the Rue Saint-Denis. Hazard had led me among those people, who all practiced commerce to dome degree, including a few artists and men of letters, so that, with regard to professions, a very mixed society was found there. I wanted to go there that same evening, with a view to procuring a few details on the manner of exchanging a banknote.

It was still daylight. I had promised myself not to stop at notices. No matter how hard I tried, a yellow paper entered obliquely into my sight and made me turn my head.

LOST…

I shivered from head to toe and red the poster feverishly. It was only a matter of a parakeet, in exchange for which a reward of fifty francs was offered. Further on, the fatal locution *lost* … caught my eye again. This time it was a matter of a greyhound bitch. The emotion was no less disagreeable. I swore not to turn my head again for anything whatsoever.

But now a voice that I could not silence made a noise in my head like all the devils, exactly as if I were cephaliloquent—the dictionary will forgive me that hybrid coinage—and said:

"What difference is there between what you are meditating and a theft? In algebraic style, finding and not returning equals stealing. *Finding* does not constitute any more right than *taking*. If I had a distinction to establish between you and a thief, it would certainly not be to your advantage. The thief employs, on occasion, cunning, skill and audacity; he knows that he is risking his liberty, sometimes his life; but you are appropriating the wealth of others basely, without risk and without peril, not even having to fear insult and suspicion. That is true to such a point that, if you were not certain of impunity, if you did not count in hundreds the means of escaping the court of assizes, if you thought for a single instant that the gaze of a judge might search your eyes and make you tremble, you would not hesitate for a moment to return the bill. Now, given that a crime is a crime regardless of punishment, you are no less a true criminal for evading chastisement."

I replied, timidly:

"This old spinster is rich and avaricious; she has ten times as much as she needs to live. Everything leads me to believe that she has obtained this money dishonestly, that she has stolen a part of it. Would it not be the height of absurdity to adopt a disinterest so unnecessary to her and so prejudicial to me, an unfortunate who does not know what tomorrow will bring?"

"Pitiful reasons! Theft is theft, whether one is poor or rich. Then too, evil cannot excuse evil. That this woman is a thief is not a reason for you to be a thief. Then again, when facing judges, there can be degrees in crime; poverty can attenuate many faults in their eyes, but before the conscience those distinctions vanish; one is a thief whether one takes a pin or a thousand-franc bill. Either you return the bill or you will be a wretch all your life in your own eyes, and you will never recover from your own scorn, a thousand times more to be dreaded than that of others."

I arrived where I was going just in time, for I was suffering greatly. I spoke just now about chance encounters and the amazement into which they always plunge me. I was about to observe another, which seemed to me to be miraculous. I had come with the intention of introducing the topic of changing bills. There was a monsieur there, a cousin of the wife of the master of the house, whom everyone called Ernest, quite simply. I had scarcely paid any attention to him before. Suddenly, his name, brought forward by an observation that he made on his cousin's coiffure, caused me a strange sensation. This is why.

In the portfolio, you will recall, among other things there was a note from a hairdresser. I had scanned it hastily. It was the paid invoice for a hair-styling, price fifteen francs, furnished by a Monsieur Ernest, hairdresser of the Rue Saint-Denis, I no longer know what number. The face, the hair, the manners and the language of the present Ernest convinced me immediately that he was a hairdresser. He must live in the neighborhood. Evidently, I was in the society of Mademoiselle Turpin's supplier and the signatory of the invoice.

That discovery gave me a profound shock; for a few moments I was completely bewildered by it. I thought how fortunate I was not to have mentioned banknotes yet, for one cannot tell what consequences that might have had.

With all possible circumspection and an icy calm, I said to Monsieur Ernest: "Do you know a demoiselle Turpin?"

"Yes indeed," he said. "I do her hair."

"What does that demoiselle do?"

"In appearance, she's a sort of second-hand dealer in clothing, who speculates on old lace, but in reality she's a usurer who lends money at interest. Her housekeeper, for she has no domestic, has told me truly fabulous things about her avarice. She certainly doesn't consume a twentieth of her income. No one knows what she does with her money..."

In my conversation with Monsieur Ernest I made an ample provision of arguments appropriate to resolve me to keep the bill, and I needed them, for the voice of which I spoke did not stop making an impression on my mind.

That old wretch, I said to myself, as I went home, *has at least twenty thousand francs of income that she has gained by illicit means. She scarcely spends two thousand a year. Lying on a heap of sterile gold, she leaves her aged relative Louise in horrible misery and pursues with humiliating threats a woman who is perhaps young, beautiful and good, whose linen she once washed. And I should have the idiocy to return to her a bill that she will hide stupidly with others in some corner, when I could obtain such a large advantage from that sum? Get away!*

But the voice recommenced its racket in my head:

"As many subtle and insidious reasons," it cried, vehemently. "Beware of what you're doing. You're in the process of digging a hole in which you'll bury yourself alive. Crime summons crime. You're thinking of nothing less than exterminating your conscience, committing moral suicide. It's the death of your liberty that you're imploring. You're going to marry a fatality that will cast you down, step by step, to the lowest rung of shame. There's only just time to repent."

I was importuned and shaken. I tried to stiffen myself. I swore that I would limit myself to that one fault, that I would live as an honest man in future.

The voice was inexorable.

"Suppose that you have enough energy or good fortune to limit yourself to this crime. Suppose that you trace your life with the most rigid Puritanism, that you become a model of purity. But the memory of your unique crime will poison your entire life. The purer you are, the more saintly you are, the more odious and hateful your evil action will be to you, and the more you will suffer. A good life has exigencies as imperious as a criminal life."

I know no image that can give an idea of what I suffered. I would have preferred never to have found the bill. Since it had been in my hands, through how many doubts, apprehensions, anxieties and cruel sensations I had passed! Before, I had been, in a sense, resigned to my poverty. It was doubtless because I understood it and felt it fully that I had been resuscitated momentarily by joy, and that I had recovered a fine passion for life.

I was plunged in dolor. What should I do? My troubled conscience suggested a host of alternatives. I attached myself particularly to that of keeping the bill with the formal intention of returning the capital to its rightful owner, with interest, at a later date. Tyrannical objections played pitilessly with the subtlety of the trap. What did I know of the future? Might I not remain perpetually beyond the means of restituting that sum? I would therefore be delivering my honor to the vagaries of chance. In reality, was it possible to commit a more dishonest action? In any case, the old woman might die in the interim. It would then be necessary for me to set out in quest of the names and addresses of her heirs. Would it not be folly to charge myself with such a responsibility, devote myself to such anxieties, and compromise my repose, for so little?

I had also thought of sending the thousand francs to old Louise, addressing the IOU for three hundred francs to Madame Laure de G*** and burning the rest. But did I have the right? I had no mission to enact distributive justice. Did I even know whether the results would respond to my expectations? In any case, only the person to whom the bill belonged could dispose of it. What had I to do with it? I imagined a man who took banknotes from a banker's safe in order to distribute them to the poor . . .

I spent a horrible night. I know nothing but jealousy that can occasion a similar one. When I got up, I was in a frightful mood and my mind was full of indecision. I went back and forth, not knowing what to do. Oh, that hesitation alone, at which I blushed, was culpable! By what tortures have I not expiated! I was convinced at that moment that I could not keep the bill without compromising my tranquility forever, but I did not have the strength as yet to dispossess myself of it.

I wanted to try temporization, to see whether my scruples might not be chimerical. In order to insulate my brain from the turbulent ideas that had been fatiguing it for two days, I went to scan the newspapers. I thought that I could procure myself some distraction by that means. The first article that hazard put before my eyes was this one:

What a lesson! I threw the newspaper away angrily, and picked up another. But I truly had an unfortunate hand. Hazard was applying itself to persecution. I did all that I could not to read this other article, but in vain; the characters drew my eyes and wrenched them from me:

A worthy worker, whose name we hasten to publish, Joseph Pidoux, resident at number six, Rue Bourg-l'Abbé, found a portfolio while returning home on Wednesday evening containing, in addition to insignificant papers, two banknotes, one of a hundred and the other of two hundred francs. Pidoux took it the following morning to the person who had lost it. That action is all the more praiseworthy because Pidoux has a numerous family and lacks work at the moment. Facts of this genre are not so rare that there is reason to be astonished about them, but one is glad to be able to record them, if only to respond to the calumnies that are constantly directed against our honest and laborious population of workers.

But I've read analogous stories a hundred times in the papers! I said to myself. And I remembered another item that had been recounted to me not a week before, concerning a poor girl who, like me, at midnight, not far from her house, had found a portfolio on the road, in which there was a thousand francs, and who had returned it without hesitation to the person to whom it belonged, even refusing the reward that as offered to her.

All these examples fermented in my head and gave me a profound scorn for myself. I ought not to have waited one second more; I should have got up, taken the portfolio and run to restitute it. I resolved once again to wait until the next day. Decidedly, I was a wretch.

I paid with cruel insomnia for that last effort of my vicious side. But it was necessary to finish it; I had had enough. I put the portfolio in my pocket, after having made a note of the papers it contained and copied the two letters, for I wanted to be able to punish myself by publishing my culpability one day, and I went to the Passage Verdeau, where I found Mademoiselle Turpin easily.

The old spinster examined me suspiciously. I told her why I had come. She pounced on the portfolio brutally and opened it with a feverish vivacity. Once she was certain that nothing had been removed from it, she looked at me insolently and said: "You've taken your time bringing it back to me."

The reproach fell so accurately that I blushed all the way to the whites of my eyes. My confusion and my embarrassed countenance made her think that I was waiting for the recompense that she had promised in posters.

"Eh!" she grumbled. "Fifty francs for the trouble of bending down!"

I went home immediately. I crushed the old witch with my scorn, turned my back on her, and left without saluting her. I am fundamentally convinced that she did not hold my lack of politeness against me.

Pardon me for the vulgarity of the comparison, but one recoils before an act of probity for fear of suffering, almost as one hesitates to have a tooth extracted, but in either case, as soon as the thing is done, one feels a profound ineffable contentment. I was at that point. As I went out, in spite of a residuum of bitter sadness, I felt more at ease and I praised myself for my action. I dare not affirm of course, that there were really any grounds for that. In fact, in all of that, of what use had my reason, my intelligence, the education I had received and the books on which I had nourished myself been? The clearest result of that intellectual development was to have reduced me to a problematic honesty, incontestably well below that of a fiacre coachman and a maintained woman.

At least I ought to congratulate myself for that adventure since, from that day on, I was radically cured of the deplorable affection common to many unfortunates that consists of passionately wishing to find something. What I endured, during three days of possession, if I can give it a cruel meaning, was more than sufficient to guarantee my future virtue.

A PARTIAL LIST OF SNUGGLY BOOKS

MAY ARMAND BLANC *The Last Rendezvous*
G. ALBERT AURIER *Elsewhere and Other Stories*
CHARLES BARBARA *My Lunatic Asylum*
S. HENRY BERTHOUD *Misanthropic Tales*
LÉON BLOY *The Tarantulas' Parlor and Other Unkind Tales*
ÉLÉMIR BOURGES *The Twilight of the Gods*
CYRIEL BUYSSE *The Aunts*
JAMES CHAMPAGNE *Harlem Smoke*
FÉLICIEN CHAMPSAUR *The Latin Orgy*
BRENDAN CONNELL *Unofficial History of Pi Wei*
BRENDAN CONNELL *Metrophilias*
RAFAELA CONTRERAS *The Turquoise Ring and Other Stories*
ADOLFO COUVE *When I Think of My Missing Head*
QUENTIN S. CRISP *Aiaigasa*
LUCIE DELARUE-MARDRUS *The Last Siren and Other Stories*
LADY DILKE *The Outcast Spirit and Other Stories*
CATHERINE DOUSTEYSSIER-KHOZE
    The Beauty of the Death Cap
ÉDOUARD DUJARDIN *Hauntings*
BERIT ELLINGSEN *Now We Can See the Moon*
ERCKMANN-CHATRIAN *A Malediction*
ALPHONSE ESQUIROS *The Enchanted Castle*
ENRIQUE GÓMEZ CARRILLO *Sentimental Stories*
DELPHI FABRICE *Flowers of Ether*
DELPHI FABRICE *The Red Spider*
BENJAMIN GASTINEAU *The Reign of Satan*
EDMOND AND JULES DE GONCOURT *Manette Salomon*
REMY DE GOURMONT *From a Faraway Land*
REMY DE GOURMONT *Morose Vignettes*
GUIDO GOZZANO *Alcina and Other Stories*
GUSTAVE GUICHES *The Modesty of Sodom*
EDWARD HERON-ALLEN *The Complete Shorter Fiction*
EDWARD HERON-ALLEN *Three Ghost-Written Novels*
RHYS HUGHES *Cloud Farming in Wales*
J.-K. HUYSMANS *The Crowds of Lourdes*
J.-K. HUYSMANS *Knapsacks*
COLIN INSOLE *Valerie and Other Stories*
JUSTIN ISIS *Pleasant Tales II*

www.ingramcontent.com/pod-product-compliance
Lightning Source LLC
Chambersburg PA
CBHW020352110726
47899CB00006B/1698